***USA TODAY* bestselling** brings you a br...

The Wallflower Academy

Miss Pike's Wallflower Academy is a finishing school designed to find even the most unconventional of debutantes a husband. And this latest cohort of young women aren't your *typical* wallflowers. Follow the girls—abandoned by their families, jilted by ex-lovers and running from their scandalous pasts—as they shed their "wallflower" status and find love!

In *Least Likely to Win a Duke*

Gwen's hopes of making an advantageous match are slim until she *literally* bumps into a duke. But Gwen knows nothing can come of their attraction... not with the secret she's keeping!

In *More Than a Match for the Earl*

Rilla doesn't want an advantageous match. And certainly not to an earl, like the one who once jilted her. Only she's quite unexpectedly found herself flirting with charming rogue Finlay, an *earl*—and rather enjoying it!

And look out for the next installment, coming soon!

Author Note

This book wouldn't exist without a great number of people. Anyone missed from the list is entirely my error, as are any mistakes that you find (please don't look).

Mary and Gordon Murdoch
My wonderful husband
Stephanie Booth
Amy Rose Bennett
Kathryn Le Veque
Awo Ibrahim
Charlotte Ellis
Ishita Gupta
Elsa Sjunneson-Henry
Krista Oliver
Ruth Machanda
The Harlequin typesetting and proofreading teams

MORE THAN A MATCH FOR THE EARL

EMILY E K MURDOCH

Harlequin
HISTORICAL

Harlequin® HISTORICAL

ISBN-13: 978-1-335-59622-2

Recycling programs for this product may not exist in your area.

More Than a Match for the Earl

 Harlequin Enterprises ULC
22 Adelaide St. West, 41st Floor
Toronto, Ontario M5H 4E3, Canada
www.Harlequin.com

Printed in U.S.A.

USA TODAY bestselling author **Emily E K Murdoch** is read in multiple languages around the world. Enjoy sweet romances as Emily Murdoch and steamy romances as Emily E K Murdoch. Emily's had a varied career to date: from examining medieval manuscripts to designing museum exhibitions to working as a researcher for the BBC to working for the National Trust. Her books range from England in 1050 to Texas in 1848, and she can't wait for you to fall in love with her heroes and heroines!

Books by Emily E K Murdoch

Harlequin Historical

The Wallflower Academy
Least Likely to Win a Duke

Look out for more books from Emily E K Murdoch coming soon!

For my bridesmaids. GB, SB, BC and SP.
And to PB, PB, BB and BB.

Chapter One

⁓⁓⊂⊃⁓⁓

The room was busy, far busier than Marilla Newell could ever remember in all the three years she had lived at the Wallflower Academy. The heady noises were bouncing off the walls, mingling with each other, worsening the weary headache after such a long day, making it difficult for her to pick out individual voices as she sat quietly in an armchair by the fire.

'Wonderful wedding, charming girl...'

'And who is her family, precisely? I have met neither mother nor father, yet Lady Devereux was telling me...'

'Never been inside the Wallflower Academy, though I have heard plenty about it! I once heard there was a blind woman here...'

The soft satin of the gown Lady Devereux had been so kind to gift her, and Sylvia, too, had small embroidered flowers upon it. They were a different style and shape to those on the bride's dress: Gwen's were forget-me-nots, Sylvia had told her, and these were daisies.

There were differences. Longer petals, a different kind of stitch. As Rilla sat silently in the melee of noise, she allowed her fingers to gently move across them. Daisies. One here... and here. A space of around two inches between them. Very delicate work.

'Is *that* her?'

'No, that's Miss Daphne Smith, nice girl, too quiet for my taste...'

Rilla sighed when the words became clearer as the speakers grew closer, then farther away, hoping that the ache in her feet would soon settle.

It would have been too much to hope that they intended to approach her. She was not the sort of woman, she knew, that any gentlemen bothered to speak to. It had not taken her the full three years at the Wallflower Academy to know that.

Why, Rilla could not recall a single gentleman actually speaking just to her since she had arrived here, which was a great disappointment to her father. What was the point in learning how to attract a gentleman, he mentioned in his latest letter, if she never put her learnings into practice?

Well, the service was over. Gwendoline Knox, newest wallflower to enter the Academy, was married—and to a duke.

Rilla permitted herself a small smile. No one would have predicted that the most recent wallflower to join the Academy would be the next to wed. But then, just because Gwen had been least likely to win a duke, that did not mean that it was impossible.

And she had.

With no father to host the wedding reception, Gwen had graciously accepted the offer to hold it at the Wallflower Academy. Which had its advantages, Rilla thought dispassionately as she sat quietly in her chair, out of the way. And its disadvantages.

Someone approached her, someone who spent far too much time with the carbolic soap and not enough time considering her words.

The smile became wry on Rilla's lips before Miss Pike spoke. It would be the same old topic, of course. The owner of the Wallflower Academy did not appear to have any other.

'Miss Newell,' said Miss Pike sharply. 'It is I.'

Rilla nodded. 'I know, Miss Pike. Please, sit down.'

She was accustomed to uttering the phrase, even though she had no idea whether there was another seat close by that would be convenient. In the murky, shadowy vision she had, it was impossible to tell.

In Rilla's experience, it did not really matter. Either her conversational partner would sit, or they would not. The only difference was the height from which the next words came.

'Miss Newell, I have something of great import to discuss with you.'

Rilla nodded but said nothing. What was there to say? Miss Pike had evidently found a chair, for her voice came from lower and to her left, but nothing Rilla could advance would prevent Miss Pike from her conversation.

It would be the same tired old conversation they had been having for above a year now. It was too much to hope, Rilla thought with a sinking feeling nestling in her stomach, that the woman would actually say something original.

And after such a day, too. Whispers in the church, the half-heard mutters wondering why on earth she was still unmarried, the desperate attempts to continuously plaster a smile on her face…

'I have spoken with your family once more, and they quite agree with me,' came the terse tone of Miss Pike above the hubbub of the wedding reception. 'You would be a marvellous tutor here at the Wallflower Academy. And with the additional help, I could open up the west corridor, welcome even more wallflowers here!'

Rilla nodded, boredom slipping into her soul as she forced herself to remain silent. An ever more frequent habit, now she came to think about it.

It was the same argument over and over, and though the Pike was not rude enough to say it aloud, her meaning was clear.

No one would marry Rilla. No one would offer for her hand. No one wanted a blind wife.

It rankled deep in Rilla's soul that Miss Pike could even think such a thing, but it was so obvious. Why else would she continuously attempt to persuade her to give up her position as a wallflower, and instead become a tutor to others?

'I think that would be a little premature, do not you?' said Rilla quietly. 'I mean, I am still young, not yet thirty. There is still a chance that I could become a wife. Have…have a child.'

She did not need to be able to see to know Miss Pike was scoffing. Rilla could hear it in her shifting movement on the chair, the way she clicked her tongue most offensively.

'Really, Rilla,' said Miss Pike dismissively. 'I am not so sure.'

'But if you were actually attempting to help me wed, to find someone to marry,' said Rilla hotly, trying to keep her voice down as she was unsure who else was around her but was unable to prevent ire from slipping onto her tongue, 'then you would know!'

There was a moment of silence. Rilla tried to hold her tongue.

'You are—'

Someone shouted across the room, blotting out Miss Pike's word. 'I beg your pardon?'

'You are ungrateful, Miss Newell.'

Perhaps she should not have asked. 'I do not ask for special treatment,' said Rilla, trying to keep her voice level. 'Just the same opportunities as the others. You see what Gwen could do, if merely left to her own devices and not prevented from success?'

Well. Gwen had perhaps not entirely been perfect in the odd courtship she and the Duke of Knaresby had entertained.

Not that Rilla was about to reveal that to the Pike.

'Here I am, running the Wallflower Academy, which is solely designed to help ladies such as yourself find husbands,' Miss Pike almost shouted over the hubbub. 'And prices go up every month, and do I ask for more funds from your family?'

A prickle of pain. 'No, Miss—'

'Five miles from London,' the proprietress was saying, though Rilla could barely hear her now. 'And close to Brighton, and as you can imagine it costs a pretty penny to…more than half…a chicken!'

Rilla frowned. A chicken? What on earth was she talking about?

'And another thing—'

The room was becoming rowdier, the noise almost deafening, Miss Pike's words were getting lost in the kerfuffle. A card table had been set up in the Orangery, Sylvia Bryant had told her earlier, and there were real fears from the servants that blows would be had over some of the hands being dealt.

'Have to sort out—'

'Miss Pike?'

Rilla received no reply. It was infuriating, not knowing whether one's conversational partner was merely thinking, hesitating, or had wished her well under the cacophony and departed, thinking that Rilla had heard her goodbye.

Though she had lived her life without sight, Rilla had a vague view of light and dark. It was not enough, however, in the chaos of this room to see whether Miss Pike had walked away.

A hand rested on her shoulder. Rilla did not jump; she was too accustomed to it. It was one of the ways the wallflowers announced their presence.

'It is me. Gwen,' said the bride. Her hand was soft on Rilla's shoulder, and disappeared though the voice continued. 'What were you talking about with Miss Pike?'

Rilla's shoulders sagged. 'She is gone, then? 'tis so noisy in here, I could not hear.'

'I believe she was distracted by Sylvia attempting to run away again.' There was just a hint of mirth in Gwen's words, enough to make Rilla believe Miss Pike had no choice but to dash after the miscreant. Typical Sylvia.

'No.'

'It…it did not appear to be a pleasant conversation between the two of you,' came Gwen's soft voice.

Rilla almost laughed. The woman married a duke not two hours ago, yet was still hesitant to speak her mind. Gwen was part empress, part wallflower. A very strange mix.

'It was not,' she said aloud. 'You may as well know—all the other wallflowers do—though I suppose you are not a wall-flower now.'

Rilla heard Gwen laugh.

'Once a wallflower, always a wallflower, I think,' Gwen's voice said, merriment in her tones. 'But you were going to tell me what you and Miss Pike were speaking of. I am sorry it was not pleasant.'

It was not, and it was surprisingly painful for Rilla to admit, but there should be no shame in it. It was not her decision, after all.

'My family and Miss Pike wish for me to give up any idea of marriage,' Rilla said quietly. A hand touched hers—Gwen's, she had to assume. It clasped hers. Somehow, it made it easier to speak. 'They wish for me to settle instead as a tutor here, at the Academy.'

Why did it pain her so much? Not only to say it aloud, but to say it to such a person: a woman she had only met a few months ago, who had already managed to find a match within that time.

And to a duke, too. No wonder Miss Pike was delighted.

'I am sorry,' said Rilla hastily. 'I should not speak of such things on such a wonderful day for you. This wedding recep-tion, it is marvellous.'

'It is altogether too noisy, and has too many people,' Gwen said dryly. 'Over one hundred people, I don't know what Percy— Miss Pike was forced to hire two men to act as ad-ditional footmen, you know.'

Well, that explained the noise pounding on Rilla's eardrums, taking away another one of her senses, making it a challenge to navigate the rooms she knew so well.

'Still. You are married now. I hope— I am sure you will be very happy.'

Gwen's hands squeezed hers. 'Thank you, but you do not need to apologize. And I certainly do not agree with Miss Pike.'

'I do not want to be a tutor at the Wallflower Academy,' Rilla said slowly, greater strength entering her voice with every word. 'I have no wish for this to be my life forever.'

The Wallflower Academy was not the worst place to live, to be sure, but to dwell in the monotony of the place for the rest of her life? To be entrapped here through a tutor position?

No. No, Rilla would not permit it.

A gentle squeeze again from Gwen, then she released Rilla's hand. 'You can do whatever you put your mind to, if you ask me. Why, you are the cleverest among us wallflowers, and without your advice and rather sarcastic comments—'

'I did not always intend sarcasm!' protested Rilla.

Gwen laughed. 'I know. And I do wonder sometimes whether…well. Not everyone understands your sense of humour.'

Rilla's stomach churned. Yes, she knew that. Had known it the moment the Earl—

'But I stand by my comment,' continued Gwen happily. 'You can do whatever you put your mind to, Rilla.'

A slow and determined sigh rushed through her lungs as she took a deep breath. 'I know. And I will.'

'Gwen? Gwen, come over here and meet—'

'I'm talking with—'

'—the Marquess of—'

'Oh. Oh, Rilla,' came Gwen's nervous voice with a touch of tension which had not been there before. 'I know you do not like being left alone, but you do not mind if I…'

'Go—meet a marquess,' said Rilla, not unkindly, as her heart sank.

'I'll come straight back,' promised her newly wedded friend. 'It's just, Percy wants to introduce me, and I…well, I'll be back.'

A quick squeeze of the hand, a rush of skirts, and Rilla was almost certain she was alone.

Alone. The word sank into her stomach like a stone. Alone, as she had ever been.

Not that she wished to be introduced in turn to the marquess, whoever he was. No, there was a special sort of awkwardness in standing before a gentleman, knowing that you were being judged, unable to see whether he approved or disapproved of what he saw.

It was intolerable.

Unless he fell head over heels in love with you, a small part of her whispered—the part of her she had tried to ignore for the last three years. And then he would marry you, and—

And then what? Rilla forced aside the thought, even as the longing for love and marriage and companionship and adventure rose in her heart.

That was not her lot in life. Though admittedly, perhaps if she took a leaf out of Sylvia's book and flirted a little…

Fear gripped her at the very thought.

Flirt? Her? She barely knew how. Just being surrounded by all these people that she couldn't see struck discomfort down her spine.

Well, she'd remained downstairs in the drawing room for long enough. Her dues had been paid, she had been perfectly polite, and now Rilla could do what she had wished to do almost the minute she had entered the church.

Retreat to her bedchamber and concoct her next defence against Miss Pike's constant demands that she become a tutor.

Rilla felt the soft heaviness of her skirts shift as she rose and grasped her cane, the reassuring warmth of the wood under her fingers. She had been placed, thanks to some manoeuvring from Sylvia, in the armchair closest to the door to the hall. Six steps—eight, in these formal shoes.

She reached out for the door as she approached it, felt the roughness of the wallpaper, the cooler wood of the door frame. It was open.

Of course it was, Rilla told herself as she carefully stepped through, listening intently for anyone stepping across the marble-floored hall, her cane making a different noise on the different floor. She had not heard the subtle click of the door, had she?

Four steps, and she would need to lean slightly to the right to avoid the plinth upon which, she had been told, sat a planter with a large overgrown something within. Rilla had felt the luscious leaves once, when she had been left alone in the hall waiting for Gwen. Springy, and warm to the touch, like the leaves of the plants in the Orangery.

Another six steps, and she would reach the bottom of the staircase. Almost free. Almost—

'Goodness gracious,' came a male voice as Rilla's cane tapped into something solid, her free hand wandering ahead of her and finding something warm.

She recoiled, drawing her hand back towards her after the sudden contact.

The memory of the touch remained. A strength, a broadness, muscles defined even through a linen shirt and soft wool jacket. A warmth, a presence, something that heated her fingers even through the gloves.

Rilla rocked for a moment on her heels. This was a contact she would not swiftly forget.

'I do beg your pardon,' she said stiffly.

Mortification poured through her chest. Dear God, she would be grateful when the pack of them left and gave her back her Academy.

'I apologize myself. I have never been here before, and I was taking some drinks over to—'

'Ah, one of the footmen the Pike hired,' Rilla said with a nod. 'It is of no matter.'

'One of the—'

'Yes, Gwen mentioned there were a couple of you,' she said, steadying herself now even as her mind whirled with the scent of the man.

Sandalwood, and salt, and lemon. A freshness and a new-ness that made Rilla tilt forward, just for a moment, to take another breath.

Oh, he smelt delicious.

Heat flushed Rilla's cheeks. She couldn't go around sniff-ing footmen!

Flirting. Well, it wouldn't hurt, would it, to flirt a little with a footman? He was only at the Wallflower Academy tempo-rarily, after all. And no one would know.

Her whole body was reacting to the man in a way it had never done before. Heat was rising, tendrils of desire curling around her heart, warmth in her chest, an aching need to lean toward him—

Rilla caught herself from falling into his presumably out-stretched arms just in time.

Get hold of yourself, woman!

'I suppose you've been traipsing about after these idiots all afternoon,' Rilla said in a low voice.

It was most indecorous to speak so, but then, he was a foot-man, and a temporary one at that. He'd be gone by the morning, taking his delicious scent with him, more's the pity.

There would be no consequences to this conversation.

'Idiots?' said the man lightly.

Even his voice was delectable. Rilla had never heard any-thing like it—like honey trickled over a spoon that coated one's lips.

She forced down the thought, and the accompanying warmth that fluttered in her chest.

'The nobility, the guests,' Rilla said softly so that only he could hear her. 'I imagine they've been ordering you about like no one's business.'

Perhaps she ought not to speak in such a manner. Perhaps the footman would be offended. She had no idea.

The noise of the drawing room was echoing around the hall, making it a challenge to concentrate on the hurried and awkward voices before her.

Half of conversation, Daphne had once read in a book and announced in hushed horror to the other wallflowers, was silent. In other words, half was not actually the conversation at all: how people looked, the sparkle in their eyes, the tilt of a head, the warmth in an expression.

All elements Rilla could not see.

She had other senses. The man standing before her had a presence that she could sense despite her lack of sight. He was mere inches from her, and though Rilla wrestled against it, she could not help but lean closer. The man was…attractive. There was no other word for it.

Yet it told her nothing about the man himself.

She was typically so wary of meeting new people. So much of who they were was invisible to her. Their opinion of her, assumed rather than known. The unspoken part of the conversation lost to her.

'You are right, these people have been absolutely outrageous,' said the man in a conspiratorial whisper. 'But don't tell anyone I said that.'

A curl of a smile tilted her lips. It was almost a flirtation! And with a servant!

It should have felt wrong, utterly unconscionable. Somehow the spark of attraction between them overrode any sense of decorum, any typical reticence with the opposite sex.

The last time she had enjoyed such a thing... Well, she could hardly recall.

Miss Pike would be horrified—a flirtation, with a servant?

But this did not matter. He would not matter in a few hours. And so she didn't even introduce herself with her proper title.

'Miss Marilla Newell,' she said lightly.

'Finlay Jellicoe,' the man said beside her in a low, sultry voice. 'And I must say, you are beautiful, Miss Newell.'

A voice, now she came to think about it, that was...warm. Amused, perhaps. A low voice, but coming from a few inches higher than her head. He was tall, then. Whoever he was.

'You flatter me, sir,' Rilla countered, her heart skipping a beat.

'Hard not to flatter a woman so elegant and so refined,' said Mr Jellicoe, his voice quiet, private, as though they were the only two in the world and were not surrounded by a cacophony of unknown voices. 'Beauty will always reveal itself, and I have to say, I am delighted it has revealed itself to me.'

And she giggled.

Giggled! What on earth?

But Rilla felt surprisingly comfortable with Mr Jellicoe; there was no other word for it. There was no tension in her shoulders, and her laugh was natural and light.

Perhaps it was because he was a servant, perhaps because he would be gone. Rilla could not explain it—but he drew something from her that no man ever had.

A longing...to know him better.

The odd thing was, she felt an overwhelming sense that he knew her already. As though this meeting was...fated. Designed.

As though she could be herself with him, as with no other.

The attraction did not hurt, of course, but it was more than that. More than anything she had ever known.

'Is there any chance that you will be retained by Miss Pike? As a footman, I mean,' she heard herself saying.

Which was a ridiculous question to ask. Her, wed a footman? The very idea!

Though a footman that spoke like this and smelt like this and who had a chest that felt like that...

Mr Jellicoe was chuckling gently, and Rilla longed to reach out and feel the movement of his joy. 'I very much doubt it. I, ah, I am not a footman, Miss Newell.'

Rilla stiffened. A half step back was easily taken as a cold chill fluttered through her lungs. 'Not...not a footman?'

'In fact, I am afraid I am one of those idiots being served,' admitted the man. He was still laughing. 'I was actually taking glasses over to my friend, Lord—'

'You rogue,' said Rilla darkly.

'You— I beg your pardon?'

A year ago—perhaps even less—Rilla would have stopped there. She would have demurred, attempted to pass off her rudeness as a jest, and hoped that the conversation would move on.

But she was tired. Tired of always being left out, tired of the Pike's assumptions about her, tired of listening to the wedding vows of other wallflowers as they stepped—or stumbled—up the aisle.

No. No longer.

Rilla was not going to put up with it any longer.

The heat of embarrassment that Rilla always attempted to avoid, and never managed to, seeped into her cheeks.

'I must say, you make a pretty poor wallflower,' said Mr Jellicoe conversationally, as though the whole thing was entertainment for his own amusement. 'Your conversation is magnificent—I'm rather disappointed.'

Rilla's mouth opened, but she was so stunned by the man's ease, she could think of nothing to say.

How dare he just come here and...and speak to her thus!

'Miss Pike tells me you'll be a tutor here before long,' Mr Jellicoe said, utterly oblivious apparently to the fact that she had ceased contributing to the conversation. 'Good for you. I suppose.'

And his nonchalance, his complete inability to understand her obvious chagrin, poured through Rilla's body like the fine brandy the wallflowers had been permitted upon the announcement of Gwen's engagement.

In the mere moments they had spent together, Rilla had felt…well, a kinship, of a sort.

Which was ridiculous, she told herself. How she could have got such an idea she did not know. It was ridiculous, foolish to the extreme.

She was feeling betrayed by a man she hardly knew…but that was rather the point, wasn't it? So swiftly into their encounter, he had presumed to know her, to speak so blandly of her future as though it did not matter…

And she had liked him. Been attracted to him.

It had been a trying day. That was what Rilla told herself later, when she looked back on what she did next.

A long day, and a trying one. She had been pushed beyond all endurance by the whispers in the church, the hushed pity of everyone she passed, the Pike's insistence she would never marry, Gwen's well-meaning but misplaced compassion…

And that was why she finally gave up all attempt at civility.

'You, sir, are a man of the lowest order and I have no wish to speak to you,' Rilla said, glaring in the direction of where the man's voice had last come from, and desperately hoping he had not stepped to the side—or worse, gone entirely. 'I am sick and tired of the boorish behaviour of men like you, and I don't care if you know it!'

And there was no response.

No spluttering. No outraged gasp. No retort that she was wrong, or rude, or disrespectful.

Instead, his voice came low, and soft, and quiet. 'Lowest order? I'll have you know I'm an earl. The Earl of—'

Rilla snorted, relishing the freedom of saying precisely what she wanted. Well, it wasn't as though she would ever encounter this earl again, would she?

'An earl? Of course. I should have guessed by your rudeness,' she said, speaking over the man. 'No manners to even introduce yourself properly. Why am I not surprised!'

'I am surprised,' said the Earl of… Rilla couldn't recall. 'As an earl—'

'I have no wish to hear it,' Rilla said curtly, fire blossoming through her lungs.

She would regret this. She knew she would; she always did when she allowed her frustrations to overcome her tongue. It was a rare occurrence, but when her temper burned, it burned bright.

To think she had believed him a footman! Had allowed herself to relax, to accept his pretty compliments!

An earl! After all she had suffered at the hands of an earl… but Miss Pike did not know that, did she? No, her father had gone to great pains to keep that within the family…

'No wish to hear it?' The earl sounded…not amused, but something else. Intrigued? 'Miss Newell, I admit I am captivated. Tell me…'

'I have no wish to tell you anything,' Rilla said, exhaustion starting to creep into her mind, demanding payment for the debts made earlier that day. 'I wish to go upstairs—alone, sir!'

The last words were spoken as a hand touched hers—a hand that was unexpected, sudden, and unwelcome.

Rilla wrenched her hand away. There was nothing more disorientating, more alarming, than being touched by a stranger when one was not expecting it.

He had probably attempted to help her, Rilla thought darkly, but naturally he didn't know. She'd lived in the Tudor manor that was the Wallflower Academy for over three years. She knew every inch: the wide hallway, the corridors, the drawing room with its sofas and armchairs that the servants and wallflowers knew better than to move, the dining room with Rilla's chair always near one end, two in from the left.

This was her world—her domain. She could, she thought with a wry smile, navigate around it with her eyes shut.

Not that it would make much difference.

'Go away, Earl of wherever you are,' Rilla said dismissively, stepping forward and reaching out for what she knew she would find.

The cool wood of the banister was a relief to her fingertips.

'But—'

'I don't want to hear it,' she said quietly. 'Tell Miss Pike I've retired upstairs. I'm not some entertainment for you, whoever you are. I'm just Rilla.'

Chapter Two

It had been, all things considered, a very long day. And now a woman was shouting at him.

Finlay stood still, as though a strong wind had just passed him and he'd had to lean into it to prevent himself from falling.

Well. That was…different.

Certainly different from Miss Isabelle Carr.

'My lord, I must apologize,' came a voice behind him. 'I had no idea you were speaking with Miss Newell!'

Finlay turned and shrugged languidly, seeing with some relief that he still appeared to have an effect on the ladies.

Miss Pike giggled. 'She is an incorrigible bluestocking that woman, my lord. You must not pay attention to a single word she says.'

Almost against his will, Finlay found his attention drifting to the stairs which Miss Newell had so recently ascended.

Not pay attention to a single word she says?

'Yes, not a single word,' he said softly.

I have no wish to tell you anything. I wish to go upstairs— alone, sir!

A bluestocking. Well, that certainly did not explain why Miss Newell had been so obviously disgruntled to discover that he was an earl. Strange. Finlay had always discovered that it aided people's opinion of him, rather than diminished it.

Most strange.

Finlay blinked. Only then did he realize that the proprietress of the Wallflower Academy was still watching him closely, evidently curious to know what he was thinking.

Not that he was thinking about much. Definitely not.

'Fear not, Miss Pike,' Finlay said, giving a broad smile which made Miss Pike flush. 'I shall not give her a second thought.'

And he truly did not. Well, he did, but it was swiftly followed by a third thought, a fourth thought and a fifth. By the time the following day had dawned and Finlay had suffered through an awkward ride with his betrothed, Miss Isabelle Carr, a monotonous conversation with his mother about the guest list for the wedding, and a dinner which he had agreed to host as a favour to his mother, he had thought about Miss Marilla Newell at least four hundred and thirty-two times.

Which was not, Finlay told himself silently as he nodded along to his friend's words as they entered his own home, technically a second thought.

'That ball was absolute rot,' Lord George Bartlett was saying with a laugh as they entered Staromchor House.

Finlay snorted. 'You always think that when they hand out subpar cigars.'

'And so I should! Outrageous behaviour,' said his friend with another snort as he strode, without invitation, into the drawing room. 'I suppose you have better here?'

It had always been their habit to finish up an evening's entertainment at Staromchor House. Finlay moved almost without thinking to the drinks cabinet, pulling out three cigars and picking up a bottle of brandy.

'A nightcap?'

'Please,' said Bartlett, throwing himself bodily onto a sofa with a groan. 'And a large one. I still have Lady Lindham's conversation ringing in my ears.'

Finlay grinned as he poured a hearty measure into three glasses and then…

'What's wrong, Fin?' came his friend's voice from behind him.

Jaw tight, stomach twisted into a knot of pain, the childhood nickname helped Finlay to speak calmly. 'Damn. I poured three glasses.'

When he turned around, there was a glittering in Bartlett's eyes that Finlay recognized. 'Damn. I thought of him again tonight, you know.'

'It's hard to go a day without thinking of him,' said Finlay heavily, picking up two of the cigars and popping them in his waistcoat pocket before lifting up two of the three glasses. 'Cecil would have hated that ball.'

'He would have loved hating it,' Bartlett countered with a wry smile, accepting the glass offered to him with a nod of thanks. 'The blackguard.'

The two men fell into silence for a moment, then wordlessly toasted their absent friend before taking a sip of the burning liquid.

'Sit, man,' Bartlett said eventually. 'And tell me how these wedding plans are going.'

Finlay groaned as he dropped into an armchair opposite the sofa, hoping the heavy movement could disguise his disinterest with said wedding plans.

Wedding plans.

It had always been this way. With his father gone for so many years, it had been Finlay's responsibility to uphold the Staromchor title in Society's eyes. That meant dinners, card parties, attending the right balls.

And now it meant ensuring that his wedding would be suitable for the Jellicoe name.

'The plans are going,' Finlay said, waving a hand. 'My mother and Isabelle are doing most of it.'

'Isabelle,' mused Bartlett. 'It's been weeks since I've seen her.'

Isabelle Carr. Finlay forced a smile back on his face. Since their engagement had been announced, he could not avoid her.

Not that he had wanted to—at least, not at first.

'How did she seem to you?' he asked quietly. 'The last time you saw her, I mean.'

'She…she looked fine.' Bartlett's voice was low, but his eyes did not waver as he spoke. 'It's strange, isn't it? She and him were so similar. When we were young, that time Isabelle cut off her hair, do you remember?'

'I remember I was blamed for it,' Finlay said dryly.

'You couldn't tell them apart from a distance,' his friend continued, a faraway look in his eyes. 'And she's grown, obviously, a woman now. And yet sometimes, in some lights, I can see Cecil in her. It's like…like a part of him is still here.'

Finlay swallowed, hard.

Bravado—that was what Cecil had always called it. Finlay's ability to move through the world with a smile and seemingly no care in the world.

Cecil had always seen right through it.

Pain.

Finlay blinked. There was pain, inexplicable pain, in his hand. He looked down.

His hands were clenched, both of them. One of them appeared to be— Dear God, he wasn't bleeding?

But he was. The pressure of his forefinger pressing deep into his palm had been far fiercer than he had expected, and a small cut, almost like a papercut, was beading blood.

Without altering his expression, Finlay casually wiped his hand on his breeches, thanking fate that his valet had chosen a dark pair for that evening.

He was not going to think of Cecil Carr again. Not tonight.

It had been his own fault for relaxing, Finlay knew. No, the illusion of laughing bravado always had to remain on his face. To admit that he felt any different, to allow himself to feel for a single second the overwhelming pain of—

'And when I last saw her, she looked…different,' said a voice.

Finlay blinked. Bartlett, one of his oldest friends in the world, appeared again before him. 'Different?'

Bartlett nodded. 'Different. I mean, I knew she wouldn't be exactly the same. I hadn't seen her for three years, not since she'd gone to Switzerland.'

'The Trinderhaus Menagerie for Young Ladies,' said Finlay with a grin.

'The Trinderhaus *School* for Young Ladies,' corrected Bartlett with a corresponding grin. 'You teased her something terrible when the Carrs told her she'd be going.'

'She didn't mind overly much,' he said defensively, pulling out the two cigars he had deposited in his pocket. 'Want one?'

His friend nodded, and it took a few minutes to cut and light them. And his mind meandered not to the Trinderhaus School, but to another place where young ladies gathered. To one young lady in particular. One with a sharp tongue and a wit that had intrigued...

When they were both blowing smoke into the room, Bartlett continued as though there had been no interruption.

'I hadn't supposed that finishing school would alter her overly. I mean, it was Isabelle. Spirited, loud, nonsensical...'

'She's changed,' said Finlay quietly.

He had not intended his words to be so harsh. But it was true. The woman who returned had not been the fourth musketeer to their little group. No longer was she the sister who had hung around the three boys something dreadful, the person who had been pretty as a child but nothing to spark desire in a man's chest.

And now...

'She has taken the death of her brother hard, Fin,' said Bartlett softly.

Finlay's stomach lurched. 'We all have.'

And somehow the tether that had kept them all together had been cut. He hadn't realized, not until Cecil's death, just how much they had all relied on him.

'She looks like her,' he found himself saying. 'She looks like Isabelle but all the warmth has gone, the joy. The mischief. She just…sits there, and lets my mother talk.'

'In fairness, no one can stop your mother talking.'

'And this whole arranged marriage…' Finlay's voice trailed away.

He was not going to think about her. Miss Newell. Most definitely not.

When he glanced up at his friend, there was a knowing look in those eyes that told him Bartlett was holding back. Which wasn't like him.

'Come on, out with it, man,' Finlay said easily, or at least as easily as he could manage while his hand stung. 'I won't be offended.'

He had meant the last few words as a quip, but he saw with a sudden dart of the man's eyes that it was apparently a real consideration.

Interesting. What was going on?

'You…you are not in love with Isabelle, are you.'

It was not a question. Bartlett spoke conversationally, as though they discussed whether or not they had fallen in love with their friend's sister all the time.

Finlay's smile held as he said, 'In love? With Isabelle Carr? Of course not.'

It was an admissionn freely made. No shame rushed through Finlay's chest as he made it, though there was a slight tension in his shoulders.

Bartlett was frowning.

'Well, I am happy to say such a thing,' Finlay said, ensuring no trace of defensiveness could be heard in his voice. 'Men of our status are not expected to fall in love, are they? And it's Isabelle, for goodness' sake. We've known her for…forever!'

He and Isabelle had been perfectly clear in their negotiation. A marriage of convenience—that was all this was. Cecil would have…well, maybe not approved. Finlay had nightmares sometimes, that Cecil would not have approved.

But Cecil was not here. Not here to go riding in Hyde Park, or play cards at White's, or—Finlay's stomach lurched—pay off his family's debts. Substantial debts.

The agreement had been made two months ago, and everything was going to plan. Someone needed to marry Isabelle, provide her with a home, protection. Pay off her family's debts—and with no dowry…

He wasn't about to reveal to Bartlett that despite his best efforts, no feelings of warmth had surfaced. None at all.

'Marriage,' Finlay said aloud into the silence, 'for people of our station, it is rarely for love. If love comes at all, that is unusual.'

'You didn't have to offer for her.'

'What, and you were about to?' he scoffed with a grin. 'Come on now—I'm the earl. I've got the income. It made sense for me to offer her my hand.'

'Out of the blue,' his friend pointed out. 'Carr…he died, and then you were gone. I didn't know where you were, couldn't find you…'

Bartlett continued as Finlay took a puff of his cigar and tried not to think about it. That time when he had desperately tried to lose himself in sorrow, certain that he could get out all the emotions and then would feel better.

As he was before. As though nothing had happened.

'And here you are, engaged to her,' said Bartlett with a snort. 'Though I noticed that Knaresby's experience of matrimony has been quite different. You must think him strange.'

Finlay leaned forward. 'No, not at all! My good man, think it through. He found love, which is all to the good. But he would have married without it, would he not?'

They all did, eventually.

And of all women in Society, Isabelle was one he actually

liked. At least, he had before the engagement, but now it was all formality and rules and never being able to actually speak to each other. And the Isabelle Carr he had known, the joyful, smiling sister of his best friend, had disappeared.

A crackle of pain shot up his side. Though he was hardly the same. Not after they had all lost Cecil.

'Before this, I would have ventured to say that Isabelle was one of the most charming women of my acquaintance.'

Finlay shrugged, placing his cigar on an ashtray. He'd lost the taste of it. 'To be sure.'

Most charming. And most changed. And nothing in comparison to—

Don't think about her, he told himself firmly. Miss Newell should not be clouding his thoughts. Should not be distracting him. Should not be tempting him to return to the Wallflower Academy and—

'I worry about you,' Bartlett said, sitting up now and leaning towards him with a serious expression. 'You… We've both lost a dear friend. The three of us, I always thought… I thought we'd grow old together. Be wittering on at White's in fifty years about the youth of today.'

Finlay snorted, mostly to cover up the stinging in his eyes.

'And I don't think you're happy offering matrimony to Isabelle,' continued Bartlett seriously. 'You…dammit Fin, you don't smile anymore.'

He was doing the right thing, wasn't he? Doing what Cecil would have asked him.

There was no way of knowing, but that certainty, though it wavered at times, was the only thing which had kept Finlay together when…when it had first happened.

His jaw tightened. His heart may be unaffected by Isabelle, but he was doing the right thing.

'And she deserves—'

'I know what she deserves, and I know what I'm doing,' said Finlay shortly. 'You don't have to mother us, Bartlett.'

His friend sighed. 'I suppose not.'

Finlay did not reply. He intended to, but at that precise moment, his mind was overcome with the memory— No, the sharp words of a woman worlds apart from Miss Carr.

I'm not some entertainment for you, whoever you are. I'm just Rilla.

His lips lifted in a rueful smile. He was thinking about Miss Newell again. Most inconvenient. What did that make it, four hundred and thirty-four?

By God, he was losing count.

'Besides, what else is a man in my position to do?' Finlay said, ensuring his voice was a mite stronger now. 'I am an earl, I have responsibilities.'

'You should flirt more.'

Finlay laughed. 'With Isabelle?'

'Well, maybe not,' Bartlett said with a shrug. 'If you don't love her…'

'I have respect for her. Great respect. Just because I have not fallen in love with her yet does not mean I shall not do so. In time.'

Perhaps. It did not matter, after all. They had agreed: it was the only way.

'But a flirtation would cheer you up,' his friend said, gesturing around the room as though there were a plethora of ladies just waiting to be flirted with. 'I'm not saying have an assignation.'

'Definitely not,' Finlay said darkly.

'But a flirtation, someone to make you smile, dust off those skills.'

'You think I've forgotten how to charm a woman?'

The very idea! He was known for it, after all. Finlay Jellicoe, the Earl of Staromchor, was one of the most charming men in the *ton*. He had been careful, even in the depths of grief—especially then—to maintain such a reputation.

'I think it's more likely that you'll realize you don't care for Isabelle enough,' Bartlett responded quietly.

Finlay bristled. Not care about her enough? He was marrying her, wasn't he? He was doing his duty—far more than old Bartlett here.

'She won't make you happy.'

'Oh, stuff and nonsense,' Finlay said sharply to the calm face of his friend. 'Don't—'

'You think the marriage will make you happy? Prove it. Flirt with another, and find them dull in comparison,' Bartlett shot back, though with none of Finlay's animosity.

It was difficult not to be a little suspicious. 'You're awfully concerned that I don't marry her—and I made a promise to her. Even if I…well, even if I did meet a woman who I liked better…'

'Now that's an interesting thought,' said Bartlett with a dry laugh as he extinguished his cigar and sipped his brandy. 'I'll throw down a wager for you, Fin.'

'A wager?'

'A wager, a bet, whatever you want to call it,' Bartlett said easily, peering above his glass.

Finlay frowned. 'Look, these wagers of ours, they never end.'

'Oh, it's not going to be as dramatic as all that,' his friend said with a wave of his hand. 'It isn't going to be like last time.'

'It had better not.' Last time had involved a bag of lemons, a dark alley, and a most inconvenient conversation with a peeler. Never again.

'My point is this,' said Bartlett with a grin. 'You need to cheer yourself up, and Isabelle… Well, you have made a commitment to her, and that's admirable. But before you launch yourself into spousal servitude—'

'You really have a way with words, you know that?' Finlay interrupted conversationally.

Bartlett threw a cushion. 'Are you going to let me finish?'

Finlay had caught the cushion. 'Your aim is getting worse.'

The second cushion caught him in the face.

'You think love is inconsequential, immaterial for marriage. I think you are hiding that fact behind your pretence of—'

'The wager, sir,' Finlay teased.

'I wager you'll feel infinitely better for a flirtation,' Bartlett said, a twinkle in his eye. 'I think it'll bring you joy, and won't betray Isabelle in any way, and you'll enter the married state far happier. If I'm wrong, you can…oh, I don't know…choose your punishment.'

Perhaps if Finlay had not been attempting to ignore the throbbing ache in his hand…perhaps if the brandy had not been so potent…perhaps if he had not been looking for an excuse to return to the Wallflower Academy and converse once again with Miss Newell…

She had been so beautiful.

The thought intruded, as it had so often since meeting the wallflower. She had been beautiful. The dark black hair that shimmered almost like starlight. The way her gown had slipped past her curves, allowing one's gaze to meander leisurely. The purse of her lips, full and shell pink, when she argued with him.

Finlay swallowed.

He was being a damned fool, he knew. Tempting flirtation or not, he had made a promise to Isabelle, and regret it he may, but that did not undo it.

He needed to think rationally. Holding Bartlett's gaze, Finlay threw out his hands and shrugged with a laugh which showed the world just how little he cared.

'A wager it is, then,' he said with a laugh. 'A flirtation—what harm can it do? And what do I win, once I win it?'

'Win?' Bartlett grinned. 'You're not going to win.'

Finlay leaned forward. 'When I win?'

His friend examined him for a moment, and a strange emotion flickered over his face. If Finlay had not been concentrating at that very moment, he would have missed it.

'You... I'll buy you and Isabelle a painfully expensive wedding present,' he said quietly. 'With my best wishes.'

Finlay's heart skipped a beat. Wedding present. His wedding, to Isabelle. The woman he had considered more a sister than a woman for most of his life. But he was doing it for—

Agony, bitter agony twisted in his heart. A pressing on his chest. Lungs constricting.

Finlay forced the grief back where it belonged, deep, dark down within his chest. Where it should not be permitted to escape.

It did not matter. He was not going to lose this bet.

Finlay rose from his seat, stepped over to the sofa, took the man's hand, and shook it hard, once, twice, thrice.

'Excellent. We have a wager.'

Chapter Three

Rilla took in a deep breath. It did not help.

'Well, it's only an afternoon tea,' came the happy voice of Sylvia, just to Rilla's left. 'We're hardly being fed to the lions.'

'Speak for yourself,' said Daphne, her tone soft. 'I think I'd rather take the lions.'

Forcing down a smile that Rilla was almost sure her friends would not appreciate, she sat quietly as the two of them chattered away.

'Never heard anything so ridiculous! Go on, wear them.'

'But I can't! They're your only pretty pair of earbobs. You'll have nothing to—'

'How long has it been since he's visited? That's what I thought, you can't remember. Here you go, let me help you.'

A gentle breeze fluttered through the open window beside where Rilla sat. She'd been placed there by Sylvia's gentle hands the moment she'd entered her friend's bedchamber. Rilla did not need to be able to see to know that this kindness was twofold. Firstly, because although she could find a seat with her cane, it was more pleasant to be guided to one without effort. Secondly, because Sylvia's habit of untidiness meant it was quite likely an unknowing foot could easily stumble.

It had only happened…what, five times before?

Rilla brushed her fingertips across the skirt of her gown. It was striped. She hadn't needed Daphne's awkward praise to tell. The contrapoint weave, lines going this way and then that, was more than enough to tell.

Her thumb stroked the weave as a sudden weight beside Rilla told her that one of her friends had sat beside her.

'You know, you don't look the least excited,' Sylvia said from close to her left. 'I thought you'd be jumping at the bit for a change.'

Rilla shrugged. 'It's not so different from any other day, really.'

And any day at the Wallflower Academy was just like any other. Day after day, trickling by like a stream. Unchanging, always the same.

It might all still be new and exciting for Sylvia and Daphne. Try getting excited about an afternoon tea after three years, she wanted to say.

And didn't. What would be the point?

Rilla was perhaps the only wallflower who truly knew what it was to feel alone here.

It had taken her a little while to grow accustomed to the monotony. After all, it was against nature for nothing to change, for the seasons to pass by without much alteration. Other than temperature and a slight difference in scents in the gardens, Rilla could not have known that time was even passing.

Not like at home. The bleats of the newborn lambs, the lowing of the cows as their calves came. The sharpness of the growing barley, the delicate scent of ale as the brewing houses began their work. The rushing of the wind through the wheat, supple then brittle as the changing—

'Rilla,' came Sylvia's voice, with just a tinge of censure. 'You're being most dull, you know.'

Rilla could not help but chuckle. 'I suppose I am right where I belong, then.'

A sudden intake of breath was all the hint she was given. For a moment, just a moment, Rilla's heart skipped a beat.

It was impossible, at times, to guess at the reactions of her fellow wallflowers. Even after a year of friendship, there were nuances she was certain she missed. Oh, they said this and that, but did they truly mean it? Were the expressions on their faces matching those in their hearts?

She could never tell.

Rilla supposed that there were liars even amongst those who were able to organize their features into pleasing shapes. She could not tell from experience. It was impossible to know.

The subtle signs that were her only clues could be so disagreeably similar. A sudden intake of breath from Daphne could mean shock. Or shame. Or embarrassment. Or just her shyness, something that Rilla had discovered swiftly in the hesitations before each of her speeches.

But in Sylvia? The same action could mean something entirely different. The precursor to laughter, a mock shock that sounded precisely the same as the genuine article.

Or something else. Of all her friends, and Rilla had few, Sylvia was the most unpredictable.

'Where you belong?' Sylvia repeated, and Rilla's shoulders relaxed as she heard the teasing tone. 'By God, are you suggesting my bedchamber is the dullest place in the world?'

'Nothing should be happening here, certainly,' Rilla teased back, her heart settling into its old rhythm. 'The Pike will have your head!'

'I… I am sure Rilla did not mean—'

'Well, even if she didn't, I choose to take offence,' came Sylvia's mischievous reply to Daphne's delicate suggestion.

Rilla could not help but smile.

The Wallflower Academy existed to take ladies like Daphne, true wallflowers, ladies who found it impossible to even look at a gentleman without collapsing into fits of nerves, and make them…

Well. Rilla's stomach lurched. Acceptable.

It was an infuriating thought, but there it was.

The trouble was—for the Pike, at least—that as far as Rilla could make out, the Wallflower Academy was packed not with wallflowers, but with troublemakers. Those who did not obey Society's rules, or fit neatly into the boxes it provided.

Daughter. Wife. Mother.

With only six wallflowers currently in residence, Rilla was almost certain that Daphne was the only true wallflower here. And that meant that when the Pike organized these ridiculous events…

Something which had been spoken some minutes ago suddenly crept forward in Rilla's mind. 'Daphne?'

She felt the warmth and pressure of a hand on her shoulder. 'Yes?'

It was a relief to have her friends approach as she preferred. A sudden voice before her was always most discombobulating. 'Did I— Did you say that your father was attending?'

There it was—that hesitation. And because Daphne had left her hand on Rilla's shoulder, she could feel her friend turning slightly. Turning in the direction of Sylvia, who was still seated beside her on the window seat.

Rilla swallowed into the silence. They were doing it again. Well, she supposed they couldn't help it. She almost thought they did not even realize they were doing it.

They were…pausing.

Being born without sight meant Rilla had nothing to explain the strange pauses which littered conversations like sudden gusts of wind across a sunny afternoon. What were they doing? How could a conversation be continued without words? What if one misunderstood what the other was saying—would you ever know?

And then the moment was over.

'Yes, my father… He…he said he would attend the afternoon

tea,' Daphne explained, her throat thick with repressed emotion. 'He said he had a…a lady friend.'

Precisely what the emotion was, Rilla was not sure. The youngest of the wallflowers had never spoken much about her parents, and her father had only visited the girl once in the last six months.

One of the Society afternoon teas that the Pike insisted on hosting, however, was hardly an intimate family affair. But it was something.

'Which means,' came Sylvia's triumphant voice, 'we will finally have something to talk about at one of these tedious affairs. Lord, why do these ladies of Society bother coming other than to gawp at us?'

Rilla's smile was humourless. 'I think that is precisely why they come.'

'Miss Pike hosts them to improve our social skills,' Daphne said quietly as a gong rang downstairs. They were required below.

Sylvia's snort was close to Rilla's ear as she helped her to her feet. 'Social skills, social skills… I have more social skills in my little finger than the Pike does in her entire—'

'You know full well that until we are married, the Pike considers us in desperate need of socializing,' Rilla said quietly, her equilibrium shifting as Sylvia led her around what must be the bed on her right. 'Gwen always said—'

'Gwen had the right idea,' interrupted Sylvia happily.

The air changed; their voices echoed louder, and the carpet changed to a thicker rug. They were on the landing.

'What, marry a duke?' Rilla asked sceptically, slipping her hand into her friend's arm.

She did not need to. If it were not for the afternoon tea, she could make her own way to the drawing room without a fuss, with the cane which was almost a part of her body in her hand.

But with guests milling about, and servants rushing back and forth with pelisses and coats and hats…

No. Much safer this way.

'Marry anyone,' came Sylvia's voice with a tinkling laugh.

Rilla heard the gasp on her other side.

'Sylvia! You wouldn't just marry—'

'To escape this place?'

'It's hardly a prison,' Rilla pointed out.

There was a hearty sniff from Sylvia. 'It's a prison! Don't you want to leave?'

'And do what? Go where?' It was not a pleasant line of conversation. 'I have been offered neither a home nor a husband, so what options do I have? What could be better than here?'

It was a damning thought.

'B-but Sylvia, you wouldn't—'

'Daphne, I'd marry old Matthews if I thought he'd take me away from this place,' came Sylvia's voice as they stepped down the wide, sweeping staircase. 'But don't you be getting any ideas, Matthews.'

'Wouldn't dream of it, Miss Bryant.'

Rilla chuckled. They were on the second-to-last step, and Matthews always kept his position just to the right, by the front door. He never had to announce himself to her as the other servants did. He was always there.

Besides, she could smell his dank, oily boot polish. He was the only footman not to use the same as the others. She could sense him a mile off.

'Now then, the drawing room,' said Sylvia, as though she informed footmen that she would not marry them every day of the week. Which, Rilla had to admit, may well be the case. 'Let's see who today's victims are.'

The victims, if such a term could be used, were surely the wallflowers themselves, though Rilla did not have time to point this out. By the shift in the rug under her feet—softer, more luxurious—she could tell they were now in the drawing room.

In the midst of Society.

The babble of voices suggested that there were perhaps twenty people in there, milling around. Just less than half were the wallflowers and Miss Pike, Rilla presumed, which left ten or twelve of London's Society who had been dragged the half an hour's carriage ride away from London to the Wallflower Academy.

'So,' she said pleasantly, as Sylvia pulled up and halted them. 'Who do we have here?'

It had become their custom since… Now Rilla came to think about it, she could hardly recall when. Attempting to speak to those who came to gawp at the wallflowers was never a very pleasant experience, and so Sylvia and Rilla had grown the habit of standing by the side of the room and carefully cataloguing those who bothered to come all this way out of London.

They were to be treated like they were in a zoo, were they? Well, two could play at that game.

'There are a few peacocks, as always,' Sylvia began.

Rilla smiled despite herself. Peacocks referred to ladies who wore outrageous outfits to ensure they were looked at. There were always a few of those.

'A tiger, but we'll ensure to avoid him.'

A tiger was a gentleman on the prowl, typically one who had got himself into a bit of bother in London and needed a swift marriage to distract from the scandal.

'A pair of sheep following a fox. Male, all of them.'

A trio of men, then. Rilla nodded. A fox was a gentleman who should not be trusted, and two of his followers who thoughtlessly agreed with anything he said were sheep.

Perhaps a year ago she would have replied to Sylvia. Certainly two years ago. But three years at the Wallflower Academy had worn her down, like waves upon a rock, and so much of herself had faded away. Been crushed.

'And my goodness, but he is handsome.'

Rilla nudged her friend. 'No animal this time?'

'You know, I'm not sure what sort of animal this one would be,' breathed Sylvia, her interest palpable. 'Very handsome, though. I wouldn't mind a little conversational practice with him—dragged here by his mother, from what I can see. A demure peacock, almost stylish.'

'You really are terrible, you know?' Rilla said lightly.

Her arm was squeezed. 'You know, I don't recognize the very handsome gentleman, but he rings a sort of bell. Attended Gwen's wedding, maybe?'

Rilla tilted her head on one side. Now that was a tone she did not often hear in Sylvia's voice. Not desire. No, it was curiosity…but something more than that. Something almost startled.

'By Jove, he's coming this way,' Sylvia breathed.

Rilla shifted uncomfortably on her feet. It was disarming, the thought that a stranger was marching towards you, with no sense at all who he was or why he may be doing such a ridiculous thing.

'Not actually towards us, though,' Rilla said quietly. 'There's no reason he—'

'You know, it does almost look as though he is making straight for us, in all honesty.' Sylvia's voice had lowered in volume, surely because the gentleman was coming closer. 'Oh, Daphne! Daphne, it's your father, and who's that with—Daphne, let go of me!'

'Wait,' was all Rilla managed to say.

And then she was gone. Sylvia's exuberance was well known by the wallflowers, which was undoubtedly why Daphne had pulled her away—as a buffer to whatever conversation Daphne did not wish to have. Sylvia did tend to act first and think later; they would both feel guilty, Rilla knew, at abandoning her here.

Because it left her…exposed.

Not exposed, Rilla thought sternly as she ensured her head did not droop with the sudden loss of her companion. She was hardly helpless, and her cane gave her the comfort she needed. Just…alone. That was all.

And besides, she was accustomed to being alone. Alone was what she did best.

A slow smile crept across her face, and Rilla saw no reason to hide it. Yes, perhaps her father was right all along. Perhaps she would be better suited—

'What are you smiling about?' asked a curious, quiet voice.

Rilla's foot hit the wall as she instinctively attempted to put more distance between her and the speaker. Pain throbbed in her ankle and up her shin, but there was no possibility of reaching down and rubbing it. Not when she could precisely tell where the mysterious gentleman who had just spoken was. Too close.

Lord, the idea of accidentally leaning down and headbutting—

'You look very well, Miss Newell,' came the strange voice.

Then the memory slipped into her mind and threw up a name.

'Very well,' he repeated.

Rilla swallowed and ensured that no hint of a grin approached the corners of her lips. She was not amused.

She recognized the scent now. Sandalwood and lemon. She had only encountered one person who smelt like that.

'The earl, isn't it?' she said as airily as possible. 'From the wedding a few days ago.'

'Impressive,' came the reply, confident, calm, collected.

Rilla snorted. 'Not so impressive. I may be blind, but I am hardly a fool. I am more than a match for you. Why, you—'

She bit down on the words just in time to prevent them spilling out. For what could she say? *You have a particular scent that marks you out?*

'Blind,' said the man quietly. Strangely. As though he were not afraid of the word, which was a most strange occurrence indeed. 'You see absolutely nothing, then?'

'I can see right through you,' Rilla muttered before raising her voice. 'Not that it's any business of yours.'

'Of course.' The man sounded…apologetic. And yet unruffled. 'You must forgive my curiosity.'

Rilla often found herself forgiving many things, and in the grand scheme of things, the man's enquiry about her sight was at least spoken with a modicum of respect.

Still. That did not mean she had to suffer his presence. Though her body was hardly suffering—it was leaning. Leaning!

Ridiculous. She was annoyed at this man, she reminded herself sternly. He had made her feel a fool. There she had been, trusting him, flirting with him…

Which admittedly, had been her fault.

Oh, God, she was still leaning!

Rilla straightened up and ensured her voice was cold and distant. 'How odd that you are here again.'

'Oh, not so odd, I assure you,' the earl said, louder now. Too loud. Would not others be turning to look? 'My mother dragged me here as part of her, and I quote, "charitable efforts." She has this ridiculous idea about the unfortunate and the lesser… Well, I saw very little point in putting up a fight.'

Rilla blinked.

Very handsome, though. I wouldn't mind a little conversational practice with him—dragged here by his mother, from what I can see…

Dragged by his mother… Well, that would account for him being here again.

An earl. Here.

Embarrassment bubbled in Rilla's chest, but she did not

permit herself to display the heated emotions firing through her body.

This man, this stranger—he was an outsider. He did not deserve to know what she was thinking. He'd already made her look the fool.

'How are you, Miss Newell?' came the earl's voice gently.

Rilla attempted again to take a step back, forgetting momentarily that her back was almost already up against the wall. It was most alarming. The man had somehow grown closer to her, far closer than was acceptable.

And they were in public, too! What on earth did the man think he was doing?

'Your name is…?' she said stiffly.

The chuckle blew warm breath across her upper arm—a fact she was most definitely not thinking about. Hardly noticing. Not at all. Not in the slightest.

'I told you I was an earl, and I was not lying,' came the cheerful voice. 'I am Finlay Jellicoe, Earl of Staromchor. For my sins.'

'And I suppose they are numerous,' Rilla said tightly.

Really, it was most unfair of Sylvia to abandon her like this. Even if the man was handsome, it was not like Rilla could tell. Or care.

Attractiveness—now that was different. There was a warmth to some people, a strange magnetic quality she could not describe but had felt once or twice. A need to be near. A pull, a tug under her navel that had caused her once to accidentally fall into that gentleman's lap and—

The Earl of Staromchor's chuckle was low, as though they were sharing a secret. Heat flushed across Rilla's cheeks, and she hoped to goodness no one would notice.

The very idea of an earl and Miss Newell, giggling together in a corner!

'I suppose they are,' said the Earl of Staromchor easily. 'But they aren't nearly so numerous as those of my mother. She's accosted a gentleman and appears to be berating him.'

'Berating him?' Rilla said, unable to help herself.

Well. She couldn't be blamed for her curiosity. She had lost Sylvia's eyes…it was only fair that she use this earl's. For the moment. Not that she wanted to.

There came a movement, the slightest of movements. It could have been a wool jacket against her skin, the very tip of her arm. Rilla's lips parted at the sudden sensation, and then it was gone. Like a whisper she had imagined.

'I think that is Lord Norbury,' came Earl of Staromchor's voice. 'He's standing with a wallflower, as far as I can make out. She looks…terrified. My mother isn't that bad.'

Even with the slightest of descriptions, Rilla could not help but identify the wallflower. 'That is Miss Daphne Smith—with her father, I think.'

'Her father,' the Earl of Staromchor mused. 'That would explain, at least in part, my mother's critique.'

'Critique?'

Rilla had not meant to say it. She certainly should not be conversing with this man, this interloper—this earl!—and most definitely not exchanging gossip. Gossip about one of her friends, no less. It was most indelicate.

Unfortunately, her wonder overcame her.

'Yes, it appears Lord Norbury has not been visiting his daughter enough,' said the Earl of Staromchor softly. 'The gossip is all over Town, as you— Oh, I suppose you may not know. I'd heard it myself, but never thought…the differences in name… My mother won't stop talking about him.'

Rilla swallowed. And that was what came of opening her mouth and allowing herself, just for a moment, to be swept up in a conversation.

Daphne's parentage was not something discussed. Not openly. And certainly not with strangers.

'Go away,' she said sharply.

There was a low chuckle just to her left, then it moved to before her. Cutting her off from the rest of the room.

'Here I am, volunteering to come to the Wallflower Academy to aid you in practising your conversation,' the Earl of Staromchor said with a teasing, lilting voice, 'and you wish me to go away?'

'I did not ask for your help, my lord,' Rilla said, pouring as much disdain as she could manage in the last two words.

'Miss Pike did.'

'Miss Pike does not speak for me,' she retorted, though immediately she regretted the sharpness of her words.

She felt heat rise from her stomach and up her chest. It did no good to critique the Pike in public, either. Good grief, she must be tired. She was not usually this...this lax.

'Nevertheless, I am happy to provide the service.'

'I do not need servicing by you,' Rilla snapped. Then the heat in her chest spread across her face. 'I... I mean— You know what I mean!'

'I certainly do. Or at least, I think I do,' came the obviously amused voice of the Earl of Staromchor.

It was an interesting voice. Oh, Rilla did not experience much variety in the way of male voices at the Wallflower Academy. There was Matthews, of course, and John, the other footman. Sometimes Cook, a man with a voice that sounded like fruit cake and spiced currants when he came into the dining room and asked opinions on a new recipe.

But this earl...his voice was different. There was a confidence there, almost no hesitation in his speech. A lilting lightness, a confidence. A warmth, like a summer breeze wafting through a forest, picking up the little scents of growth and life.

It was doing that thing to her stomach again.

It was all Rilla could do not to push past the man and storm to the door. She knew the way; it was but eight or nine steps from here, and other people would simply have to move out of the way, that was what.

But she wouldn't allow this earl to win. She just wouldn't.

'Besides, if anyone needs practice for their conversation, it is you,' she said sharply. 'You are the one who failed to introduce himself when we first met. Allowed me to make a fool of myself with Miss Pike gone. And you…'

You're an earl, she wanted to say. *You're not to be trusted. I know your sort.*

She detected a soft noise, perhaps the shifting from one boot to another.

'You are the one with the exemplary conversation skills, are you?'

Rilla held her head high. At least on this ground, she was stable. 'I don't depend on titles or good looks. I may not be exemplary, but I'm a damned sight better than you.'

She had expected an almost immediate reply. Strange, in a way, she was a tad disappointed to stand in the silence after her bold comment.

It wasn't that she was starved for conversation. Far from it. Sylvia and Daphne were perhaps her closest friends, but there was not a person in the Wallflower Academy that Rilla did not have a passable friendship with.

And that was the trouble, wasn't it? Three years in the same situation, the same place, with the same people. Oh, a few arrived but they left just as swiftly. Look at Gwen, married within months.

'I… You don't… I… I didn't…'

And then Rilla smiled. She had ruffled him. She had ruffled an earl. 'I'm sorry, is this your example of excellent conversation?'

The Earl of Staromchor cleared his throat, and he was close, far closer than she thought possible. 'How did you get here, Miss Newell?'

'Why, through the door after descending the stairs,' Rilla said sweetly, joy twisting around her heart as she imagined how irritated she could make this man.

Well, serve him right. Coming here to help wallflowers practise their conversation, indeed!

'No, I meant—well, before the Wallflower Academy. Where do you come from, who are your people?'

Immediately the joy started to melt away. She was not going to tell him—no. He didn't know her title, he didn't know her father, and it had to stay that way.

If he caught whiff of that scandal…

She had her sisters to think of, Rilla thought sternly, pressing her hands together as though that would prevent her from spilling any secrets. Any details. Or any information whatsoever.

No, this man may jolt her off balance, make it completely impossible to think clearly, and smell absolutely divine…

She was not thinking that an earl smelt divine!

'Your people are, Miss Newell?'

'My people,' Rilla said stiffly, 'are the Newells.'

'And where are they?'

'I don't actually have to tell you, you know,' she said as calmly as she could manage. Where on earth was Sylvia? 'Besides, I have no time for earls.'

'No time for earls? Why the devil not?'

Rilla silently cursed her inability to keep her mouth shut. Just when she had decided that she was not going to reveal any of herself to this stranger—this earl!—she had to go and make a comment like that. It was infuriating.

Most upsettingly, it was herself that she was annoyed at.

'Good day, my lord,' she said curtly.

She made it almost six steps. That brought her within touching distance of the door frame that led back into the hall, and she would have made it, too.

If it wasn't for the most maddening hand on her wrist. A hand whose touch should not have burned, should not have sparked a tingling heat that travelled up her arm.

'Let me help.'

'I know the way,' Rilla said, attempting to step around him.

The trouble was, the Earl of Staromchor had the advantage of her, quite literally. Just as she moved left, she could hear him, feel him mirroring her, stepping in her way. A step to the right and there he was again, her hands outstretched and brushing up against the silk of a waistcoat, the cold metal chain of a pocket watch.

She halted, cheeks burning. What must the rest of the room think!

'All I asked was—'

'Are you here to choose a bride?' Rilla interrupted, hoping to God that her deflection would be sufficient. 'The Duke of Knaresby did, but you know that, since you attended the wedding. So, here to pick a wallflower bride?'

Apparently, it was an excellent deflection. The Earl of Staromchor hesitated just a moment too long before he said, 'I have no need to come to the Wallflower Academy to choose a bride.'

Rilla swallowed, and remembered what Sylvia had said.

And my goodness, but he is handsome.

If this Earl of Staromchor was as pleasing to look at as Sylvia said, then evidently he knew it. Knew that any lady in the *ton* would be pleased to receive his attentions.

All earls were the same. They were interested in what they could get, not what they could give.

'I have no desire to plan a wedding at present,' the Earl of Staromchor continued, his voice low as though they were sharing a private conversation. 'Or, in truth, to be married. In fact—'

'Fascinating as that is,' Rilla said curtly, 'I—'

'Staromchor, come on, we'll be late back to London!'

The woman's voice was loud and rich, sounding like how plums tasted. Rilla turned her head just for a moment to the left where the voice came from, but as she did so, a voice replied.

'Coming, Mother.'

It was the Earl of Staromchor. Footsteps, shifting away. Rilla swallowed. So. He was gone.

And she was glad, she told herself firmly. No good could ever come out of speaking with an earl.

Chapter Four

❧⁓❧⁓❧

Good weather drew Londoners out like bees, and like bees, they swarmed.

The place they swarmed to, Finlay always thought, was Hyde Park, which was as central as one could be to the fashionable part of London. The tall, towering trees shone green light down on everyone who passed beneath them.

And today, that was a great many people.

Safe atop Ceres, the mare he'd brought to Town, Finlay looked out at the crowds of people.

Ladies, as far as the eye could see. Farther. Ladies with tall bonnets that demanded to be seen from a distance, some bearing feathers, some bearing lace. Ladies with gowns that swept along the bone-dry paths, scattering fallen leaves and dust in their path. Ladies wearing blues and greens and yellows, pastels and prints, stripes and even in some cases, spots.

Finlay was not exactly an expert in the world of fashion—quite proudly not so—but even he thought the spots were a bit much.

Though the gentlemen were hardly any better. Some of them were following what he considered to be the Beau Brummell line of things, dark colours, little velvet or lace. Others appeared to be wishing to gather as much attention as the ladies, if not more. They sported gloves lined with fur, top hats that were creeping up to the heavens, canes for those who really wished to make a statement.

And children. Governesses. A few people exercised their dogs, others wandered with their pets in their arms, as though their little feet could not make the ground. Carriages rolled past, trimmed with silk and with golden paint across their wheels. Horses whinnied as they clopped through the place.

Hyde Park was a veritable sea of colour, ever changing, swiftly moving. The streams of people constantly shifted, their colours intermingling then clashing then separating. It was enough to give even the rainbow enthusiast a headache.

Yet despite all those before him, his thoughts did not tend to those he could see, but rather to one of the few ladies who did not appear to be taking the air in Hyde Park today.

Miss Isabelle Carr.

Finlay's stomach twisted painfully at the thought, and not because Ceres had stepped awkwardly across the path to get out of the way of another man who was galloping as though he were late for an appointment.

Isabelle. The shell of the woman she had been before. She had to stop hiding away from the world. It wouldn't— Nothing could bring him back.

She was slipping far from his thoughts. The space in his mind, in his heart, was unfathomably being replaced by a fiery gaze and a delicate figure.

Miss Newell.

He was dragged away from pleasant musings—such as the exact tilt of Miss Newell's head as she castigated him—only by the most important of topics.

Like the Carr debts.

Just that morning when he had stepped downstairs to break his fast, he had been halted from entering the morning room by a dour Turner.

'Turner?' Finlay had asked the butler curiously. 'Don't tell me my mother has given you a wild instruction again. Demands for strawberries?'

'I wish it were that simple,' replied the loyal butler quietly. 'Here.'

From a pocket in his livery, Turner removed a small bundle of letters, tied together with what looked like garden string.

And Finlay's heart had sank.

He had known precisely what they were. He had not needed to take them to the study—the one room that was his own in his mother's townhouse—and break the seals and read them.

'To the sum of fifteen pounds,' Finlay had read aloud, keeping his voice low just in case his mother did what she so often did, and barged into his study to see what he was up to. 'A debt of three pounds, but with interest…six pounds four shillings. Another one, yes…eighteen pounds and thruppence, though as unpaid for several months, rising to…'

It had been all he could do, when Cecil had died so suddenly, to track down the bulk of the debts.

Oh, every gentleman lived right to the edge of his means; that was expected. When Finlay had first met Cecil, up at Cambridge, the two of them had never exceeded their income but often danced right along the edge.

But Cecil and Isabelle's father had been a famous spendthrift, and Cecil's untimely loss came barely a month after their father had died. Finlay's friend was only halfway to understanding how the estate had got into such a mess, and Isabelle was left alone. Penniless.

The trouble was, as Finlay's friend had always said when he had lived, there was always so much more expense when it came to living in London than one expected—and his father had never known when to cut back and economise.

The upkeep of the house, yes—servants, and food. But also clothing. Keeping the horses, stabling the carriage. Keeping it running. And there were dinners to host; one had to host dinners. And parties to attend, and card parties included their own awful debts. Art to buy. Wallpaper to import. Statues to commission.

And then there were all those costs one did not expect. Lawyers and accountants and tradespeople—more tradespeople, Cecil had always said, than could reasonably be expected to even be found in London.

Finlay's smile was pained as Ceres turned a corner in Hyde Park.

Cecil has a way with words.

Had. Had a way with words.

And that was the trouble. For as soon as Finlay was certain that he had paid off the debts of the Carr family, more seemed to turn up. And the worst of it was, Isabelle had no dowry. All had been spent by her father, without her knowledge.

A flash of dark, almost black hair, a laugh.

Finlay's head turned so suddenly he actually cricked his neck. Lifting a hand from his reins to rub at the offending sore spot, he blinked after the woman who had so suddenly caught his attention.

And his stomach settled. It was not Rilla Newell.

Not that he should be thinking of Rilla Newell, he told himself most firmly as he took his reins back in hand and nudged his steed forward. He was engaged—though he'd realized how foolhardy offering a marriage of convenience to Isabelle was about five minutes after the matter had been concluded.

If only words could be taken back…

Though now he came to think of it, Finlay thought ruefully, he hadn't learned. Now there was that ridiculous bet with Bartlett.

And still his mind meandered to Marilla. Miss Newell. Though after such a damning conversation at the Wallflower Academy only a week ago, he supposed he should give up thinking about her altogether.

I don't actually have to tell you, you know. Besides, I have no time for earls.

The trouble was, she intrigued him. Finlay had never encountered a woman with such a visceral reaction to his title.

Well, perhaps a few—but those ladies had smiled, simpered, shot him looks that told him in no uncertain terms that they would be rather pleased to accept his advances.

Meeting with a woman who heard the title and baulked... it was unheard of.

What was even stranger was how the pain in his chest had wavered, no longer pressing on his lungs like...

Finlay blinked. That had only happened when he had been speaking with Miss Rilla Newell.

Now that was worth thinking about.

'...plenty of pleasant ladies to converse with here in Hyde Park,' a man was saying to his companion as they walked past. 'Just don't bother heading towards the Serpentine, the Wallflower Academy chits are there.'

Finlay swiftly turned in his saddle towards the ornamental lake and his eyes widened.

By Jove.

A line of ladies was meandering with purpose through Hyde Park. At the front was quite clearly Miss Pike, pointing up and around them as they went. The wallflowers followed her in pairs, arm in arm, heads down, evidently not enjoying the public outing.

And at the back...

It was Miss Newell. Finlay blinked, hardly able to believe it.

But a flirtation would cheer you up. I'm not saying have an assignation but a flirtation, someone to make you smile, dust off those skills—

He had an opportunity to charm Miss Newell. Just the thought of it made his body hum, his loins spark with heat.

Because charm he would. True, Finlay had not had much

of a positive start with the wallflower, but all that was about to change. He was well dressed, and they were in public but had been introduced so it was perfectly acceptable, wasn't it, to approach her…

And this time, he was going to turn up the charm so high, she wouldn't know what had hit her.

Metaphorically speaking. Of course.

The main trouble was Miss Pike.

Dismounting from Ceres as nonchalantly as he could manage, Finlay followed the trail of wallflowers as they snaked through the Hyde Park crowds.

'Great architecture to be seen throughout London, but today we are focusing instead on nature,' came Miss Pike's voice from the front of the crocodile. 'Over here, if you look up, you'll see a huge oak tree, one of the finest…'

Miss Newell was right at the back of the line of wallflowers, a cane in one hand and the other tucked in with that of a Black wallflower Finlay could not recall the name of. Cynthia? Simon? No, that couldn't be right.

Following them so close that he was almost surprised that they did not turn to berate him for his ill manners, Finlay considered what his next move should be. The blind wallflower was being led by her companion, and would instantly notice any approach by a strange gentleman.

As would everyone else in Hyde Park.

Perhaps this was a mistake. Perhaps he should just retreat home, admit to George that he didn't care for Isabelle as he should but he had no choice but to go through with the marriage now he had offered it, and…

'Ridiculous idea to leave my cane in the carriage. You know I hate being without it when away from the Wallflower Academy. And to bring me on this nature walk, honestly!' Miss Newell was saying.

Her friend snorted. 'What, you have no other senses?'

'Oh, I can hear the wind through the trees and smell the flowers,' said Miss Newell, breathing in deeply. 'And—goodness. The Earl of Staromchor. Sylvia, why didn't you say?'

Finlay stiffened as the two wallflowers turned their heads. Sylvia, that was her name, looked startled, and Miss Newell…

Miss Newell looked remarkably pleased with herself. As well she might.

'Rilla, I had no idea he was there, but you're right,' said Sylvia, a curious gaze raking over Finlay's features. 'How did you know?'

It was an important question. Finlay would not have described himself as an expert, but by God, he hunted. It should have been easy for him, in the melee of Hyde Park on this sunny Sunday afternoon, to follow the wallflowers with ease without being detected.

And for some reason, pink was blossoming across Miss Newell's cheeks. Most prettily, pairing with the soft, inviting pink of her lips in a way, Finlay was certain, she could not know.

'I… I just knew,' Miss Newell said lamely.

Finlay wasn't convinced, and neither, it appeared, was Sylvia. 'Knew? Poppycock, you must have—I don't know, smelled him or something.'

Sylvia continued chattering away and so she did not, unlike Finlay, spot the sudden dark red that splotched across Miss Newell's face—nor how she turned away from them.

Dear God, was that truly it? She had…smelt him?

Attempting surreptitiously to sniff the lapel of his collar, Finlay was startled by the ladies' sudden movement. They were continuing on with their walk, rejoining the gaggle of wallflowers.

Irritation sparked in his stomach. What, they were just going to walk away from him?

But it appeared Miss Newell had no compunction in brushing off the attentions, however slight, of an earl. By the time Finlay had caught up with them again, leading Ceres by the reins, he heard her say, 'No need to talk to him, that's all.'

'No need to—he's an earl!' Sylvia hissed.

'I am, you know,' Finlay said helpfully, casting an eye over Miss Newell.

She was beautiful. Strange, in a way, that he had not noticed before. Oh, he'd noticed the pleasing shape of her mouth, the delicate way her hair swept across in its pins, inviting hands to—

Dear God. Get a grip of yourself, man!

'Here, you take her,' Sylvia said suddenly, removing Miss Newell's hand from her own arm and placing it unceremoniously onto Finlay's. She met his eye with a grin, and gave him such a theatrical wink, he was astonished he wasn't seated at the Adelphi Theatre. 'I'll distract the Pike with a question about aqueducts. Miss Pike—'

'Wait!' cried both Finlay and Miss Newell together.

His heart skipped a beat as he glanced at her, now walking stonily by his side in silence, refusing to turn to him.

Sylvia evidently believed the two of them to be in cahoots, though to what end, he struggled to imagine. Surely she did not think…?

Finlay swallowed hard and ensured he kept his head high, ignoring the curious glances that were being shot his way by other pedestrians in the park. He was walking in public with a woman. It was perhaps a little unusual, but not entirely scandalous…was it?

This was what he had wanted, wasn't it? The chance to charm Miss Newell.

To win a wager, Finlay reminded himself. He was engaged to be married to Miss Carr. Not a love match, certainly not, but one he was going to see through to the bitter end.

So. Charming. He could be charming. The bet depended on it.

'May I fetch you a drink, Miss Newell?' Finlay attempted with a laugh. 'I am afraid I am a poor footman, but…'

'Spare me your pleasant nonsense,' came the curt reply.

His laugh died on the wind. Ah. Well, perhaps that was not the best idea. It wasn't as though they had parted on the best terms the last time he had the pleasure of her company.

So. Where to begin?

'Miss Newell, you look radiant today, did you know that?' Finlay said with a wide grin.

Only when the words were out of his mouth did his face fall. *Oh, hell…*

Miss Newell's twisted expression contained no mirth. 'You know, funny you should say that, but no, I can't say I've had much use for my looking glass of late.'

Finlay swallowed. Well, that perhaps wasn't the best opener. But that was of no matter. He had others.

'And what a splendid day it is,' he said cheerfully, waving his free hand about to gesture at…

At what she could not see. Hell on earth, but he was going to have to think harder than that.

Miss Newell's face was a picture of restrained mirth. 'You're not very bright, are you, my lord?'

'I just… I forgot… Well, it is pleasant to be walking with you in Hyde Park, Miss Newell,' Finlay said, pretending to be utterly undone by her wit.

It wasn't particularly hard to pretend, in truth. Not that he would have ever admitted it.

Yet still she kept him at a distance, as she appeared to do with the whole world, as far as Finlay could tell. It wasn't the cane. It was her very demeanour.

Silence. It appeared Miss Newell had no interest in responding to his words, no matter how polite they were.

'And are you enjoying your time in London?' Finlay continued as he steered her gently along the path, which curved to the left.

There was a slight pressure on his arm, and then it returned to the light touch it had been before. A tingling feeling crept up to his shoulder, something warming and unknown, unusual and unfamiliar.

Finlay swallowed. It was a feeling he could dismiss. It meant nothing, obviously.

'Yes,' said Miss Newell dismissively.

He waited for a moment, expecting her to continue, but when she did not he found himself unreasonably lost. Well, how did one make conversation with a woman who evidently had no interest in said conversation whatsoever?

Well, he'd told old Bartlett that he had the charm. Time to butter her up.

'You are clearly a very intelligent woman, Miss Newell,' Finlay said firmly as he followed the wallflowers, wishing to goodness he could sit Miss Newell at a bench where he could accidentally on purpose brush his leg against hers. That always worked. 'In fact, I—'

'I'm not that easily impressed, you know,' Miss Newell interrupted with a blank look that she cast his way. 'I'm not like Sylvia. I don't desire to be admired everywhere I go. Nor am I like Juliet, who accepts compliments so prettily.'

A twisting discomfort was making itself at home in Finlay's stomach, precisely where he did not wish it to be. Though he attempted to distract himself by looking at the plethora of beautiful ladies around them in Hyde Park, he was most bewildered to discover that none of them held the simple elegance that the woman on his arm did.

'I don't want you to be like any of those other ladies,' Finlay said, hardly certain which one Juliet was, and not particularly caring. 'I just—'

'What?' Miss Newell shot back, causing tingles of anticipation, warm and alluring, to shoot up his spine. 'You just what?'

It would be a great deal easier to converse if he were not so damned attracted to her.

She was…unlike anyone else he had ever met. Oh, Finlay had met a great number of people; as a member of Society, it was impossible not to.

And none of them glared like Miss Newell, spoke to him so cuttingly as Miss Newell, made him feel as though speaking to her was a privilege he had not yet earned.

In anyone else, it would be off putting.

But there was a warmth to her, one she evidently could not fully contain. Finlay could no longer ignore the desire she sparked in him, the need to know her better.

To touch—

Steady on there, he told himself firmly. *You're in public. And you don't go around touching young ladies against their will!*

'You're very quiet,' Miss Newell said.

There was a look almost of disappointment on her face.

Warmth crept across Finlay's face. Try as she might to argue the opposite, she wanted to talk to him.

The knowledge buoyed him as nothing else had, and the shot of excitement and joy was unparalleled.

I wager you'll feel infinitely better for a flirtation. I think it'll bring you joy, and won't betray Isabelle in any way, and you'll enter the married state far happier.

Or not at all.

Dammit. He may have to tell Bartlett he was right and lose the bet. What was the penalty for losing, again?

'And it's not like I care,' Miss Newell continued stiffly. 'Your conversation leaves much to be desired at the best of times, when you're not lying about who you are or making a fool of yourself at afternoon tea. But you are preventing me from conversing with Sylvia, and—'

'Look, I'm trying to butter you up here,' said Finlay before he could stop himself, the foolish admission slipping out. 'The least you could do is—'

'Enjoy it?' Miss Newell said, tilting her head towards him. Something blazed in her expression, something he could not fathom. 'And why are you buttering me up, pray? Not exactly the charming opening I thought earls were supposed to have.'

Finlay took a deep breath and attempted to regather himself.

Well. It was exasperating in the extreme, not to be immediately liked. Worse, it was most unpleasant to discover within yourself an expectation of being liked.

If only she could see the amiable tilt of his jaw, his dazzling smile, the way he carried himself. He was even wearing one of his newest waistcoats and jackets, elegant and cut remarkably close to his figure. A figure that, Finlay would previously have boasted, had got more than one woman in a tizzy.

But none of that mattered. Not to Miss Newell, anyway.

Fine. Charm hadn't worked. Time for direct questioning. 'Why don't you like me, Miss Newell?'

Evidently she had not been expecting that. She almost tripped over her own gown, and Finlay reached out and placed a hand on her waist to steady her.

And unsteady himself.

Rapid thoughts of molten desire that were most unsuitable to be thinking and feeling while standing in the middle of Hyde Park rushed through Finlay's body. Unbidden, uncontrolled, all inspired by the merest contact with a woman who pulled herself free of him the moment she had regained her balance.

Finlay almost stepped back, but he managed to keep his presence of mind and retain hold of Miss Newell's arm. For her benefit, he told himself, mind whirling as he attempted to understand what precisely he had just experienced.

'It's not you,' Miss Newell said curtly. 'It's the fact that you're an earl.'

'An earl?' Finlay repeated blankly.

They were standing still now, the train of wallflowers disappearing off along the path. But Finlay didn't care. How could he, when such a beautiful enigma was staring up at him?

Miss Newell's eyes were a startling grey. It was the first time he'd noticed that. No wonder he hadn't realized she could not see the world as it was when they had first met. One could almost be forgiven for not noticing, such was her beauty.

And she hated earls?

'Forget I said anything,' said Miss Newell awkwardly. 'And return me to Sylvia. The Pike will soon notice.'

'I'll return you to Sylvia safe and sound once you've answered me,' Finlay stated far stronger than he intended.

He was not, after all, a cad. They weren't that far behind another pair of wallflowers. He wasn't alone with her. Not really.

What, a small voice muttered in the back of his head, *would Isabelle say about that?*

Miss Newell bit her lip, her head turning, her cane moving as they started again slowly along the path. Was she listening for Sylvia, for the other wallflowers? Was she wondering just how far from them she was?

Evidently she would not risk it. Dropping her head and speaking so quietly that Finlay could hardly hear her, she said softly, 'I'm not actually Miss Newell. Well, I am.'

Finlay blinked. 'Well, that sorts that out.'

There was brief flash of a smile, then it was gone. 'I'm actually the Honourable Miss Marilla Newell and I was… I was once engaged to the Earl of Porthaethwy.'

This time Finlay did let her hand slip from his arm.

Engaged before? Honourable Earl of Porthaethwy?

He blinked, the sunlight of the day suddenly dazzling—or was that her? Miss Newell was a woman far above the station he had assumed for her. What was a woman of that breeding doing in a place like the Wallflower Academy?

'Was once engaged?' Finlay repeated the one part of Miss Newell's statement that gave him the most pause.

Once engaged? A scandal, then?

Miss Newell shrugged, though there was evidently more pain in that expression than she knew she was revealing. 'He broke off the arranged marriage the day he met me. I was sent to the Wallflower Academy the following week. There. Now, will you return me to my friends?'

But Finlay could think of nothing but the outrage that was curdling around his heart.

Broke off the arranged marriage? The cad, the lout, the—

'The very idea!' he said hotly, words breaking out against his will. 'I don't see what— I mean, why should he care about… about…?'

Finlay swallowed.

Rilla was glaring just past his ear. 'He didn't care that I was blind. He knew that—everyone knew that. I was born that way. No, he broke it off for quite a different reason. Only earls know how to end a match.'

And he understood that, didn't he?

It was that annoying voice again, and this time, Finlay swallowed hard and was unable to ignore it.

Because it wasn't entirely wrong. There had been moments, hadn't there—more frequently with every day that passed— that he considered breaking off his arranged marriage with Isabelle?

Not because there was anything wrong with her, no, but because…

Well, he didn't have a good reason. Something in him just rebelled at the idea of wedding a childhood friend. Particularly when she was so…so altered. So lost.

'Are you going to return me to Sylvia or abandon me here?' Miss Newell said darkly, cutting through Finlay's thoughts.

'Though you are an earl, I wouldn't be surprised if you chose the latter.'

And that did it. Finlay pulled himself together, puffed out his chest, smoothed back his hair…then realized that every single one of those motions was lost on the woman before him.

Blast.

'I shall return you to Miss Pike now,' Finlay said quietly, deflating. 'And I hope I shall soon—'

'Oh, no,' said Miss Newell firmly, reaching out and deliberately placing her hand on his arm without a hesitation. 'No, Your Lordship. I wouldn't bother to hope.'

Chapter Five

'And she will be here any moment!' declared Miss Pike, a froth of excitement in her tone. 'A duchess visiting the Wallflower Academy is hardly a run-of-the-mill event, and some of you—yes, you, Daphne—are dreadfully unprepared. So please, for goodness' sake, be on your best— Sylvia Bryant, put that footman down!'

Hurried footsteps grew louder then fainter as the Pike traversed the drawing room, moving from the polished floorboards to the rug then out to the hall. Muffled laughter. A muttering in a low voice, embarrassed, contrite.

Rilla smiled.

Well, as there was no telling what mischief Sylvia would get into next, she had ceased attempting to predict it around four weeks after the woman's arrival.

After all, had she not orchestrated a most unpleasant encounter with *that earl*?

Try as she might, she could not conceive why the blackguard had sought her again.

It was irritating. He was irritating. And much against her wishes, the true vexation was that he had not appeared the last five days at the Wallflower Academy.

And why would he? Rilla asked herself darkly.

Besides, she didn't want him to. The delectable-smelling man, the one whose presence raised her hackles and made it impossible to concentrate, why would she want him here?

Dragging herself away from remembrances of strong hands on her arm and the sense of danger, of being separated from the other wallflowers, Rilla returned to the conversation in the room.

And immediately regretted it.

'Duchess here,' Daphne's voice whispered, sotto voce and filled with terror. 'Why she would want to come here—'

'No need for that, now!' Sylvia's voice was half mirth, half frustration. A sudden weight dropped onto the sofa beside Rilla. 'I don't see what was so bad about—'

'I think you know precisely what the problem was here,' came the Pike's stern yet steady tone. 'Leave the poor footmen alone, you know they can't— Ah, here she is. Now, let me go and greet our honoured guest.'

Rilla's nerves prickled as chatter rose up once more about the arrival of a duchess.

A duchess.

What on earth was she coming here for? She certainly couldn't be meeting with a friend, and they were just too far out of London for this to be a coincidence. Besides, the Pike had been informed in advance. That meant planning.

Another one of the nobility coming here to peer at us to see what a wallflower looks like, Rilla thought darkly. *And they wonder why the London Tower menagerie is so popular...*

New footsteps. Light, measured, definitely coming from the hall.

Rilla's spine stiffened, her stomach tightening into a knot. Could she avoid notice? It was always a challenge, being the one who could see naught but a vague sense of light and dark. Avoiding unwelcome conversation was just that much more difficult.

And there was no time now to retire to her room. That would require crossing the hall, and there was no possibility she could avoid—

'Her Grace,' intoned Matthews's voice from about ten feet from Rilla, 'the Duchess of—'

Her heart sank.

And then it rose.

'Gwen,' Rilla breathed.

She was nudged none too gently in the side.

'Now how on earth,' muttered Sylvia as the footman droned on, 'did you know that?'

There was only one person in the world, Rilla was certain, who still scrubbed the back of their neck with carbolic soap out of habit, but also now wore the delicate rose scent her husband had presented her on their wedding day.

It was a jarring medley, and it was altogether Gwen.

'Gwendolyn Devereux, wife of the Duke of Knaresby.'

'Yes, yes, we don't need any of that nonsense,' came the ruffled voice of Gwen. 'I only came to see Rilla and Sylvia. We don't need all this.'

'But Your Grace!' The Pike was obviously rattled, though Rilla could hardly comprehend why. She'd managed to get a duchess to cross the threshold, hadn't she? 'Visiting all the wallflowers, it would do a great deal for their reputations, elevate them.'

'I'm here, and you are fortunate I came at all,' shot back the determined voice of the duchess.

That was Gwen. She may have been sent to the Wallflower Academy, but she was no shrinking violet.

'Yes, move a chair here.'

A scraping noise jarred Rilla's nerves and a hint of worry fluttered around her mind. It was always so much more difficult to navigate a space like the drawing room once something had been moved.

'Don't you worry, Rilla, I'll ask him to put it back,' came Gwen's voice, closer now, and lower. She was seated on the chair opposite her. 'I know you like sitting in the sunshine there.'

Despite herself, Rilla smiled. 'Thank you.'

It was a kindness not everyone offered, and as chatter erupted around the drawing room, she surmised most of the wallflowers had returned to their conversations, embroidery, and reading.

Still. That did not mean they could speak freely.

'The Pike's gone,' came Sylvia's carefree tone with a laugh. 'Lord, Gwen, when she was banging on about a duchess, I never conceived that it could be you.'

'I sometimes get surprised myself when I'm announced into a room.' Gwen's words spoke of shyness and surprise, but Rilla was not fooled. She could hear the pride, the delight, the joy.

Did anyone else hear it? Was she perhaps the only one who could tell, who was concentrating on the slight shake in the vowels, the hesitation of the consonants?

Sylvia snorted. 'Don't be daft, you love it!'

'I certainly do not.'

Rilla allowed the words to wash over and around her. It was like bathing in a pool of warm light. Or at least, what she presumed it would feel like.

She was so…so lonely.

Perhaps it was only when surrounded by chattering ladies, like now, that she noticed it. Alone with her thoughts, never truly sharing them, never wanting to share them. Lost in a sea of wallflowers.

Though she had hardly noticed it before, she had missed her friend. Gwen had been a part of the Wallflower Academy for a mere matter of months, but Rilla could not deny that she had grown to truly like the woman.

The woman who was now, apparently, the toast of the *ton*.

'So kind, so affectionate,' Gwen was saying in that lilting, carefree tone. 'And he is just…'

Wonderful, by all accounts. Try as she might, Rilla could not entirely attend to the words of her friend. No, she was altogether distracted by a thought which, once made, could not be unmade.

Gwen had made love to her husband.

Heat sparked in her cheeks, but Rilla could not dislodge the revelation from her head. What was it, to be touched by a gentleman? To have him love you, to connect to that most intimate place? To bear oneself and never worry again that you would be alone?

Shifting awkwardly in her seat, she tried not to consider it. It was not as though she would ever be blessed with such knowledge.

One night, one encounter would surely be enough to satiate her appetite. One—

'But you've hardly spoken, Rilla.'

Rilla allowed herself to nod. 'I suppose not. I suppose I have nothing new to offer because…'

Because she could not see.

Those were the words Rilla did not say aloud, but they hung in the air, heavy in their unspokenness. All three of them knew what it was she had not said. She had never feared being open with them, her friends.

The way people spoke to her, or did not speak to her. The way they presumed she was helpless, useless, ignorant! The assumption that no one would wish to marry her.

Why were they treated as prospective brides, and she treated like a dried-up old spinster of a teacher? The very idea of staying here at the Wallflower Academy, helping others to marry when no one wished to wed her…

How she longed to find someone who knew her, truly knew her…and loved her.

Rilla had hinted at as much when she had spoken briefly to

Gwen at her wedding, but this was the first time she had admitted to so much in front of Sylvia.

The sudden intake of breath to her right proved her expectation correct.

'But she can't do that!'

'She can do whatever she likes, she's the Pike,' Rilla opined wryly.

She was nudged in the shoulder.

'Don't be ridiculous,' Sylvia said, and the merriment and teasing had left her voice now. 'You can't actually be considering— she can't force you to leave!'

Rilla sighed, reached into her corset—an excellent place for keeping things, it was a misery that true pockets were not the province of the lady—and pulled out the letter that had arrived that morning. The paper was expensive; she could feel the delicacy of the grain. 'Here. You can read it. I don't mind. Sylvia already has.'

The hand that took the paper approached as a waft of rose water confirmed it was Gwen who had taken it.

'Keep it,' said Rilla with as airy a manner as possible. 'I know it by heart.'

It had surprised people, when she had first arrived at the Wallflower Academy. Her ability to memorize things once spoken to her was astonishing, apparently.

Rilla could not think why. How else was she supposed to enjoy things? She was hardly going to always find someone to read her letters to her, over and over again.

Under the genteel chatter around the drawing room about the right thread for this next portion of embroidery, and where someone's missing book was, and just how precisely Sylvia thought she was going to get away with her next adventure, Rilla heard the unfolding of the paper.

Her fingertips unconsciously moved to the seat of the sofa. The velvet underneath was soft, comforting, warm, a balm compared to the words shortly read aloud by the newest member of the aristocracy.

"'My dear Marilla,'" Gwen began to read softly. 'Oh, it's from your father.'

She must have glanced to the end, or perhaps there was a difference in the handwriting between men and women. Rilla did not know.

'Yes. My papa.'

"'My dear Marilla,'" Gwen repeated. "'Thank you for your last letter. Do consider speaking to Miss Pike about opportunities to better yourself.'"

'Better yourself?' Sylvia's voice dripped in resentment. 'I hate that he wrote that. I thought you were rather splendid already.'

Rilla reached out, lifting a hand, and her friend knew to take it and squeeze it. A lump came to her throat and though she had intended to say something witty and amusing, nothing came.

Sylvia squeezed her hand back and held on to hers, dropping their clasped fingers onto the sofa.

She must have nodded at Gwen, or indicated somehow to keep going, for the duchess continued.

"'I will admit, my child, that it would be a relief to us if you did consider leaving the Wallflower Academy and taking up a position somewhere that indicated that you had resolved not to marry.'"

'Not to marry?' Gwen's voice was startled as she repeated the words, but then she continued reading. "'Your two younger sisters—'"

'I don't want to hear this again,' Sylvia cut in. 'It was bad enough reading it the first time.'

'Keep going, Gwen,' Rilla said, her heart contracting painfully. 'Or I can recite it, if you wish? "Your two younger sisters are unable to attend Society events, not with an elder sister out and unmarried. If you wish them to ever find suitors of their own, then you will need to take a step of kindness and move out of their way. You know the estate is entailed, and you know I have to marry off as many of you as I can. And if you are so fortunate as to meet an earl again, do us all a favour and steer clear. Yours faithfully, your ever-loving Papa.'''

Silence fell after this pronouncement. At least, silence between the three of them. Daphne and Juliet appeared to be bickering good-naturedly over a skein of red thread in another corner.

Sylvia's hand squeezed hers. 'It's outrageous.'

'It's certainly not a letter I'd wish to receive,' said Gwen quietly. 'Though I must admit, marriage to Percy has put paid to the unpleasant missives my mother was sending.'

'Another benefit of winning a duke, I suppose?' Sylvia quipped.

Rilla sensed Gwen's smile, imagined the tilt of her head which had once been described to her, the flush upon her cheeks.

Whether she was correct or not, of course, was quite another matter.

'Oh, I cannot imagine not being Percy's wife,' Gwen said, happiness radiating from every syllable. 'Being loved, being adored in the way that he loves me—one reads about such things, but you never expect it to happen to you. Why, the other day...'

Rilla did not attempt to reach out for the return of her letter. She did not need the paper back to have the awkward words of her father ringing through her mind.

And it was hardly her place to interrupt the happy words of a newly wedded wife.

Envy was an unpleasant emotion. It prickled and stung as it meandered through the chest and into the heart, poisoning everything as it went.

It was not as if two people could not be happy at one time,

or that Gwen's happiness marked or prevented her own. It was simply that Rilla could not help but feel sad. There was something unpleasant about the idea that she herself would never—

'And have you met Rilla's earl?' Sylvia's voice said, cutting through her thoughts.

Rilla opened her mouth immediately. 'He is not my—'

'He approached you right in this room,' said Sylvia, with a triumphant air that was most disconcerting. 'And at Hyde Park—the cheek of the man! He must admire you greatly to do such a thing.'

'An earl?' Gwen's voice was all curiosity. 'Who is your earl, Rilla?'

'He is not my—'

'Well, he's certainly not mine,' chortled Sylvia. 'I think you've made quite an impression there.'

Nausea blossomed up in Rilla's chest.

I think you've made quite an impression there. Her father's words echoed through time. *And His Lordship wishes to end the engagement. What in God's name did you do?*

'Rilla? Rilla, are you quite well?'

Try as she might, Rilla could not force down the sickening feeling sweeping over her chest. Her fingers gripped Sylvia's tightly, a mooring stilling her in a storm.

'Rilla? Should we send for a doctor? She's awfully pale, and she's not responding…'

'I am quite well,' lied Rilla, hoping she had injected sufficient warmth into her voice. 'Quite well.'

End the engagement. Well, the Earl of Porthaethwy was perfectly entitled to walk away, since they had not yet wed. It was just a betrothal. Just the sum of her hopes and dreams. Just an insult to herself and her family when he walked away, right there, at the altar. Just—

'Oh, bother, there's my coachman,' Gwen declared. Rilla

heard a trace of anger in her voice. 'And I had hoped to tell you— Blast. I'll have to go.'

'Go?'

'Do not ever marry a man without meeting his mother. That's all I'll say, Sylvia,' Gwen said in a dark tone as her voice shifted. She had stood up. 'I'm expected back for dinner, and I'll need to change and—'

Rilla allowed her friends' chatter to wash over her. The moment had passed. Their attention was no longer fixed on her.

Which was all to the good, she attempted to tell herself a few hours later, as she was putting the final touches to her toilette before one of the Pike's official dinners. Attention on her was never good.

Especially when offered by arrogant earls who thought they could merely walk up to a woman and have her swoon into his arms…

Look, I'm trying to butter you up here. The least you could do is—

Enjoy it?

'Another Wallflower Academy dinner,' Rilla said with a sigh as she gently lifted a long string of jade beads over her head, arranging them over the bodice of her gown. 'Another chance for the wallflowers to impress. Or, as the case may be…'

It was a good idea in the main, she supposed. The Pike had instituted six official dinners with members of the *ton* during the Season, hosting them at the Academy itself.

All in the attempt to marry off her charges.

Rilla did not wait for Sylvia this time. She knew the way well enough, and Matthews, judging by the scent of boot polish, was holding his usual station at the bottom of the staircase. The chatter in the drawing room was loud, but Rilla did not bother to approach.

Why should she? There would be naught but awkward conversation, loud chatter masking the sound of her footsteps, and the chance that some fool had moved a chair.

That was the last thing she needed—to fall flat on her face.

No, the dining room was safer.

Only twice did Rilla wonder, as she stepped across the hall and made her way to the dining room, whether Finlay was in the room filled with all the noise.

Only twice. Which was impressive, Rilla decided as she opened the door and stepped forward, hands reaching for the chair at the end of the table. The warm wood met her fingertips. Because she had thought about Finlay almost constantly while dressing for dinner.

One, two, three...

Rilla counted the chairs as she moved down the left-hand side of the table. Ten—a large dinner then, at least twenty-two.

Pulling out the chair right at the end of the table, so as to keep out of the way as best as possible, she sat and waited for the gong.

It was not long. The sonorous noise echoed around the house and the door opened. Footsteps, many and heavy, laughter and hands clapping on backs, mutterings and noise...it was overwhelming.

Rilla was relieved she had chosen to seat herself before the racket assaulted her ears. It was so much harder to concentrate on navigating, on finding her way around—

'Miss Newell,' said a voice that was far too familiar. 'We meet again.'

Rilla's stomach dropped out of her chest, through the chair, and into the floor. 'Sylvia.'

The word had slipped from her mouth before she could stop it.

The Earl of Staromchor cleared his throat. 'N-no, it's not—it's Finlay.'

Trying her best not to panic, sheer irritation driving her forward, Rilla snapped, 'Where is Sylvia?'

'Don't get your bloomers all knotted up,' came a clear voice across the hubbub, causing gasps from some and mutters of, 'My word!' from others. 'I'm coming!'

Rilla suppressed a smile. Well, no matter what else happened in the world, there was always Sylvia. Always the same.

'Get out of my— I live here, you know. If you don't move—'

'What on earth is she doing?' breathed the gentleman now seated beside her.

Rilla stiffened, a cold wash of terror flowing over her again.

Had he not taken the hint? Had he truly seated himself beside her?

'Sylvia is my...my...'

The words were impossible to say as shame poured into her chest.

All she had to do was squash down all feeling, she told herself sternly. Force away all hints of desire, pretend she didn't want to converse with him...

But it was no use. The man intrigued her, most annoyingly, though she would be mistress of herself. She would focus on the dinner, and not the dinner guest.

Oh, how she hated these dinners. She had asked the Pike again and again if she could be excused from them, yet the woman had not accepted her more than reasonable request. And so she had made a bargain—an agreement, with Sylvia.

A Sylvia who was panting as she sat on Rilla's other side. 'Honestly, the state of some of these men. I would hardly call them gentlemen!'

'Neither would I,' Rilla said pointedly to Finlay—to the Earl of Staromchor, she corrected herself—before turning back to Sylvia. 'You...you will assist me?'

'Always,' came Sylvia's prompt response without any hint of embarrassment.

Some of the tension that had crept into Rilla's shoulders melted away. There was no one she could depend on quite like Sylvia.

And besides, she could feed herself, and dress herself, and walk confidently with a cane; she was no child! It was, however, helpful if someone arranged the food on her plate in a set way, so she could easily find it, and then place the cutlery in her hands. Sylvia had sat beside her for every meal at the Wallflower Academy for just such a purpose.

'I actually wished to speak to you privately,' came Finlay's voice on her right.

Rilla ensured that her expression remained perfectly still. 'And yet you cannot.'

'But I—'

'We are at dinner,' she pointed out coldly, hoping the man would take the hint.

Honestly, were all earls this dim-witted?

'Privacy is impossible.'

Thank goodness.

In the quiet of her own mind, Rilla knew how deeply she was tempted. There was something about this man. Not merely his persistence, which made no sense before one even started.

No, it was something else. When she had first spoken to him, believing he was nothing more than a footman…

Well, it had been like talking to Matthews. And yet nothing like talking to Matthews. There had been warmth, and ease, and comfort.

And now she would have to forget all that, push it away most decidedly, and concentrate on what was before her.

What was before her?

'Some sort of meat and vegetables,' said Sylvia's voice, as though she had heard the silent question. 'Smells good, if you ask me.'

'Chicken,' said Rilla nonchalantly. 'Seasoned with dill, sprigs of rosemary from the garden to garnish. Honey-roasted parsnips, burnt slightly, I believe, along with winter peas and what I believe are boiled potatoes. Yes, definitely boiled.'

Well, it was hardly difficult. They all had noses, didn't they?

She reached out for the napkin she knew would be just to the left of her plate.

It was not there.

'Allow me,' came a quiet voice she was attempting to ignore.

Rilla's fingers splayed out in a futile attempt to stop the inevitable. Finlay merely moved around her. The sudden sensation of her napkin on her lap was intrusive, but so much more was the sense that he had leaned forward, invading her personal space...

Bringing a scent of sandalwood and lemons. A warmth, his breathing fluttering on her skin. The sense that if she just leaned forward, just an inch, she would touch—

'I just wish to talk with you,' came Finlay's soft voice. He must have leaned back, for the sound was not as loud as she had expected. 'There is no crime in that, Miss Newell.'

Rilla snorted. *No crime, indeed.*

'I have no interest in talking to an earl.'

'If I could take off the title to please you, I would,' came the sardonic reply. 'But as that isn't possible, do you think you could remove your prejudice?'

It was most difficult to glare at someone you could not see, but Rilla attempted it nonetheless.

The whole dining room was filled with chatter now—mostly the gentlemen to each other, as far as she could hear. The wallflowers of the Academy were not known for their comfort in the presence of so many people.

Hoping to goodness her words would be hidden under the noise, Rilla said darkly, 'I don't want to talk to you, my lord.'

'Finlay.'

'My lord,' Rilla repeated, gripping her hands tightly together in her lap. 'And I'm hungry. Sylvia?'

Feeling exposed as she always did when it came to mealtimes, but a thousand times more now that she had such a brigand to her right, she parted her lips.

And waited.

'She's talking to the gentleman on her left,' came Finlay's voice. 'M-may I?'

The hesitation in his voice sounded genuine, but Rilla's stomach lurched. How could one tell? How could any gentleman be trusted when she could not look into their eyes and know, for certain, their intentions?

Her stomach growled.

Oh, this was ridiculous. It was only food, wasn't it?

'You may cut up the chicken,' Rilla said stiffly. 'And…and then place the fork in my hand.'

There was a noise on her plate. Then the scraping noise on the crockery ended, and Rilla waited.

The arrival of the fork in her hand was gentle. Then came the brush of a thumb over her palm, and a rush of heat poured up her arm.

Don't think about it.

She speared a piece of chicken and lifted the fork to her mouth, chewed, and swallowed her mouthful in silence, relieved yet slightly surprised that the earl had not spoken. Her heart thundered, her stomach churned—because of the chicken, Rilla tried to convince herself—and she forced her breathing to remain regular.

'More?' His voice was soft, intimate, his breath warm on her neck.

He must be leaning close to her, Rilla thought as her head spun. Oh, God, but it was so sensual. So intimate.

'Y-yes, please,' she breathed.

This time she waited expectantly as he cut more chicken and returned the fork to her. Waited for his fingers brushing against hers. Her breath caught in her throat. And then his fingers returned, lingering this time, sliding against hers.

Rilla knew she shouldn't be enjoying this, shouldn't be permitting a man, any man, to do this.

And in public!

So why did this feel so...so...?

Good grief.

She wasn't starting to...to trust him, was she?

'I've never gained so much enjoyment,' came Finlay's quiet voice, 'from food. Not ever before.'

Rilla hastily swallowed as her fingers tightened around her fork. 'If you think I'm going to let you—'

'Don't you enjoy this?'

Damn and blast, the man was incorrigible.

'If you don't want to be thrown out by the—by Miss Pike,' she amended swiftly, 'I would recommend stopping.'

'You don't like it when we touch?'

Heat blossomed in her chest and Rilla knew it was too much to hope that the colour, whatever it was, had not reached her décolletage. The man was...was flirting with her.

Flirting! With her!

'If you can't behave, I shall have to ask Sylvia to—'

'I can behave,' came Finlay's quiet voice, and Rilla felt the loss of his presence as he moved back, a sense of emptiness around her. 'I can behave.'

Very much doubting that, yet unable to stop herself, Rilla sighed. 'Then...then you may help me.'

'And...?'

'Don't talk to me,' Rilla said darkly, wondering what on earth she thought she was doing. 'Consider it a compromise.'

Chapter Six

I can behave.

Then...then you may feed me.

And...?

Don't talk to me. Consider it a compromise.

Finlay jerked away as the half dream, half memory faded into immediately obscurity.

Damn. It had been remarkably pleasant, too.

'And that is why the modiste absolutely has to be a Frenchwoman,' said the Dowager Countess of Staromchor sternly, the carriage rocking the three of them side to side. 'In truth, Miss Carr, I do not see how you can advocate any other.'

Finlay blinked blearily at his mother, seated directly opposite him in the Staromchor carriage, and then his gaze slid to the woman beside her.

Miss Isabelle Carr.

She was not flushing at his mother's rudeness, nor stammering her objection to the woman's demands.

No, she was just looking out of the window as the carriage rattled down the Brighton streets. No expression tinged her face, nothing at all. It was curiously empty.

'Miss Carr?' Finlay's mother said sharply.

Finlay winced as Isabelle turned to his mother with a blank, almost confused expression.

'I beg your pardon,' she said quietly. 'Did you say something?'

He had known it would be a bad idea from the very start.

Of course he had; it had been his mother's. The dowager countess had been absolutely certain that all he and Isabelle needed to spark more romance between them—her words—was time together. Time to enjoy each other's company. Time to fall in love.

Poppycock.

She had insisted, however, and Finlay was hardly in a position to deny her. It appeared that Isabelle had been unable to argue with his mother, either. That, or she simply did not care.

And so a trip to Brighton was decided. A week there, no more. A chance to take the waters, enjoy the sights, see Prinny if they were lucky, and attend the Assembly Rooms. Brighton was a place, his mother had assured both of them, that no one would suspect the engagement. It was easier to keep it quiet, she had said. There had been enough gossip about the Carr family, in the dowager countess's acidic tone, to last a lifetime. So, Brighton it was.

Which was where they were headed now.

'Hard to believe the wedding isn't that far away.' His mother beamed with a knowing look. 'And once your happiness is all tidily sorted, I can see to my own.'

Finlay rolled his eyes at that. As though his mother did not prioritize her own happiness already. Why, from the bills that had arrived from the modiste last week, and that dinner she'd thrown—

'Don't you roll your eyes at me, young man.'

He smiled weakly. 'My apologies, Mother.'

His mother sniffed. 'I should think so. Here I am, a widow.'

Finlay groaned this time, though with a wry smile. It wasn't as though he hadn't heard it all before, after all.

'Losing your father so long ago, and here I am, without the continuation of the line,' the dowager countess continued with a glint of steel in her eye. 'Something you are, at least, going to finally correct in the near future.'

It took all Finlay's self-control not to look at Isabelle, which unfortunately meant that he had little left over to prevent his cheeks from reddening.

Well, really! Talking about such a thing before Isabelle!

'You look troubled, Miss Carr,' said the dowager countess with a raised eyebrow. 'Why, I would almost say that there was something on your mind. Pray, tell.'

Finlay looked again at the woman he would be marrying in just a few short months. Not that the *ton* knew that yet.

His mother was right. Isabelle did look distracted. At least, she did not appear to be attending to those she was seated with in the carriage.

Cheeks flushing, the younger woman reached into her reticule, pulled out what appeared to be two letters, seals broken, and offered them to Finlay with a trembling hand.

He couldn't help but notice the tremble. Dear God, what had happened to her? The Isabelle Carr he had known before she had disappeared off to that godforsaken finishing school had once trounced him so hard in chess, she had crowed all day and been sent to her bedchamber for unsportsmanlike behaviour.

Isabelle had argued that as she was not a sportsman, it did not matter. Then she had climbed out of her window down the wisteria and made faces at him, Cecil, and Bartlett through the dining room windows.

Where was that woman now?

'I… I am afraid… Well, I did not expect any more, but…'

Isabelle pressed the letters into Finlay's hand as he wished to goodness she would just call him Fin, as she'd used to.

The letters were cold against his fingers. He did not need to look to see what they were.

More debts.

'Oh, dear, how frightfully uncomfortable for us all,' said his mother, quite unnecessarily. She whipped out her fan and fluttered it, as though that would make the unpleasant sight of bills disappear. 'Dearie me.'

Finlay quickly pocketed them. 'Thank you, Miss Carr,' he said formally, as was required of him. 'I will pay them the moment we return to London.'

Isabelle did not reply. She had already turned away, hands clasped together in her lap, gaze directed out the window.

It was not as though she could see much. The autumnal evenings had drawn in faster than Finlay had expected and night had fallen early that afternoon. Grey clouds had gathered on the horizon, and though the expected downpour had not yet occurred, he would be surprised if they returned to their lodgings in the dry.

But between now and then...

'Ah, here we are,' announced the dowager countess, all hints of debts and money forgotten. 'The Assembly Rooms. I have heard the food is much improved since we were last here—not that it could be much worse! Indeed, as I told Lady...'

Finlay allowed his mother to witter on as he stepped from the carriage and offered a hand to Isabelle. She took it, descended without meeting his eye, then waited silently on the pavement for the dowager countess to descend.

For a moment, he was tempted to say something.

Do you miss him?

Do you wonder why? Why him? Why us?

Do you ever think...?

'I see they haven't lit the place any better,' sniffed the dowager countess.

Finlay jumped. Evidently he had helped his mother from their carriage without noticing.

'Not nearly enough candles,' his mother continued, striding forward without waiting for either of her two younger charges. 'I shall have to speak to someone about that.'

Finlay had never liked Brighton, and he was reminded of why as he entered the Assembly Rooms with Isabelle on his arm.

The place was crowded. Once again more people had been

admitted than was proper, and they were all paying the price for it. Not a single person appeared comfortable in the crush, and the multitude of candles and smoke from the many cigars heated the room up something terrible.

And worst of all, there was no one of his close acquaintance to be seen. It was to be expected. They were not, after all, in London. And yes, it was mollifying in part to see so many pretty young ladies immediately turning to him and smiling, beaming at his handsome features, the expensive cut of his coat, the way he was immediately at home in any room.

But for some reason, the typical pleasure Finlay gained from being so admired…it felt lacking. Not that there was an absence of it, but it lacked the potency of the past.

Don't talk to me. Consider it a compromise.

An unbidden smile crept across his face as warmth flickered through his chest. A teasing remark from Rilla was suddenly far more pleasurable than the sycophantic expressions of a dozen women. Which did not make sense.

Fawning was already occurring ahead of him. Evidently someone had realized that a dowager countess had entered the place, for there were two gentlemen already offering his mother food, drinks, and likely as not the chance to redesign the decor of the place.

Finlay glanced at Isabelle. Her eyes were downcast. Her lips were pressed together, not pursed in an attitude of judgement or thought. They were merely closed, with no expectation that they would open.

When had it suddenly become so difficult to speak to the woman? If he had met Isabelle now, he would have described her as dull.

Dull? The woman who had, at the age of seventeen, smeared her father's telescope with ink and paid off all the servants not to tell him for three whole days!

Dull? The child who had learned to swim by pushing Cecil into a river and been forced to rescue him!

Dull? The woman who, when she had written to her brother upon first arriving at the Trinderhaus School for Young Ladies, had described her companions with such boldness that he had almost split his waistcoat laughing!

Where was that Isabelle?

Finlay's gaze flickered over the woman who would in a short time be his wife, and he felt nothing. What on earth was he doing? This was madness: he'd had doubts about the suitability of this match the instant he'd offered it. Did it really help Isabelle to be tied to a man who could not love her?

Surely there was a way to… Well, end the engagement. Only a few people knew about it, so the scandal would not be overtly disastrous. Did…did she wish to end it?

'Isabelle,' he said awkwardly.

'George,' Isabelle breathed.

Finlay frowned. 'What do you— Oh, thank God.'

Shoulders relaxing the instant he saw a familiar face, he steered them towards a table covered in canapés and slapped the arm of the man with his back to them.

'What the devil are you doing here?'

Lord Bartlett turned, mouth full, and sprayed pastry all down his front. 'Isabelle!'

Chuckling as his friend reddened, trying to put down the canapés he was holding and brush the pastry from his front at the same time, Finlay felt a surge of relief. Well, at least there was one person here he could speak to. And, if he were careful…

'Didn't expect you to be here, Staromchor,' Bartlett was saying, his tone easier now he was no longer covered in flakes of pastry. 'Isabelle—Miss Carr, I mean…'

'I did not know you were in Brighton,' Isabelle said in a rush, voice low and eyes downcast.

And Finlay saw his opportunity.

Well, it wasn't as though they didn't know each other. They had grown up together; they all had! And it would give him a chance not to speak awkwardly to his betrothed for five minutes together. That was a risk he had to take.

'Bartlett, you wouldn't mind taking care of Isabelle for me for a few minutes, would you?' Finlay said, speaking over the two of them.

Both Bartlett and Isabelle were staring.

'Taking care of her?' Bartlett said.

'A few minutes?' repeated Isabelle.

'Excellent,' said Finlay firmly, lifting her hand from his arm and placing it on Bartlett's. 'I just need to— I have to…'

His voice trailed away as he stepped from them, hoping Bartlett would forgive him for abandoning Isabelle in his lap.

There was just a small twinge of guilt as Finlay helped himself to a glass of wine, downed it, then gave it back to the footman who had offered it.

Cecil would not have approved.

It was a painful thought, and one he could not ignore. He had attempted to do what was right by Isabelle, and he was certain Cecil would have approved of that. The marriage, that was.

The abandoning Isabelle because Finlay just didn't know what to do with a woman so changed…

Probably Cecil would not have approved of that part.

He had attempted to be honourable. He was doing the best he could. What else could Finlay do—just watch his best friend's sister fall into penury?

No. No, he had taken steps against that. These thoughts that pained him, that reminded him Isabelle was hurting just as much as he was, that eventually the name of Cecil would have to be mentioned between them, that if he entered into a marriage like this he would be lonely for the rest of his life…

Finlay would certainly have done something about those

thoughts, rattling through his mind like a barouche without any concern for its passengers, except for—

Except for a flash of something in the corner of his eye.

It was just a movement. A moment. If he hadn't spent so much time in the carriage thinking about Marilla, perhaps the genteel movement of a woman ten feet away would not have caught his interest.

But he had been thinking of her, and so Finlay did look around when he saw a woman who looked remarkably like her. The same dark black hair, the same figure, the same bearing. So similar, in fact, that a twinge of guilt crept into his heart as he looked over.

Isabelle deserved better than that—better than him. If he didn't get his act together...

Finlay blinked.

It wasn't a woman who looked like Marilla.

It was Marilla.

'I said,' came an irate voice with the force of a gale, 'are you going to ask Miss Carr to dance?'

Finlay blinked for a second time. This time his view of Marilla—*Marilla! What on earth was she doing here?*—was blocked by a woman of more advanced years and significantly advanced irritation.

'Mother,' he said weakly.

'I have been attempting to speak with you for nigh on five minutes,' said the Dowager Countess of Staromchor with a glare.

An exaggeration, Finlay was sure. Certainly he could not have been so lost in his thoughts that he had... Well, perhaps it was five minutes. It couldn't have been!

'And you're not listening again,' intoned his mother darkly. 'What are you thinking about?'

Finlay swallowed, and knew he could not tell the truth. And so, unusually for him, he told a lie. 'Cecil.'

His mother's face immediately softened. 'You dwell too much on the past, my dear.'

'It is hard not to,' he said honestly.

'And yet you have the future to look forward to, a future with a good woman,' his mother pointed out. 'Honestly, Staromchor, anyone else would hope that you had romance on your mind!'

She fluttered her fan suggestively and waggled her eyebrows over its ribbon.

Finlay's stomach lurched. It wasn't possible, surely, that his mother had guessed… But then, he had acted in a most outrageous way at the latest Wallflower Academy dinner. It had occurred over a week ago, and he had half expected the scandal sheets to mention the disgraceful way that he had been seen feeding Marilla.

It wasn't his stomach that lurched this time, but something a little further down.

Flirt. That was what Bartlett had said. Was there anything more flirtatious than that?

And the man was right. He did feel better for it.

'I must say, I am delighted Isabelle is starting to finally worm her way into your heart,' Finlay's mother said with an approving nod.

Finlay's jaw dropped. Then he cleared his throat and closed his mouth swiftly, as though he had always intended to do that.

His heart—Isabelle?

How could his mother be so wrong?

'And while on the subject of your betrothed,' the dowager countess said with a beady eye, 'I think you have been remiss.'

Finlay frowned. 'Remiss?'

Had he not done everything in his power to sort out the tangled mess Cecil had left? Had not every debt been paid? Had he not offered marriage, the one thing left in his power, to the woman who would otherwise be left alone in the world with no one to—

'You have barely spoken to her since we arrived, you know,' his mother said sternly. 'You palmed her off to that Bartlett boy!'

'That Bartlett boy' had a moustache, was over six feet tall, and had punched a man clean out in the boxing ring last Tuesday.

Finlay said none of this. 'Bartlett knows Isabelle just as well as I.'

'But he is not engaged to be married to her,' his mother pointed out sharply. 'You are.'

He was. And Finlay was going to do precisely what was required of him, as soon as he stopped staring past his mother's shoulder at Miss Newell.

Miss Newell, who was alone. How was that possible? Where was Sylvia, the Pike, others from the Wallflower Academy?

'Outrageous that you aren't dancing with Miss Carr,' the dowager countess was saying, half to him, half it seemed to herself. 'What people will say, I don't know.'

'I don't care what people will say,' Finlay said before he could stop himself.

It was now his mother who was in the corner of his eye; all his attention was taken up with the radiant Miss Newell. A Miss Newell who was wearing a gown of elegant blue silk, a foil to her hair and her colouring, one hand clutching that cane of hers.

'Society will talk,' his mother was saying. 'It's the look of the thing that we have to worry about. If it looks—'

'I don't care how things will look,' Finlay said, ignoring his mother's outrage and incoherent splutters. 'It would be abominably rude of me not to greet an acquaintance.'

His heart almost skipped a beat as he waited for his mother to respond.

The dowager countess was biting her lip. 'I suppose that's true.'

'I wish to speak to Miss Newell.' And before he could

change his mind, before any hesitancy could enter his chest, he pushed past his mother and approached...

Marilla.

She was standing on her own at the side of the Assembly Rooms. Evidently her companions, whoever she had come with, had been asked to dance. Marilla Newell, however, was clasping a dance card utterly unmarked with pencil, her gaze downcast.

Finlay cleared his throat and, fighting the urge to put his hand on her arm, said quietly, 'It is I, Miss Newell. Finlay Jellicoe. Earl of... It's Finlay.'

Why, precisely, he did not wish to speak about his title, he could not fathom. Well. Marilla—Miss Newell—had given him plenty of reasons to cease speaking of such a thing. Her broken engagement, a topic which he dearly wished to speak on, had to play some part of that.

But to despise him so utterly merely because he shared a peerage with a cad?

'Staromchor?' Rilla's eyes widened, her cheeks flushing most prettily.

And she had no idea, Finlay realized with a strange lurch in his chest. No idea how tantalizing she looked to him in that moment. No idea how close he was...

Although apparently she did. Miss Newell took a step back, thankfully missing a footman who was transporting a silver tray of empty glasses, and frowned.

'What...what are you doing here?' she breathed.

Finlay tried to smile, then remembered she could not see the expression, and shrugged.

Damn and blast, but he was a fool.

'It's the Assembly Rooms,' he said feebly. 'In Brighton. Much of the *ton* is here.'

'But this is Brighton,' Miss Newell said, most unnecessarily. Her voice caught.

Did he make her breathless?

'It is indeed,' Finlay said, his smile finally natural. 'I might ask you what you are doing here, far from the safety of the Wallflower Academy.'

Miss Newell scoffed. 'I need no such safety. I am hardly about to be ravished by a passing gentleman.'

Fighting all his instincts to tell her that she was indeed most ravishing, and he would be more than happy to offer his services, Finlay instead accidentally bit his tongue.

God in heaven—he was supposed to be flirting with her!

Say something, man!

'And what are you doing here?' Miss Newell asked, bearing the conversational burden. 'Not in the Assembly Rooms, I mean. In Brighton.'

Finlay hesitated. There was so much he could tell her. So much. About Cecil, and his death, and how much it hurt. About Isabelle, and the Carr family debts, and how he was trying to do the right thing but it was a millstone around his neck and every moment he thought about it the rope grew tighter.

About how changed Isabelle was, and their marriage of convenience, and Bartlett's words a few weeks ago about a flirtation and joy and a last hurrah before succumbing to the drudgery of the married state.

About how his mother had dragged him here, and there was nothing he could do but allow himself to be swept away by the storm of the decisions he had made. Decisions he had made before he had ever met Miss Marilla Newell.

'S-Staromchor?' Miss Newell's sightless eyes flickered over him, around him, her voice uncertain. 'You...you are still there, aren't you?'

There was a flinty sharpness in the depths of that voice. Here was a woman, Finlay was starting to see, who assumed the worst of people. Did she really think he would just walk away without declaring the conversation at an end?

Or was this merely another method of hers to keep people away?

'I am still here,' he said softly.

Something like a shadow of a smile flickered across Miss Newell's face. 'I thought so.'

'How could you tell?'

'The world is different when you are close.'

Heat evidently blossomed over her cheeks and was mirrored by the heat in his own. Finlay could never have hoped for such a sign of her regard, but—

'I should not have said that.'

'I am glad you did,' returned Finlay, his heart skipping a painful beat. 'And I wish you would call me Finlay.'

He did not have to listen for the shock; he could see it on her face and in the way her breasts rose with the sudden intake of breath. Every part of his notice seemed attuned to Miss Newell.

'Why on earth would you wish that?' she said softly.

Finlay grinned, wishing to goodness she could see him. This whole conversation would be so much easier if he could reply with a mere sparkle in his eyes, a look of wicked mischief.

As it was, he was forced to say aloud, 'Because…because I wish to call you Marilla.'

It was an intimate request—but then, when a man had fed a woman by hand, in public, such things ceased to be so wicked. At least, in his mind.

Evidently not in Miss Newell's. 'And why on earth would I give an earl permission to do that?'

'You know, the least you could do is attempt to see past my title,' Finlay said with just a hint of irritation.

It wasn't until Miss Newell raised a sardonic eyebrow that he realized his error.

'Ah. Erm…figure of speech,' he mumbled.

Damn and blast it, he would have to go and say something

like that! Attempt to see past his title? He had to say that…to a blind woman?

'I know what you meant,' Miss Newell said softly, and there appeared to be real understanding in her voice. 'Lord knows, you aren't the first to fall foul of a slip of the tongue.'

And a roar of anger, unbidden and uncontained and most unexpected, rose in Finlay's throat.

'Who the devil has done that?'

'Oh, most people,' Miss Newell said, seemingly misunderstanding his ire. 'Do not concern yourself, my lord. I do not take offence, not any longer. I am more than a match for them.'

Yet there was a tired lilt to her voice that suggested something else. Some other kind of injury.

'You don't have to push people away all the time.'

'Yes, I do,' she said firmly, a renewed strength in her voice. 'I always do, and I always will. Besides, I like being alone.'

Finlay had not intended to speak the obvious truth, but there it was. 'No, you don't.'

A flicker—just for a moment, it looked like she was about to say something. But she could not deny it, even if the flush in her cheeks suggested she did not appreciate him stating it.

Finlay swallowed. 'I still wish to call you Marilla.'

The words had slipped from his mouth before he could stop them, but Finlay saw to his surprise that Miss Newell did not shy away from his tenderness.

Her lips curled into a smile. 'I suppose you do. But the people I like call me Rilla.'

Oh, hell. What did that mean?

'So,' said Finlay, desperately attempting to calculate precisely what the best approach here was. It would be so much easier if there weren't so much noise in this place, the music and the chatter rising to such a pitch that his ears seemed full. 'So…'

It appeared for a moment that she was not going to put him out of his misery. Then she dipped her gaze to her hands.

'You may call me Marilla, I suppose,' she said airily, as though she had bestowed a great gift. 'I am still not sure about you, Finlay Jellicoe.'

A barb of boiling-hot steel pierced his heart as Finlay grinned like a dolt. Hearing his name on her lips—it was almost as potent as being given permission to speak her name.

Almost.

'Marilla,' he breathed, wishing he were closer to her. 'Marilla…'

'But you must wish to return to your party,' Marilla said, the stiffness which had momentarily melted away now returning to ice over her expression. She turned to look towards the dancers, her face impassive. 'Do not let me detain you.'

Finlay closed the gap between the two of them. Perhaps it was not very politic. Perhaps others would stare, and gossip would arise, and Isabelle would see and break off the engagement.

He stepped back. 'I have no wish to return to my party.'

Marilla raised an eyebrow. 'You…you do not?'

Finlay shook his head, muttered a curse under his breath that was thankfully lost in the thrum of applause and warm laughter as a dance ended and the assembly applauded both dancers and musicians, and knew what he was about to say was a dreadful mistake.

A mistake he wanted to make.

'I would rather spend time with you, Marilla,' Finlay said softly. 'I find that lately, I would always rather spend time with you.'

Chapter Seven

But really, this was a most ridiculous idea. Of all the people who could be chosen for such an idiotic, unthinking, preposterous—

'I know I can rely on you,' said the Pike sternly as a wall of noise hit Rilla in the face.

It was almost unbearable. Like losing another sense. The barrage of noise was heavy like iron, a painful medley of sharp and soft. Sharp like the clack of heels on marble, the slam of a door, the clink of a glass hitting stone, shattering. Soft like the rush of fabrics, the gentle laughter, the susurration of a thousand voices murmuring.

Rilla staggered slightly, putting out her hand to she knew not where, the other grasping her cane. Damned cane. All it did was remind her of her difference.

Oh, God, she had known this would be a mistake. She should have put her foot down, refused point-blank to come. One would think, after all, that her almost complete lack of sight would protect her from such nonsense.

How on earth would she navigate such a situation?

'I've got you,' came Sylvia's quiet voice.

There came a hand on her arm, a steadying sensation, the world righting itself…but the noise was still incredible.

Where had the Pike brought them, a cattle market?

'The Assembly Rooms at Brighton are most impressive,' the Pike's voice continued, as though she had neither noticed nor cared just how unsettled Rilla had become. 'You can see, Miss Smith— Miss Smith, are you attending?'

From the fractious tone of the woman, Rilla presumed Daphne was not.

'I am sorry, Miss Pike.'

'I did not choose the three of you to attend me on this trip to Brighton merely for my own benefit,' snapped the curt voice of the Wallflower Academy proprietress. 'You three have been my charges the longest, and it is time you put what you have learned in my lessons to good use—in public!'

'And yet here I am, and I can't think of a single thing I've learned in that damned lesson of hers,' Sylvia muttered in Rilla's ear.

Rilla attempted to nod. They were no longer moving, which was a great relief, but it was still highly disconcerting.

She did not like leaving the Wallflower Academy. Not because its environs were particularly pleasing. No, it was that once Rilla had grown accustomed to the layout of a place, it was highly unsettling to be dropped somewhere entirely unfamiliar. The corridors of the Wallflower Academy were well known to her, her seat in the drawing room, her place at the pianoforte, her knitting bag. Even the gardens held no surprises for her.

It was all hers, and everything right where she expected it to be.

But this…venturing out to Brighton, of all places, a carriage ride away and with none of the certainty she relied upon…

Rilla's jaw tightened.

To be reduced to a dependent.

Sylvia's hand had remained on her arm. 'Let's find a quiet place near the wall, shall we?'

Rilla attempted to show her gratitude through her lack of complaining, though wasn't sure whether her friend understood the great effort.

Miss Pike chattered on with every step. 'And as chaperone,

I am expecting you, Miss Newell, to provide a careful examination of—'

'Miss Pike,' Rilla said, her tongue loosening as she and Sylvia came to a stop. Yes, she could feel the sense of a wall behind her. Good. That would reduce the approaches that strangers could make. 'What on earth did you think you were doing, bringing me here?'

There was a hesitation, a momentary silence. She presumed the proprietress of the Wallflower Academy was looking, bewildered, at the two other wallflowers.

Rilla had once asked Sylvia to explain what bewildered looked like. Oh, she knew how it felt. That strange dizziness in one's mind, the sense the world was shifting, an inability to understand what on earth had happened.

But what did it look like?

'Why, I brought you to act as chaperone for Miss Bryant and Miss—'

'And how precisely do you expect me to do that,' Rilla interrupted, as sweetly as she could manage. 'Considering I cannot see?'

It was perhaps a tad harsh. Lord knew, Miss Pike had never treated her poorly due to her lack of sight. But still, Rilla had had enough. Wrenched from the one place she felt comfortable, suffering motion sickness all the way along the coastal road, then forced out of their snug lodgings to attend a gathering in which she could not participate?

No. Not without protest.

'Ah,' came the voice of the Pike.

Rilla heard what appeared to be a snort. It came from Sylvia's general direction.

'I suppose it will be difficult for you to—'

'Miss?' said a new voice. A low one, a dark one—a man's voice. 'Though we have not had the pleasure of being introduced, would you do me the honour of dancing with me? Mr Jones is the name.'

Rilla forced down a smile. Well, it was equal odds which of her friends the man had approached. Both Daphne and Sylvia, apparently, were very pretty. Refined. Elegant.

The response of the Pike, on the other hand…

'Not properly introduced!' she was saying, in full flow. 'No, no, I am sorry, young man, this simply won't do. Come on, we'll find the master of ceremonies. You too, Sylvia.'

'But—'

'But me no buts,' uttered the woman grimly. 'Miss Newell, you stay there. You…you just stay there.'

Footsteps sounded, hurried and accompanied by the continued muttering of the Pike, and started to drift away. And then they were gone, and Rilla was left alone.

Letting out a large sigh, she supposed it wasn't the end of the world. She had no difficulty in standing for long periods of time, and all she had to do was wait for the Pike's feet to tire and they would all return to their temporary lodgings.

In fact, it was pleasant to be left alone with her thoughts for five minutes. After that carriage ride and Sylvia's incessant chatter—

And then he was there. Before her. Finlay.

Words slipped from her mouth without much intervention from her mind, and before she knew it, Rilla had blurted out, 'But this is Brighton.'

If only her voice could remain steady and that she was not alone.

Oh, but that isn't true, is it? whispered a voice just in the back of her mind. *You haven't been able to stop thinking about him, have you? Why, in the carriage ride here when Sylvia was enumerating the multiple ways the Wallflower Academy had injured her, you allowed yourself to imagine—*

Their conversation meandered and Rilla found herself struggling to pay attention sufficiently to speak. Words that she was most certainly not going to say continuously threatened to burst from her lips.

I've never gained so much enjoyment from food. Not ever before.

If you think I'm going to let you—
Didn't you enjoy it?

What did he want from her?

None of that was appropriate to say. Admitting such a thing to anyone was shameful indeed, but to disclose to the very object of her desire that she was so conscious of him, so warmed by his presence? For that was what this was, wasn't it? Rilla had never felt anything like it before, and she had run the gamut of emotions in the past.

Fear, anger, joy, bitterness, regret…she had known them all.

But not desire. Not this delight that he was here, Finlay, in Brighton. Not this wish she could step closer to him, feel his skin against hers.

And then she was giving him the opportunity to leave, and he did not take it, and Rilla could not understand why he was being so…so odd. So attentive. So—

'I would rather spend time with you, Marilla.'

Rilla's lips parted.

How could he say such a thing, with calm, and equanimity, and a sense he was telling the absolute complete truth?

'Besides, I want to dance.'

A cold chill rushed across her collarbone. 'I am not stopping you.'

'No, but I'll need your hand,' returned Finlay with alacrity.

This time Rilla really did laugh. 'You are jesting.'

'Not in the slightest.'

'But…' He had to be jesting. Rilla could not see the man,

but honestly, he was being ridiculous! 'I... I don't know how,' she said quietly.

Admitting such a thing was an unpleasant experience. Rilla knew well the limitations the world placed upon her, and it was galling to admit that there was something she could not do.

Dancing was all very well at the Wallflower Academy ballroom, with the Pike shouting out instructions and no one likely to get in her way. That was different.

But here? In public? In the Brighton Assembly Rooms?

'My cane... I cannot possibly...'

'I'll give it to a serving woman. Here...'

It was pulled gently from her hands, her one anchor to time and space, and then she was at sea, utterly lost, ready to be buffeted back and forth in the noise and the clamour.

A hand rested on her arm, then came a tug. Rilla stepped forward, unable to resist the pull.

'Finlay...'

'You know, I do like it when you call me Finlay,' came the low, guttural voice of the man who appeared to be pulling her through a crowd of people. Rilla could feel fabrics brush up against her arms, just past her gloves. 'Though you should probably call me "my lord" now that we are in the line.'

And he was gone and Rilla panicked, flaring dread rising as she stood somewhere in the middle, she presumed, of a room filled with people.

'One step forward, curtsey,' Finlay said quietly.

It was not an order. Not quite.

True, there was a certainty in his speech that brooked no opposition. Here was a man who spoke and was accustomed to being obeyed.

And it wasn't as though she had much choice.

Rilla did not have to think. Her feet obeyed, her knees bending as she curtseyed towards a gentleman she could not see in a rush of other skirts either side of her.

'And back,' came his command.

A shiver of something hot and delicious rushed through Rilla's back. People did not order her about! She had her own thoughts, her own determination, her own—

And wasn't it wicked, being told what to do by such a man as this?

The music continued and for a moment she froze, unsure what to do, conscious of the many eyes now following her.

'Step left, right hand up,' came the now expected instructions. 'And back…'

It was a slow dance, for which Rilla was thankful. A fast dance would have made it impossible for Finlay to give her moment-by-moment directions, but her ear was so attuned to his voice now, she could make out even the slightest hint through the din of the dance.

And what a dance. Each time Finlay's hand touched hers, every time his presence thrummed beside her, Rilla could not deny the sensual attraction that flowed through her.

He was…

And she was…

In danger.

That was the thought that rose to the top of her whirling mind as Finlay promenaded her, slowly, down the set.

Feeling like this was not safe. Feeling like this about anyone was…was a weakness. It was a chance for them to hurt her, to disappoint her. To reduce her to something she was not.

Caring for this earl was only going to bring her pain, and she most certainly should not permit it.

When the dance ended, therefore, Rilla told herself sternly that her heart was thundering in her chest due to the efforts of the dance, and no other reason.

'Some fresh air?' Finlay's hand had taken hers again, placing it on his arm as her cane was pushed into her other palm.

She did not pull away.

Because I require someone to navigate for me, Rilla thought sternly.

For no other reason.

The Brighton Assembly Rooms surely had a balcony. That was her first thought after Finlay had woven their way through the hubbub of people—no sign of the Pike, thank goodness—and opened a door to reveal fresh air.

But when Rilla was guided down steps instead of onto a terrace into the night air, she started to realize they were not stepping outside, but leaving.

Leaving the Assembly Rooms. Alone.

The sharp scent of salt and the crunch of pebbles under her feet revealed a very different story.

'You…you have taken me to the beach!'

'Well, when in Rome. Brighton,' Finlay amended, and she could hear the laughter in his voice. 'Here, sit on my coat.'

It was most disorientating, lowering oneself not to a chair or sofa but to the crunch of pebbles. But there was something intoxicating about the sea breeze tugging at her curls, the smell of the sea and driftwood piercing in her nostrils, the gentle lapping of the sea not too far away.

And the warm presence of Finlay beside her.

'Now, tell me,' he said jovially, as though he frequently escorted wallflowers out of public places to interrogate them on beaches. 'What's next for Miss Marilla Newell?'

Rilla was nonplussed. Well, it was hardly an exciting question. 'The Pike will probably tire in an hour or two, and…'

'I don't mean tonight,' came his quiet voice.

'Oh,' she said, a mite unbalanced. 'Well. We do not intend to stay long in Brighton, and Sylvia—'

'No, I don't mean— I mean the future. Your future,' said Finlay. His voice was gentle, encouraging. 'You cannot intend to stay at the Wallflower Academy forever. Not a woman of your beauty and wit.'

Beauty and wit.

When was the last time someone had described her thus? Rilla could not recall. She could not recall it ever happening.

And perhaps it was the unseasonably warm breeze, or the lull of the tide, or the fact that her heart was still fluttering from the dance. Perhaps it was the rebellious nature of leaving the dance, the scandalous nature of being alone with an earl.

Whatever it was loosened her tongue. Rilla found herself saying, 'Well, whatever I intend to do, I can't… I won't go back home.'

A subtle sound was accompanied by a movement. Finlay appeared to be leaning back on his hands. 'And why is that?'

Rilla wet her lips.

How was it possible to feel so safe with a gentleman, and yet so in danger?

'I… I do not believe they would welcome my return. My sisters—one is married, and I have two younger who are unmarried—are awaiting my marriage or admission into spinsterhood, and then they can enter into Society.'

'I do not see why.'

'You know how it is The elder must marry before the younger enters Society. And in truth, I do not think my parents ever fully recovered from the scandal of my broken engagement,' Rilla said, more harshly than she had intended. 'With no brothers and an entailed estate, something has to be done and I am not the daughter to do it. A Newell wedding would blot all that out. My sister Nina's two babies have already done some of the work, bless her.'

The words had flowed before she could stop them, and she was not surprised at the silence from the gentleman beside her.

Yes, sometimes you just had to speak, and that speech would drive away the only man who had bothered to pay more than five minutes of attention to you. What had she been thinking? There was no reason for—

'That is…that is outrageous!' Finlay spluttered, voice breaking with seemingly suppressed emotion. 'Your broken— I am most certain it was not your fault, so why should you be punished for some brute's…? Damn. Oh, damn. Oh, fiddlesticks.'

Rilla was laughing now.

How could she not be?

'You do not have to fear. Sylvia swears like a sailor. There are few curses I have not heard.'

The almost inaudible chuckle made her heart skip a beat. 'I do apologize. It's just… Well, you are the most interesting woman I have met in…in a long time. And beautiful. The idea of not wishing to— I mean, any man who has eyes in his… damn.'

She did not even have the wherewithal to be offended.

What was Finlay trying to say? Was he…? No. He couldn't be.

'You are trying to seduce me.'

'Can you be seduced?'

'No,' said Rilla, perhaps a mite harsher than she had intended. 'So I wouldn't bother if I were you.'

'But half of the fun is the flirtation,' came Finlay's teasing voice. 'More than half, if the flirtation is of any calibre.'

Despite herself a slow smile crept over her face. 'And you believe you offer flirtation of a high calibre?'

It was a foolish thing to say. What did she know? How could she compare Finlay Jellicoe's flirting to any other man's?

No man had ever bothered.

There was a shifting movement beside her. Even if she had not felt the pebbles move, she would have known Finlay had moved to be closer to her. His scent was stronger, and she could feel the warmth of his chest as his shoulder touched hers.

And even without those two senses, she would have known. How, Rilla could not explain, but she would.

There was something about Finlay that made it impossible not to know when he was close.

'I only offer flirtation of the highest calibre.' His voice was warm, soft, smooth, enticing. It was a voice a woman could grow painfully accustomed to. 'And you may attempt to deny it, Marilla Newell, but you like me.'

She did like him, and she would deny it, if pushed.

This man—any man—was not supposed to charm her so utterly, so quickly. She was not supposed to think about that dance as shivers of heat shot through her body. She should not want to feel his hands on hers once more. To know his touch.

Well, there was only one way to nip that in the bud. Some good old Rilla Newell sarcasm.

'I knew you would be attracted to me,' she said airily, as though she said such things all the time. 'But you do not have to make it so obvious, my lord.'

Rilla expected a laugh. She expected a denial. At the very least, she expected him to rise, brush off the dirt from his breeches, then coldly suggest he return her to the Assembly Rooms.

What she did not expect was for a warm hand to graze her cheek, a thumb to part her lips, and a low voice to say, 'I'm going to kiss you now. Unless you want me to stop.'

Rilla wet her lips, mouth dry, and before she could speak, Finlay Jellicoe, Earl of Staromchor, was kissing her.

And oh, what a kiss. With searing heat and delicate power, his tongue teased her lips apart and lavished pleasure on her mouth such as Rilla could never have imagined.

Every part of her body had come alive. She could sense herself on the beach, kissing Finlay, in a way she had never known herself to feel. The temptation to lean back, pull him against her, feel the crush of his chest, the weight of him—

And then it was over.

Rilla blinked, her eyes dry.

Had she just...? Had he just...?

'Well,' she said with a long, low breath. 'As long as you don't fall in love with me, Your Lordship, I suppose I shall chalk that up to high spirits.'

It was a foolish thing to say. The moment she had said it, Rilla cringed.

She cringed even harder when the man seated beside her chuckled, a low rumble in his chest making her think of heat and the way he seemed to know precisely how she wanted to be kissed.

'I wouldn't worry about that,' came Finlay's low voice. 'I have no intention of falling in love with anyone.'

Chapter Eight

It was not a long walk from the Brighton Assembly Rooms to his lodgings, but after kissing Marilla Newell senseless on the beach, Finlay decided not to take a carriage back. The cool of the evening was required.

His thoughts meandered back to those stolen kisses, causing him to almost slip off the pavement as his footsteps came too close to the edge.

'Watch it!'

Finlay turned, slightly stunned, to see a barouche driver shake a fist in his general direction. He merely grinned.

How could he do anything else? He had shared what was perhaps the most incredible evening with a woman, one he could never have predicted. Just a few short weeks ago, Marilla was nothing to him. He had not even known that she had existed.

Dear God, a world without Miss Marilla Newell. How had he managed to stand it?

It had been a wrench to leave her, but as Miss Pike had started to look for her wayward charge, there had been no choice. Not after being informed by a strangely morose Bartlett that Isabelle and his mother had called the carriage to return to their lodgings an hour ago.

Finlay knew precisely what would happen if he stayed. He would offer to escort the Wallflower Academy party to their lodgings, and before he knew it he would start to declare nonsense about love and affection and marriage.

And he couldn't do that, could he?

Finlay's wandering feet should have taken him straight to the rooms his mother had taken. It was but a five-minute walk.

But in the gloom of the evening, with partygoers dressed in their finery, pie sellers yelling their wares, and a great deal of noise and excitement on every street, Finlay found calm in the midst of them.

And in that calm he knew he had to ask himself one question.

What was he going to do about Marilla?

Finlay passed the building which held his mother and Isabelle but did not turn aside. He could not go up now. He needed to think—and he could not help but feel that the presence of his mother would hardly help matters.

Instead he continued on, passing a lamp lighter, two gentlemen clearly already deep in their cups, and a woman who was attempting to solicit their interest.

I knew you would be attracted to me. But you do not have to make it so obvious, my lord.

Finlay's manhood stiffened at the mere memory of what they had shared together, what he had wanted to share with her. All his thoughts, his feelings, his emotions.

His heart.

For all that this had started out as a bet, a jest between himself and Bartlett, Finlay knew it could go so much further than that.

No, this was getting out of hand. Try as he might to convince himself that his heart was not getting entangled, he could no longer pretend it was something else. That meant he had to act; he had to speak to Isabelle.

Guilt crushed his chest but Finlay could see no other alternative. He had to break off his engagement with Miss Carr, break it to his mother that he had made another choice, and break all Society's expectations by courting Marilla.

Oh, it would hardly be an enjoyable conversation. There

was nothing more that he wanted to avoid, now he came to think about it.

Isabelle would be alone, unprotected, unguarded.

But she will have no debts, Finlay tried to console himself as he stepped across the road and walked around a corner.

Almost all the Carr debts had been paid, had they not? He had done that for her. True, it would be a challenge to find a husband without a dowry, yes, but there were no outstanding arrears to drag her down.

'You did that, at least,' Finlay muttered.

'You talking to me, fine sir?' said a newspaper seller, gazing up at him.

Finlay blinked. 'What? Oh, no. No, my apologies.'

'Least you could do is buy a paper,' sniffed the young man.

Now that he came to look properly, he was nothing more than a child, really. Finlay stuffed a hand in his pockets, pulled out a sixpence, and gave it to him. Then he kept on walking.

'Oi! Oi, doncha want ya paper?'

Finlay ignored him. His mind was already whirling with too many thoughts, too much information. Too many decisions.

And the thing was, there wasn't anyone he could go to for advice.

He knew what his mother would say. He had made an offer to Miss Carr, and he should honour it. A gentleman should have nothing less expected of him—and an earl? His word was law. His word was supposed to be trustworthy.

He couldn't go to Bartlett. Oh, how Bartlett would crow over him, Finlay knew, if he made the mistake of going to his closest friend. After all their talk about a flirtation, Bartlett would find it most amusing that Finlay had managed to lose his heart—and to a wallflower, of all people.

Finlay's stomach lurched.

The trouble was, the one person whose opinion truly mattered to him was…was Cecil.

Brushing away an errant tear that Finlay was not going to permit to fall, he could not deny that it was Cecil's advice he craved. A rush of guilt poured through him every time he considered breaking off his engagement with the man's sister—but then, Cecil had never asked him to offer a marriage of convenience to Isabelle, had he?

Finlay had done so because he had thought it right, but had Isabelle expected such a thing?

He tried desperately to remember her reaction when he had first, awkwardly and stiffly, proposed the match.

Had she appeared in any way excited? Joyful? Relieved, even?

No. No, there had just been a sort of stoic acceptance.

Relief sparked in his chest, removing some of the twisting doubts around his heart. Well, Finlay had to speak to her, break it off. Why, for all he knew, she would be delighted to be free. She hardly cared for him, as far as he could tell.

And she was a pretty sort of woman, he supposed. There would surely be someone else willing to marry her.

Finlay's shoulders lightened immediately as the load bearing down on them melted away.

He was going to marry Marilla.

Well, first he had a little work to do on that front, he supposed. Marilla may welcome his kisses, but marriage—that was quite another thing entirely.

Granted she was a member of the Wallflower Academy. Surely she would accept the hand of any passable man to get out of that place?

And to be sure, he had the slight inconvenience of a fiancée. That was nothing that a quiet and delicate conversation couldn't solve.

And then, Finlay thought as his heart rose, he could start the charm offensive. Show Marilla that earls were not all blackguards—that this earl, at the very least, was not.

The fluttering in his chest was growing, paired now with the warmth he had felt on the beach.

Yes, it was sudden. But when one knew, one knew. That was all there was to it.

All he had to do was break off an engagement a few weeks before the wedding, try to calm his mother from her hysterics—he knew she would have them—then propose to Marilla and convince her to marry an earl.

Finlay sighed as he approached the front door that led to his lodgings. Simple.

Shutting the door behind him and leaning against it heavily, Finlay congratulated himself on his decision. After all, it wasn't as though he had to do anything about it now. He could relax this evening, perhaps have a long bath to soothe his aching muscles, and then tomorrow—

'Ah, Your Lordship,' said Turner politely, stepping into the hall. 'I thought I heard you enter.'

Finlay stifled a smile. It was Turner's pride that he always was there to welcome the Earl of Staromchor back at all hours. It had become a form of competitiveness with the most senior footman, and once again, the older man had triumphed.

'I have placed your guest in the drawing room, and your mother is entertaining her,' said Turner, his frown still lining his forehead.

Finlay's heart skipped a beat.

Guest? Her?

Surely it was not possible. Why on earth his mother would invite Rilla he had no idea. He had never mentioned—

'Miss Carr, I believe, has rung for some supper,' said his butler delicately. 'Apparently the fare at the Brighton Assembly Rooms tonight was insufficient.'

The slight slump of his shoulders was, Finlay hoped, covered by the debonair shrug that he swiftly forced. Oh, of course.

Technically, he supposed, Isabelle was their guest. Foolish of him. 'Oh. Oh, I suppose so?'

'Shall I announce you?'

'Thank you, but I am almost certain my mother and my betrothed know who I am,' said Finlay, frustration seeping out. 'That will be all, Turner.'

Whether or not his servant appreciated the abrupt dismissal, he was not sure. Finlay did not look up when his butler marched away, and dropped his head in his hands when he was certain he was alone.

Oh, God. He had to face her—though perhaps this was for the best. The conversation had to be had, and it was far better to do so in private with his mother in attendance so that she could accept the change in their plans.

Now all he had to do was find the right words.

But as Finlay approached the drawing room, it appeared there were already plenty of words already being spoken in the elegantly apportioned room. The door to the corridor was ajar, and just as Finlay reached out for the door handle, some of those words caught his ears.

And he froze.

'I care deeply about his happiness, of course, but I cannot help but feel—'

'You will make him very happy, I am sure.'

Finlay hesitated, guilt searing through his heart.

It was his mother and Isabelle, talking in quiet voices. Their voices were full of restraint, somehow, as though they were talking around a particular topic for fear of disturbing it.

For fear of what it could reveal.

'His happiness is… It is the most important thing to me,' Isabelle was saying, her voice warm and full of affection. 'There is not a single day that does not go by when I do not think of him.'

Finlay's mouth fell open.

He had never heard Isabelle speak in such a manner. There

was more than warmth and affection in those tones—there was love.

And he knew damned well it was love, because that was how he knew he sounded whenever he thought of Marilla.

Surely...surely he had not been so blind? Surely Isabelle Carr had not fallen in love with him?

'You do not speak with him about it, I suppose?'

That was his mother. Finlay leaned closer to the door, careful not to push it open any farther, desperate to hear more.

'Speak to him about...?'

'About how you feel,' came the dowager countess's voice. It was serious—far more serious than Finlay could recall her ever being.

Well, this was a serious business, he thought darkly. This marriage of convenience was about to become something entirely different.

'Oh, I could never speak to him about the depths of my feelings.' Isabelle's voice almost sounded apologetic. 'Besides, I do not think it would be appropriate. He does not expect it. He would not... I do not think he would wish it.'

And the guilt Finlay had been pushing aside as much as he could all evening, from the moment he had decided to take Marilla to the beach, roared through him like a dam had broken.

How had he been so—well, there was no other way to say it—so blind? All this time, he had been operating under the assumption that Isabelle was as nonchalant about their engagement as he was. She had never shown much interest in him, hardly spoken to him since Cecil had died, had never suggested she felt any joy in becoming his wife...

And now he was to learn that this was merely because of the depths of her feelings?

'Love is a strange thing,' the dowager countess was saying. Even through the door, Finlay could hear the power of her words. His mother was someone who always knew her own mind. 'A person may think they are in love, but in fact all they have is admiration and affection borne from childhood.'

Finlay swallowed. Had Isabelle ever shown any preference for him when they were children? He could not recall…but then, he had hardly been thinking of such a thing, had he?

'Oh, but this is far more than mere preference.' Isabelle's voice was direct, determined; she was absolutely sure of herself. Finlay could not recall ever hearing her speak so—not since she had returned from the Trinderhaus School for Young Ladies. 'I love him, my lady. Everything he says is music to my ears, everything he does is the best thing a man has ever done!'

Finlay's eyes widened. *Oh, hell.*

'Whenever I am with him, I can think of nothing but the pleasure I gain from being in his presence,' continued Isabelle, her voice warming with every word. 'Whenever I am not with him, I am overcome by longing, by counting down the days, the very hours until I can be with him again.'

Hell's bells.

'I do not believe I have ever met a man who has so perfectly attuned himself to my needs, my wishes,' said Isabelle tenderly. 'The kindness he has shown me—'

'He is a very kind man,' the dowager countess agreed lightly. 'I suppose.'

Finlay almost snorted, but managed to stop himself in time. Well, that was hardly high praise from a mother, but as it was his mother, it was rather more than he had expected. She never was one for over-the-top declarations of affection.

Very kind, indeed.

'He is the very pinnacle of manhood,' Isabelle said, her voice lowering. 'I love him, my lady. He is the only person I could ever conceive of marrying. Being his wife—'

'Your wedding is in a few weeks.'

'Y-yes. Yes, I know.'

Finlay allowed a long, slow breath to escape from his lungs

as the two women continued chatting. He did not listen to the words, not any longer. He did not need to.

Well. Isabelle Carr was deeply in love. It could not be denied— he did not need to see her to sense the depth of her feeling.

How she had managed to keep such powerful affections so hidden, he did not know…but then, Finlay was starting to realize that there was a great deal about the feminine psyche that had passed him by.

Perhaps Bartlett knew about all this?

'I am not sure what to do.'

Finlay tried to slow his breathing as Isabelle's words cut through his mind.

'Do? I do not believe there is anything to do. You are getting married.'

'And marriage is a very important thing, yes,' came Isabelle's soft voice. 'I would not wish to—'

'You love him,' said the dowager countess sharply.

Finlay's heart rose to his throat. His fingers were clutching the door handle so tightly that even in the shadowy darkness of the corridor, he could see the whites of his bone pressing through the skin.

'I love him,' came Isabelle's voice, and it was bolder now, sharper. More like the Isabelle he had known.

Was she still in there somewhere?

He heard his mother sigh. 'Well, in that case, there is nothing for it.'

Finlay straightened up, resolve stiffening in his chest.

Yes, there was nothing for it; his mother was completely right. How precisely he had managed to entrap himself like this, in a cage, he did not know, but the point was that he had.

Isabelle Carr loved him.

It was not a love he had wanted. He had not demanded it, nor attempted to gain it. He had not courted or wooed; he had believed the whole thing to be a marriage of convenience that benefited her, yes, but did not touch her heart.

Well, now he knew he was wrong.

Finlay had only tried to do what was right, to care for Cecil's sister. Now he would have to do what was right, even if it kept him from the woman he…he felt something for. What it was, he would not yet name.

Not yet.

Whatever it was, it was hotter and far more tempting than the staid loyalty he felt for Isabelle. But he had to put that aside.

He stepped into the room.

'Finlay!' exclaimed Isabelle, cheeks suddenly splotched with red.

'There you are,' said the dowager countess, a frown on her face but a similar concern in her eyes.

Finlay attempted not to notice. He really should not have been eavesdropping, and he was hardly going to admit he had done so.

Still. There was one way to put Isabelle's mind to rest, and he was going to do that right now. Even if every word would have to be dragged from him. Even if Marilla's face swam in his mind, her laughter, her joy. Even if she was a woman he was now divided from forever.

The two ladies were seated on a sofa together near the fire. The drawing room had, until this moment, been one of his favourite rooms in these lodgings. The place was decorated in the French style—not too French, because Napoleon had made it far too unfashionable thanks to his ridiculous antics. But the paints were that delicate blue that the French so preferred, and the chandelier was designed to the French taste. The paintings on the walls, however, were distinctly British, the pianoforte in the corner Italian.

It had been a room where Finlay had spent a great deal of time. They always came here, whenever it was time to indulge his mother with a trip to Brighton. He had always been happy here. There had never been anything to connect it with sadness.

Now it would always hold the memories of this moment. This disaster. This decision.

'Miss Carr,' Finlay said formally. 'I wish you to know I am completely committed to this marriage. Our marriage.'

Isabelle was blinking furiously.

Dear God, was she blinking away tears of joy? Finlay thought wretchedly.

'That…that is… Well, I—'

'And I want you to be sure of this,' Finlay continued, hating every word but knowing she needed this reassurance. Lord knew he had hardly given her much over the last few weeks. 'There is nothing, nothing that will prevent our marriage from going ahead.'

'Staromchor,' his mother said quietly. 'I would wish to have a small word in your ear.'

Finlay glanced at his mother, almost irritated she was interrupting this very important conversation.

After all that she had just heard from Isabelle, did his mother not understand that this was crucial? That the poor woman evidently needed to be reassured, that she wanted to hear some sort of warmth from him?

The Dowager Countess of Staromchor was frowning. 'Staromchor. I really must speak with you about—'

'This is not the time, Mother,' Finlay snapped, turning away and back to Isabelle.

His future bride, for that was how he must consider her, was a beetroot red. 'Actually, my lord, I—'

'Look, I know you have expected more from me, and I suppose most of that is my own fault,' Finlay said in a rush, forcing the words out now in the hope that if he said them quickly enough, they would not be so painful. 'I have been an inattentive fiancé, I am afraid, but that changes from this moment on.'

Isabelle blinked, evidently confused. 'It…it does?'

'This marriage is important, and it will go ahead,' Finlay said firmly, as though there were nothing he wished for more in all the world. 'You deserve a wedding, Isabelle, and…and affection. I will do my best to give it to you.'

Even if I cannot match the depths of feeling you so clearly have for me, Finlay thought wretchedly. *Good grief, what did a man do when his wife was head over heels in love with him, and he was just…nonplussed?*

Well, he would have to learn. In a month or so, he would have a wife, and he would have to make it work.

Isabelle was still stammering. 'I… Well, I—'

'You can be assured of that,' said Finlay stiffly, walking over to her and bowing low.

Would it be too much to kiss her cheek? Yes, probably.

'You will be my wife, and I will be your husband, and we… we…'

He saw Isabelle swallow hard as she looked at her hands.

'We will live,' she said softly to her fingers, 'happily ever after.'

Nausea rose in Finlay's chest as the enormity of what he had done began to overwhelm him.

He was going to marry Isabelle Carr. He could no longer see Marilla, not in that way. Not as a woman who entranced and inspired him.

And he was instead to be wed to a woman whose insipidity had somehow come from nowhere, despite the fact that she apparently loved him.

'Happily,' Finlay said, his mouth dry. 'Happily ever after.'

Chapter Nine

It was a feeble protest that Rilla had put up. So feeble, in fact, that she had been slightly concerned that the Pike would suspect something.

As it was…

'I knew you would finally come around to my line of thinking,' Miss Pike declared importantly, rustling in the carriage as though she were a leaf in the wind. 'And Miss Smith is grateful, I am sure, for the companionship!'

If she knew Daphne, Rilla thought darkly, and she did, the woman was about as miserable as it was possible to be. She was a true wallflower, one who would have escaped this evening's entertainment if she could.

'So kind of the dowager countess to invite you, Miss Smith, to her card party this evening,' trilled the Pike as the carriage slowed to a jolting stop.

Rilla's wry smile must have gone unnoticed by the proprietess, for there was no reprimand. To the contrary, the Pike was unusually gracious to her, helping her down from the carriage without so much as a complaint that it delayed them from entering wherever it was they were, and placing her cane carefully in her hands.

'Now, this is a big night for Miss Smith,' the Pike hissed in Rilla's ear, as though Daphne was not standing right beside them. 'Heaven knows why she was invited.'

'I do believe she can hear you, Miss Pike,' said Rilla in a calm voice.

Her cane tapped on the ground experimentally. It was most irritating, having to depend on such a thing. The Wallflower Academy grounds were so well known to her now, she did not need a cane. She barely needed an arm to traverse the gardens, or even make her way to the stables. Not that she had much cause to.

A warm and slightly shaking hand took hers and then placed it on an arm. Daphne.

Guilt seared through Rilla as the three ladies moved up a small flight of steps. She was just as ignorant as Miss Pike as to why Daphne—Daphne Smith, of all people!—had been invited to such a thing.

Still, she could hardly complain. The Pike had demanded that Rilla act as chaperone, a ridiculous request yet again, but this time she was hardly going to argue.

She was going to see Finlay again.

Pushing aside the thought as best she could, Rilla submitted to having her pelisse taken off her by an unseen footman, her heart hammering.

The last time she had been with him, he had been kissing her furiously.

What on earth would he say when—

'Ah, Miss Smith, Miss Pike— Oh.'

Heat rushed to Rilla's cheeks. She had presumed she would have at least a few moments at the dowager countess's card party to collect herself before being thrust into the presence of the man she—

Of the man who had kissed her, Rilla attempted to tell herself. Nothing more.

Well. A little more.

Parts of her were unfurling like leaves which had closed during the cold of wintery night, desperate to feel the sun again.

The parts of her which had been subdued by the long sojourn in the Wallflower Academy were awake again.

She was ready to open her heart.

But the expected joy was not accompanied with the heat that was suffusing her lungs, drying out every breath, making it impossible to talk.

Because when Finlay had spoken there was such…such coldness.

'Oh, my lord, such a wonderful evening, I know we shall have a pleasant time,' Miss Pike was trilling in her best fawning voice. 'And to think, Miss Smith has caught your mother's eye! I did speak to her once about her acting as a sort of guide, or sponsor, you know. Almack's is such a wonderful place to find suitors, and I wondered…'

'My mother is in the room to the left,' came the short reply from Finlay. 'Please, Miss Pike, Miss Smith. Do go on in.'

Something settled a little in Rilla's stomach, making it less likely that her luncheon would be making an appearance.

Of course, he had to be stiff and sullen before the Pike. The last thing they wanted was for her to think that they…

They what?

Rilla had been unable to untangle precisely what it was that she felt for the man, and had most studiously avoided interrogating it. What good would that do?

Still. It was pleasing to be here, to be around him. The moment the Pike and Daphne were gone, they could—

'What are you doing here?' Finlay said, voice tinged with shock.

Rilla took a step back, her cane tapping on the ground instinctively to ensure she did not fall down an unsuspecting step.

Even with the cane, her head reeled.

What the—

'I don't know what you—'

'My mother's invitation was for Miss Smith, with Miss Pike as her companion.' Finlay's voice was distant.

Discomfort prickled against her temples. 'Miss Pike said—'

'Trust Miss Pike to take it upon herself to invite another. And you, of all people.'

Of course, came the sinking thought that nestled painfully in her heart, weighing it down like a lump of lead. Of course.

What had Rilla been thinking? She should have known that nothing would be different. That he wouldn't be different. That an earl couldn't be trusted.

All expectations of warmth and connection, of perhaps a repeat of the florid kiss he had poured down on her—all was forgotten.

She had to leave.

'Where do you think you're going?'

'Out,' Rilla snapped, unable to bear it. She had turned to what she recalled was the direction of the door. 'My pelisse, if you please.'

'You cannot think to—'

'Why stay? I am clearly unwanted, though that is hardly a new sensation and so I do not know why it bothers me so,' Rilla said, the words spilling out before she could stop them. 'My pelisse, please.'

Footsteps. The rustle of silk.

And yet no pelisse was placed in her hands or around her shoulders. To the contrary, Finlay spoke in a low voice, and not to her.

'Give it to me, and return to the door, please.'

Irritation sparked in the edges of Rilla's eyes. Trust an earl to order people about and just assume they would follow. What had she been thinking?

'This is why I shouldn't have trusted an earl,' she said in a low voice as presumably the footman returned to the door-way. She'd just have to hope he would follow the precept of most servants and pretend he could not hear a single thing. 'Just when I thought—'

'Thought what?'

Rilla struggled to articulate what was more a sensation than a thought, a feeling not a meaning.

She thought that there had been something between them. Something different. Something that meant her first kiss was going to mean something, go somewhere, though where precisely, she did not know.

Oh, she felt so foolish. How could she have come here, to his mother's house, and expected a welcome!

No, women like her were for kissing on a beach out of sight of the world. Not for actually acknowledging in public.

'You cannot out-argue me, you know,' came the irksome tease.

Her temper once again flared. 'I think you will find I am more than a match for any earl!'

'I will not deny it. Any earl would be lucky to—'

'Forget I said anything. Forget I came.' Rilla moved forward, pelisse or no. The very thought of staying here was unbearable.

'Rilla, wait!'

A hand on her arm. She jerked away violently. 'I told you. I hate it when—'

'And I suppose I should have just let you fall down the stairs and break your neck?' Finlay snapped, pulling her roughly back so that her arm burned. 'You might just have to accept that sometimes people are actually trying to help you!'

'And you might just have to accept that sometimes people don't want your help!' Rilla had attempted to keep her voice down, cognizant that other guests could arrive at any moment. And that blasted footman was still there. Oh, well, at least it would be something to protect her reputation.

Though she was not entirely sure, Rilla thought Finlay swore quietly under his breath.

'You are making this impossible.'

She had to laugh at that. 'I am? You are the untrustworthy one. The last time I saw you, it was kisses and—'

'Keep your voice down!'

But Rilla was fired up now, heat burning through her veins, shame and embarrassment coursing through her. To think she had let this man kiss her! Kiss her, and on a beach, in the dark!

And now he did not even want her here?

'Why is my presence here so odious to you?' she demanded, trying to keep her voice low. 'Why?'

There was a moment of silence. The silence grew longer and longer, and eventually what broke it was Finlay clearing his throat.

'I... I cannot say.'

Rilla snorted. 'What a surprise.'

'I don't like keeping secrets.'

'And I don't like being one!' she retorted, her cheeks burning at the merest hint of a suggestion. 'I mean, it's not like I am... I am not your... I won't be...'

'You do not have to sound so mortified,' came Finlay's quiet voice. 'Nothing happened.'

And just when she did not want them, tears promised to burn in the corners of her eyes.

Nothing happened. Oh, no, to an earl, she supposed nothing had happened. Just a fervent kiss on a beach. Just a sharing of herself in a way she had never done before. Just a connection formed that was heightened by the secrecy, and the smell of the sea, and the knowledge that such an assignation was forbidden.

Just Finlay, a man she had thought...

'I should have known,' Rilla said, her voice thick as she attempted to control her emotions. 'It's always the same. You know, I comforted myself when I was a child, and the maids were teasing me behind my family's back—they denied it when confronted, of course, and were permitted to stay—I comforted myself by telling myself that things would be better when I was older. Better!'

There was an odd sort of noise from Finlay. A sort of— could a grimace make a noise?

'You were teased by...by your family's maids?'

'Oh, yes, the maids, a footman. Once our housekeeper changed all the furniture in our drawing room so that I couldn't navigate by myself. I got a black eye, in the end,' Rilla said, the words pouring from her like water, righteous anger launching them forward. 'A village boy almost drowned me in a pond. Once, our vicar pulled me up to the front of church to demonstrate how the blind would no longer exist in heaven.'

'The bounder!'

'And that's nothing compared to what I endured when I was sent to school!' Now tears were threatening to pour down her face, but Rilla did everything she could to hold them back.

And she was well practised at such an art. Her life had required her to be.

'And yet again, and again, I told myself that when I was a woman, I would at least be respected,' Rilla continued, her fingers gripping the top of her cane as though it were the only thing rooting her to the earth. 'And I was engaged to the Earl of Porthaethwy.'

'I was going to ask you about that.'

'But of course, God forbid that I be happy,' she shot back at him, speaking over the quiet question with a rapid hiss of her own. 'I've never felt wanted, or safe, never known who to trust, and you are the perfect example, Finlay Jellicoe, of why—'

'Rilla...'

'Don't call me that,' Rilla said sharply. 'You haven't earned the right.'

Her words hung in the air, weighty with meaning and caught in the web of tension between them.

It wasn't supposed to be like this. A kiss like that, on the beach, was meant to be the beginning of something. Not the end of something.

Were her desires, her dreams, truly so odious to anyone she encountered? Once again Rilla forced back the tears, holding herself upright and ensuring her head did not drop.

There was no shame in wishing to be married—unless one was a wallflower, she supposed. And it wasn't as though a kiss was just a kiss, to some gentlemen at least. She had not expected, nor demanded, promises of happily-ever-after.

Even if her heart had longed for them.

'I'll call your carriage,' came Finlay's quiet words when the silence was eventually broken.

And the last remnant of hope—that he would fight for her, that he would try to convince her—died in Rilla's heart.

'Thank you,' she said stiffly. 'I'll wait in it.'

'And I will visit you at the Wallflower Academy to…to apologize properly.'

'I won't hold my breath,' Rilla said darkly, as the harsh fabric of a footman's livery brushed against her arm. She was being guided now, and not by Finlay. 'Do not bother to lower yourself, my lord, by coming to the Wallflower Academy unless you are certain—absolutely certain—that you can bear to be seen with me.'

A part of her hoped that Finlay would accompany her out to the carriage. A part of her hoped he would help her into it, and then be overcome with remorse and longing, and enter the carriage after her, and—

But they were foolish hopes. Hopes that were proved wrong.

And as Rilla waited for what felt like hours in the Wallflower Academy carriage, waiting for Miss Pike and Daphne to be finished at the card party, she told herself the same thing again and again.

You are not a match for an earl.

Chapter Ten

The Tudor manor rose beautiful and golden in the afternoon sun. With winter drawing ever closer, the sun was low enough to cast glints of sparkling gold on the windowpanes in the three-storey building.

And as Finlay rode along the drive and glanced at the formal gardens to his left, he saw two women. One he immediately ignored. The other was Marilla Newell.

And that was when he almost fell off his horse.

'Oh, damn!'

The rest of his curse was silenced by the unsettled neighing of Ceres, his horse. The two women turned, both staring curiously in the direction of the man who evidently couldn't control his own steed.

Finlay swallowed the embarrassment.

At least she hadn't seen him make a complete prat of himself, he told himself as he dismounted—shakily—and straightened his riding coat.

'I think your earl has fallen off his horse,' came the murmured whisper of the woman holding on to Marilla's arm.

Oh, for the love—

'I didn't fall,' Finlay called over the ten-yard gap between them. 'I… I dismounted.'

'He's not my earl,' he heard Marilla mutter into her friend's ear.

It wasn't Sylvia. This was a different wallflower: Miss

Smith, if he remembered. Not that he had much interest in her. It was the woman she was guiding around the formal knot garden he wished to see, though he could not have hoped to orchestrate such a perfect meeting as this.

Well. Discounting almost falling from Ceres, that was.

If only he could separate them, Finlay found himself musing as he stepped forward, hands hanging by his sides.

Were hands supposed to hang by your sides? What on earth did hands do, anyway? What had he ever done with his hands before? Had he ever had damned hands in his whole—

'My lord,' gushed the wallflower, dipping in a low curtsey that far exceeded what his rank demanded.

Finlay did not look at her. He looked at Marilla.

She was radiant. A delicate blue gown with a cream spencer jacket matched the bonnet which partially hid her dark rich curls. There was a frown on her forehead, a pained one that should have told him immediately he was not about to be welcomed.

And he did not care.

Staying away from Marilla Newell had proved impossible. So putting aside his guilt, and telling himself most firmly that there was no law against an engaged man talking to another woman, here he was.

Like a fool.

Finlay swallowed. The last time they had been together, he had refused to give any explanation as to his rudeness and aloofness, and she had revealed…well, some rather awful things about her past, and just how deeply he had hurt her.

Could hurt her again.

And yet…

'Would you be so good as to leave us to talk, Miss Smith?' Finlay asked with one of his most charming grins.

Miss Smith. Well, it was an innocent enough name for the illegitimate daughter of Lord Norbury, he supposed. His mother hadn't been able to stop wittering about the man all week. Apparently he—

Miss Smith immediately stammered, in a rush of red cheeks and downcast eyes, 'Oh, b-but that wouldn't do at all, m-my lord, I c-couldn't possibly.'

'Do you want to ruin my reputation?' came the expected hiss of Marilla.

'Just for a few moments, thank you, Miss Smith,' said Finlay smartly, as though the very idea of opposition was preposterous.

Miss Smith had dropped Marilla's arm in apparent shock. 'Oh, that won't be—'

'Excellent,' said Finlay brightly, taking the abandoned arm of Marilla just as swiftly as Miss Smith released it. 'My, there appears to be a very pleasant walk about this knot garden, Miss Newell. Will you favour me with your company?'

Miss Smith had already walked a great distance by the time he had finished his pronouncement, and was not surprised when Marilla instantly wrenched her arm from his.

'No one is impressed by your posturing,' she said tartly, turning away.

There was no real malice in her words. At least, Finlay did not think there was. He was still learning the contours of Marilla's moods, the changes so instant he could barely keep up.

But he wanted to. By God, he wanted to.

'It's not posturing,' Finlay said as he watched her. 'And you were the one who announced me with my title, I didn't— How are you doing that?'

He hadn't intended to actually ask the question, but it was impossible not to.

It was a miracle. Despite the complexity of the garden, the multiple low hedges weaving around in intricate knots, Marilla was walking around them seemingly without a care in the world.

How was she not falling over?

Marilla glanced back over her shoulder. 'Doing what?'

'That!' Finlay knew he should have explained himself better, but he could barely articulate it. Stepping forward, he tried to take her arm. 'Let me help.'

'It may surprise you to learn that I don't need your help,' said Marilla tartly. 'And I don't appreciate people just touching me whenever they feel like it. If I want help, I'll ask!'

Her voice rang clear and sharp across the garden. A pair of ravens squawked unhappily and rose from a nearby oak tree.

Finlay bit his lip.

Well, when she put it like that...

'I am sorry.'

Marilla turned her ear to him as though attempting to take in every facet of every syllable. 'I beg your pardon?'

'I apologize. I shouldn't have touched you. I just—' He caught himself just in time. 'There is no excuse. I am sorry.'

She stared at him, those delectable lips parted in shock.

'And while I'm at it, I suppose I have a few more apologies to offer,' Finlay said quickly, before she could send him away. 'I—'

'If you are going to apologize for that kiss,' Marilla said in a warning tone.

His shoulders slumped, though he was momentarily heartened by a flashing thought.

She wants to be kissed again.

'No,' said Finlay quietly. 'No, I am afraid it is far more serious than that. It's... Well, I should not have been so abrupt with you. At my mother's card party.'

'No, you should not.'

There was a hardness to her words which concealed her true thoughts. Her face, too, was difficult to read.

Finlay swallowed. 'I cannot pretend to share all, Marilla—

Miss Newell, apologies. I am not a perfect man, and I make no claim to be. I would, however, like…like to be a friend to you.'

More than a friend. But he had committed to Isabelle Carr, so a friend was all Marilla could be.

Perhaps the tension and the regret seeped into his voice as Finlay added, 'Lord knows why you would forgive me. I'm not sure I would forgive me. I… My mother has expectations of me.'

Expectations that I will marry a completely different woman.

And quite unexpectedly, a slow smile spread across Marilla's face.

'Well. That's the first time I've heard an earl admit to being unforgiveable. And you are… Well, you are not the only one whose parents have expectations. You are forgiven. This time.'

Continuing to pick her way through the complex knot garden, she did not forbid him from joining her. That was the rationale Finlay offered himself, at least, for moving to walk by her side.

They continued in silence for a few minutes, until Finlay said, 'I still don't know how you're doing it.'

'Doing what?'

'Walking. I mean, without your cane,' he explained. 'Navigating sight unseen.'

Marilla said softly, 'I know this garden well. I helped plant it when I first arrived, three years ago.'

Three years?

Finlay had not realized that the woman—that any wallflower—had been here quite so long. 'And so…so you know it off by heart?'

'Do you learn the corridors of your home "off by heart"?' she chided him gently. 'Just because I cannot see, that does not mean that I cannot recall where I walk. And I walk here often. I like it here.'

Finlay looked about them.

It was a pretty enough garden. Most of the flowers were over by now, and a few weeds were starting to break through the soil at the borders. Precisely why it was so beloved to Marilla, he could not fathom.

'The feel of the box, the scent of the bay and the lavender,' Marilla said, answering his unasked question. Her hand trailed into the border, brushing her fingertips on the plants. '*Buxus sempervirens. Laurus nobilis. Lavandula.* They are beautiful.'

'You are very clever.'

'I have a great deal of time on my hands,' she returned with a laugh. 'And I like learning. It is why the Pike—excuse me, Miss Pike—believes I should be a governess or teacher. Believes no one will ever care enough for me to…to offer for my hand.'

And that was when Finlay knew he was in danger.

In danger of caring, of admiring this woman too much. In danger of allowing the desire he felt for her, the attraction that such a bold and intelligent woman sparked in him, overwhelm him.

In danger of wishing to be here more often, to be beside her more often, to be a part of her life.

'You are very quiet.'

Finlay's gaze jerked up, and he saw a curious expression on Marilla's face. Wasn't that interesting—that a woman who had never seen a curious face could still offer one?

'I was just admiring your knowledge of Latin,' he lied.

Well, there was absolutely no possibility he could reveal the truth.

'A true bluestocking, if ever I saw one,' he continued.

'You say that as though it were an affront,' Marilla said lightly, turning a corner as they crunched onto a gravel path and leading him into what was evidently the rose garden. The bushes had been cut back hard, though a few petals still rested on the cold soil.

'I do not know many ladies who would relish being described as a bluestocking,' Finlay pointed out.

'But I am not a bluestocking. Not really,' she shot back. 'What, because a woman is not traditionally beautiful and she has a passing understanding of books, she must be a blue-stocking?'

Marilla laughed. It was a light laugh, a teasing one, one that rang through the air like music.

Finlay's stomach lurched.

'Don't you project your feelings of inadequacy onto me, Finlay Jellicoe,' Marilla said, nudging him in a way that made Finlay's heart skip a beat.

Swallowing hard and telling himself he had absolutely no desire to kiss her again, no, not at all, Finlay said, 'Look, Marilla…'

'No,' she said softly.

Finlay halted. She had come to a stop beside a climbing rose by the wall, her fingers outstretched, brushing up against the prickly stem as though to see what efforts the gardener had made.

And there was an inscrutable expression on her face.

'What do you mean, no?' Finlay said quietly. 'When I asked— I mean, at Brighton, you said I could call you Marilla.'

Don't think about that kiss don't think about that kiss don't think about—

'I said that my friends called me Rilla,' she said without turning to him. 'I think it…it is time for you to call me Rilla, don't you?'

Finlay swallowed hard. 'And you should call me Finlay.'

'And you'd like that.' Rilla's voice was soft, and they were the only two people in the entire world. 'It would bring you happiness, and that…that is something in short supply in your life, isn't it, Finlay?'

His jaw fell open.

Dear God, how could she possibly spot that? He hadn't told her about Isabelle—not that he was sure how he would explain that—and she was blind. She couldn't see him, couldn't know how often his face fell into melancholy or know how frequently he only appeared to be attending to what was going on around him.

So how the devil did she know?

'I can sense a great sadness in you,' Rilla said, turning around and once again answering his unasked question. 'I can't explain the perception, but I do have it. Even if you do not speak sadly, even if you have no wish to tell me about it—you are not obliged to. But you are sad, aren't you?'

Finlay hesitated. He could tell her. He could attempt to explain about Isabelle, about how the girl he had known had transformed into a stranger, a woman he did not understand.

Finlay had realized that morning, in horrendous clarity, just what his life was going to be.

His married life.

Isabelle, there but not there. And himself. And he was trapped; he couldn't get out. He had made a commitment to her, a promise to care for her. How would he, in all honour, escape it? Escape her?

And now he was here, standing in a dead rose garden, being told by a blind woman who he was starting to truly care about that he was sad.

Finlay brushed away the tear that fell. Thank God no one was here to see it.

'You cannot see me,' he said aloud, awkwardly. 'You cannot possibly know if I am happy or sad.'

'That's where you are wrong,' Rilla said softly. She had turned from the rose now to face him, and took a step forward as she spoke. 'Do not misunderstand me. Those who are blind are not magically able to "read" a room. And yes, I cannot see you. I have only a vague sense of light and dark, and it's not something that has ever changed. But I don't need to see to know.'

'How, then?' Finlay asked quietly.

After all, he'd done his damnedest to keep his gloom away from Society's prying eyes. Grieving Cecil…it was best done in private.

But it appeared there was no private when it came to Miss Marilla Newell.

There was a sad sort of expression on her face as she tilted her head. 'I have learned to pay attention to the unspoken words, as well as the spoken ones.'

A lump formed in Finlay's throat. Somewhere, a robin started to sing.

'Besides, there is so much more to communication than mere speech,' Rilla continued. 'Tone of voice, inflection, hesitancy. The way people move—I cannot see it, but with you…you are a very physical being.'

Finlay was not the only one to flush a dark red.

'You know what I mean,' Rilla said into the silence. 'You… Well, you know what I intended by that.'

He did. It was just a little startling that she could be so perceptive, so understanding of him after just a few encounters. Even if each one had felt intense, and deep, and far more meaningful than anything he had ever shared with anyone else.

Finlay brushed his hair from his eyes as though that could bring him some sort of equilibrium, but it did not. And that was when he found himself opening his mouth and saying something he had not said to anyone.

'My friend died.'

Rilla stepped forward, but then halted, as though she were not sure if her presence would be welcome.

Oh, how he wished she had continued, that her hands had been outstretched and he could have taken them, grounded himself with her touch.

For he was exposed now. Naked, as though he had peeled off all his clothes and bared himself for the world to see.

'What was their name?'

The lump in Finlay's throat made it almost impossible to speak, but he finally managed to say, 'Cecil. Cecil Carr. Well, I suppose he was Lord Carr, but I always knew him as Cecil.'

Speaking his name… Finlay had expected it to be painful. He rarely permitted himself to do such a thing, after all. His heart could only take so much.

Yet speaking it here, in the quiet and the gentleness of the rose garden, with only Rilla as his audience…

The lump in his throat lessened.

'I am sorry for your loss,' Rilla said softly. 'Losing a friend…that is awful.'

Finlay found himself nodding. 'Yes. Yes, sometimes…sometimes I wake in the night. It's dark, and I'm alone, and it's cold, and I wonder why I have woken. Nothing seems to have happened, no noise to startle me, and—'

The words ceased, almost immediately.

There was a pain in his chest, a tightening around his heart he knew all too well. This was the grief, this was the agony that prevented a single syllable being uttered.

He had been a fool to think he could speak of Cecil.

'And then,' Rilla said softly.

She was closer now, just a few feet from him. Almost close enough to touch.

And though he did not feel her contact, Finlay was heartened by her closeness. The sense of peace she brought him was unlike anything he had ever known.

The hand squeezing his heart relented. It began to beat again. His lungs relaxed.

'And then I remember. He is gone, and to a place where I cannot bring him back,' Finlay said quietly, his voice taut. 'And I think, how could I have forgotten? Forgotten Cecil, my closest, my very best friend, how could I forget that he is gone?'

It did not require an observant person like Rilla to hear the self-loathing in his voice. Finlay knew every word was dripping with it.

What sort of a person was he—what sort of a man forgot such a thing?

'I believe it is natural,' Rilla said softly. 'In our dreams, we wish—we long for the things we have lost. The people we have had to say goodbye to.'

Finlay's dark laugh filled the small garden. 'Say goodbye—I didn't have time to say goodbye. I didn't even tell him…there was never any need to tell him how much his friendship meant.' He cleared his throat. 'An accident. A hunting accident, one the fool was too tired to go on but too polite to decline the invitation and… I should have been with him.'

He could have saved him. If he had been there—

'Being there wouldn't be enough,' came Rilla's soft words.

Finlay flinched, the strange sensation of hearing her speak what he had just been thinking hotly jarring in his chest. 'You speak as though you know.'

There was silence, but only for a moment.

'My mother,' Rilla said, in a dry, matter-of-fact tone which quickly cracked as she continued to speak. 'I was with her, and yet you think you would know what to do, you think you can save them, but when it happens…'

Finlay stepped closer to her, needing to feel her presence. It soothed, just as much as it burned. 'My father died when I was small, but so long ago that to be honest, I barely remember him. I have my mother, of course.'

'Who is formidable.'

It was difficult to disagree. Finlay breathed out a laugh, the stinging in his eyes ignored as best he could. 'She means well, and so do I, and so we've got on rather well over the years. But she doesn't understand me like…like Cecil did.'

Rilla brushed the top of a lavender bush with her fingertips, and the scent burst into the chilly air. 'My mother was my champion. Losing her—it was more than losing a parent. Like losing my sight, all over again.'

'Yes, that's exactly it. Like losing a sense, one you could not realize was precious until it was gone.' Finlay tried to take the bitterness from his voice, but it was difficult—though perhaps it was the only thing preventing him from weeping.

There was silence between them, but it was not painful. In fact, now Finlay came to think about it, the tension and unbearable pressure on his chest were fading. Melting.

Bearable, once more.

'I don't know how you do it,' he said with a breathy laugh, desperate to close the gap between them but knowing that if he did so, the warring tears would finally win. 'Speaking with you, it's like…it's like speaking to myself. I haven't…haven't been able to talk about this, with anyone. Not like this.'

Rilla's smile was rueful. 'Loss speaks to loss without the need for manners.'

Finlay snorted. 'I suppose so—another thing I've lost with Cecil's death. There's something special about a friend like that, and not knowing it was coming, no way to tell Cecil how important he was, had always been. We were meant to…'

Oh, God, he was going to cry. And the tears came, just a few, and they were silent and so he hoped to God that Rilla would not notice.

The hearty sniff he was forced to take, however, could not be ignored.

'We were meant to grow old together, reading newspapers and complaining about the youth of today,' Finlay said, trying to laugh but there wasn't enough air in his lungs. 'Talking politics and moaning about the cold of the winters. And now he's just…gone. Just like that? How is that possible?'

He had not expected an answer. There was no answer, as far as he could tell. There never would be a rational explanation for Cecil Carr not existing and the world continuing on without him.

When the answer came, it was as soft and as silent as the tears running down his face.

Rilla took his hand.

How she had done it, he did not know. Finlay did not care. The comfort of her skin against his, the warmth, the knowledge that she was standing with him just letting him feel, letting him say all the things he had not said to anyone else…

They stood there together for a few minutes. Or an age. Finlay wasn't sure. It did not matter. Every second was precious.

Eventually he squeezed her hand, and Rilla squeezed back. When he tried to speak, it was on a breathy laugh as though he could sweep all the true emotion away. 'H-how did you know that I needed comfort?'

'I didn't know,' Rilla admitted softly, her voice thrumming with a warmth he had never heard in her before. 'I just guessed.'

Finlay's chuckle lightened, ever so slightly. 'I suppose I should not presume on your powers of deduction too heavily.'

'No, you shouldn't. I was wrong about something.'

'Which was?' he asked.

Rilla did not speak immediately. She appeared to be considering whether or not to speak. When she did, it was hesitant, unsure. Finlay would almost guess she was…ashamed?

'I thought… Well, you have always sounded very carefree. I admit, I did not think you had such depths to your character.'

Finlay shook his head wryly, then recalled she would not sense such a motion. 'If you don't care, then it can't hurt.'

Rilla's laugh was dark, and it pained him right to his core. 'Perhaps we are not so unlike after all.'

'What do you mean?'

She had already stepped away. 'Nothing.'

'Do not give me that. I know you better than that,' Finlay shot after her.

He had not intended his words to be so aggressive, and now that they had been spoken, he regretted them.

Rilla had halted, however, and she did not continue to move away. 'Yes. Yes, you do, don't you?'

Finlay swallowed.

'And yet we are so different,' she continued, a dark humour in her tones. 'I am a wallflower here only because no one bothers to take much of an interest in me. I have no choices, no power, no options for my future.'

'I know all about no choice and no power,' Finlay said without thinking.

It had been a foolish thing to say, but his marriage had been on his mind and the words had slipped out before he could stop them.

Rilla frowned. 'What on earth would an earl know about a lack of power?'

Finlay hesitated. He was dancing along a dangerous line here now. The flirtation had been wonderful—Bartlett had been right—but they were verging on something else here, weren't they?

More than a kiss stolen on a beach. More than a walk together, fingers slipping by each other, hearts skipping beats.

He had shared with her now, and she had with him. He knew her better than any lady in the *ton*, and somehow all the other ladies of the *ton* were dull in comparison.

He needed to tell her about Isabelle.

The thought was sharp and unpleasant, but he could not deny its veracity. This had gone on too long now. Rilla deserved to know—and Isabelle deserved to have his full attention. They may not care about each other in that way, but she was to be his wife.

And yet he couldn't. How could he utter Isabelle's name when Rilla had returned to him, her fingers reaching out for him, splaying across his chest?

Finlay's heart skipped a painful beat. 'Rilla…'

'Finlay…'

'There you are, Miss Newell, I— Oh, goodness! My lord!'

Finlay did three things in very rapid motion.

Firstly, he released Rilla's hand, though it cost him a great deal to sever the tie to comfort which he had only just found.

Secondly, he raised his other hand swiftly to brush the remaining tears from his eyes. There could be no evidence that Finlay Jellicoe, Earl of Staromchor, had done anything so pedestrian as crying.

And thirdly, he turned with a charming smile that he knew always worked and bowed low. 'Miss Pike.'

When he straightened, it was to see the proprietress of the Wallflower Academy looking aghast.

'Miss Newell—and my lord—speaking privately in the rose garden? It's outrageous!'

'Miss Pike,' Rilla began stiffly. 'It's only—'

What precisely it was 'only', Finlay was never to discover. He was too fascinated by the way all Rilla's warmth, her softness, her comfort had disappeared. The chill had fallen and she was now as reserved and as aloof as she had been when he had first revealed his true identity.

Lowest order? I'll have you know I'm an earl. The Earl of—

An earl? Of course. I should have guessed by your rudeness.

How did she do that?

'And here I am, attempting to make good matches for all my wallflowers, and—'

'There is nothing to be concerned about. We have only—'

'I was looking for you, Miss Pike,' Finlay interrupted hastily. 'And then I was walking with Miss Smith and Miss Newell, and now I am delighted to find you.'

The two women halted their words immediately.

Yes, the mention of Miss Smith had immediately cooled the proprietress's concern; he could see that.

Miss Pike blinked. 'Me?'

'You,' he said warmly, stepping towards her and ensuring that he added a brilliance to the smile and a glitter to his eye.

That was it, be the roguishly charming man that everyone in the *ton* knew him to be…

'Oh, my lord,' said Miss Pike, a pink flush covering her cheeks.

'I was hoping to gain your permission to take a pair of your wallflowers riding,' Finlay said smoothly, as though nothing would make him happier. He ignored the snort of ridicule behind him. No matter how sensitive Rilla was proving herself to be, there was always an undercurrent of mischief. 'Three days hence—perhaps the Misses Newell and Bryant?'

Chapter Eleven

〜〜〜〜

Nothing else smelt like the local village church. Nothing.

'In the name of the Father, and of the Son…'

Rilla breathed in deeply, finding comfort and solace in the dependability of the little church that sat just outside the Wallflower Academy.

Beeswax candles. Heavy starch in the vicar's vestments. The hardness of the pews, lightly scratched along the seats. The cool of the stones beneath her feet. Snowdrops. It must be the Wallflower Academy's turn to provide flowers, for the place was heady with their scent, and they were the current favourite of their proprietress.

In a world in which Miss Pike attempted to change her fate, and in which gentlemen bared their souls to her without her quite knowing what she had done to receive such intimacies, the building was another one of her anchors.

'Amen.'

Rilla swallowed, attempting to follow the church service rather than get carried away by the memories of two days ago.

But it was a challenge. Finlay had—they had never spoken like…

It was more than she could ever have imagined.

H-how did you know that I needed comfort?

I didn't know. I just guessed.

'The reading today is taken from…'

Rilla heard the rustle of pages as fifty or so of the congregation rustled through the Bibles provided on each pew. She heard the genteel cough of someone just behind her, the shifting of someone who was evidently uncomfortable.

It was just another Sunday morning. One which would surely pass just as all the others had.

Except that she had a man on her mind, and Miss Pike was seated next to her and determined to—

Well. Irritate her.

'I suppose your father has written to you,' breathed the woman on her left.

Rilla did not permit a single inch of her face to alter. What on earth was the woman thinking—and after her etiquette lesson only yesterday! 'We are in church, Miss Pike.'

'It's very important. The moment I read it this morning I knew I had to speak to you about it. I merely wondered—'

'Then Moses said to the people, "Commemorate this day, the day you came out of Egypt…"'

'If you had heard—'

'"The land he swore to your ancestors to give you, a land flowing with milk and honey—you are to observe this ceremony in this month—"'

'The news!'

Try as she might, Rilla could not bring herself to grace the woman with a glare. She had worked on her glare for many years, her sisters assisting her at times, and Sylvia had aided her in perfecting the raised eyebrow.

The trouble was, none of those attitudes seemed particularly appropriate for church.

Even if the vicar was, apparently, almost as short-sighted as she was blind.

'Miss Newell,' murmured Miss Pike, nudging her with her elbow as though that would incentivise her to respond. There was tension in her tone that Rilla had never heard before. 'Have you heard from your father?'

Rilla sighed heavily. She would much prefer to indulge in memories of Finlay nudging her, Finlay taking her arm, Finlay revealing his heart to her in such a manner...that of a friend.

No, not quite a friend. Sylvia and Daphne were perhaps her closest friends at the Wallflower Academy, and neither of them had ever wept on her shoulder.

But it was not as though Finlay had said anything about... affection.

'Miss Newell!'

'I heard from my father two weeks ago,' Rilla murmured under her breath, not bothering to turn her head to the side. The woman had to learn.

No, Finlay had said little of affection—nothing about it, in fact. His attention had been fixed, quite rightly, on the friend he had lost.

Besides, earls could not be trusted.

The little voice at the back of her mind which had sought to keep her safe, protected, isolated all these years finally managed to break through the chattering in her head about charming young earls.

He was an earl. Finlay was of that class of gentlemen who thought not only was the world beneath him, but it was supposed to do his bidding. He was part and parcel of the whole nobility, a part of Society that looked down on mere gentry like herself.

'And he mentioned the end of next month?'

And yes, Finlay appeared different from many of the gentlemen of that set she had encountered, Rilla had to accept. He had a...a depth to him no other man had ever revealed to her. And yet...

'You know, then, about the change of circumstances coming?'

Yet it was all too easy to deceive her.

It had been Rilla's greatest fear, ever since that awful encounter with that boy, years ago. She had known the village pond was closer than that, yet he had still called her forward.

And she had believed him. He had said they were friends. Did not friends trust each other?

The subsequent soak had been terrifying. Pond weed inhaled, water clogging her lungs… If her father had not been there…

Rilla blinked. 'End of next month? Change of circumstances?'

Now that Miss Pike's words had finally caught up with her mind, she had probably spoken too loudly. There was an awkward cough from Sylvia beside her, and Rilla heard with a twist in her stomach that the vicar's sermon had momentarily halted.

'That…that is to say… Where was I? Ah, yes. That is to say, when we examine this passage closely…'

'I was not aware of a change of circumstances,' Rilla said quietly, now desperate for the previously loquacious Pike to speak up. 'Miss Pike?'

'I had presumed your father had informed you.'

Now the older woman's voice sounded unsure, unsteady. Most unlike the woman Rilla had known for the last three years.

Oh, how she wished they were no longer in church. It would be easy, then—or relatively easy—to encourage Miss Pike to reveal what awkwardness was to hand, and then Rilla could acclimatize to it. She always did. Always adapted, always found a way through.

Though it was all too easy to deceive her, Rilla had ceased to be so trusting a long time ago. The worry at the back of her mind that she was being taken advantage of never truly disappeared, but there was little she could accuse the Pike of.

Arguing in favour of her becoming a tutor, yes.

But actual cruelty?

No, the woman didn't have a cruel bone in her body. It wouldn't even occur to the Pike to—

'I refer, most unwillingly, to the fact that your father will cease to pay for your place here at the Wallflower Academy at the end of next month,' Miss Pike said in a soft rush.

Rilla was suddenly very aware of her body. Of her buttocks sitting on the pew, her spine against the back rest, her fingers clasped together in her hands, her lungs tight and painful. Her lips parted in shock. Her breath became ragged.

Cease to pay for your place here.

The idea that she would have to one day leave the Wallflower Academy…

It was home. In a way, it was more home than home had ever been. Oh, her father meant well—she was almost sure of it—but with her mother gone and the estate entailed, Rilla had learnt from a young age not to consider Newell Place as her true home.

No, it was here. The Wallflower Academy. It was the place where she had been permitted freedom, the first friends she had made, her escape from—

And now they were going to make her leave?

'And as we can see from the verses that follow, we notice that…'

'I… Cease to pay?' Rilla breathed.

Miss Pike shuffled awkwardly beside her as she whispered, 'I cannot just keep people forever, Miss Newell, you know that. Your father has paid for my help for three years, and you have never…'

Ah, this old tune.

Rilla allowed it to wash over her. She knew this speech, had heard it many times. It was the standard Miss Pike 'I've done everything I can to help you get wed, and you've done nothing' speech. Sylvia was often treated to a variation. Daphne, too.

But though the repetitive phrases may have comforted her

in the past, perhaps even made her smile, Rilla could not do so now.

What was she to do? Where was she to go?

Surely not back home, back to her father. His latest letter had been most clear. He had no wish for her to return; her sisters needed a chance to enter Society without the mark of her past hanging over them. And besides, Nina was still living close by.

So where did that leave her? Where…where could she go?

'And as you are welcome at home—'

'I am not welcome at home,' Rilla said through gritted teeth. Not after they'd all taken Nina's side.

Another elbow in her ribs from Sylvia. She was being too loud again, but she couldn't help it.

She had nowhere to go.

What was to become of her?

'Sort something out,' Miss Pike finished in a low murmur.

Just then the vicar said, 'Hymn number forty-two.'

The congregation rose and Rilla rose with it, moving on instinct instead of any rational thought.

Her mind was buzzing, attempting to take in what she had just been told—and the infuriating thing was, she noticed as the organ started up and voices rose in song, that she couldn't stop thinking about Finlay.

You are clever.

Here she was, about to lose her home, her sense of place and purpose…and her mind instead decided to meander down the trail that led not to solutions, but to an earl who could not be trusted?

An earl who kissed her like the devil on a beach in Brighton, and then simply did not mention it again, as though it had never happened?

The rest of the church service was a blur. Rilla was certain that it had happened; it would have been most strange if it had not. But if she had been asked about it later, there was not a single detail she could have provided.

When the processional music struck up and the congregation bowed their heads as the vicar and the sexton passed by, Rilla found her heart was thundering along with the heavy bass of the organ.

What was she to do?

'Are you coming, Rilla?'

Sylvia's voice cut through her panic and she jerked her head. Somehow the music had ended. The chatter of the end of church had begun.

Her friend's voice was light and airy. She had evidently not heard the shocking revelation from the Pike, Rilla realized, and so was ignorant of the coming disaster. And she would keep it that way.

There was no need for more people to worry.

'I… I will, presently,' said Rilla quietly. 'Don't worry, I can find my own way home.'

The final word she uttered stuck momentarily in her throat. Home? Where was home? If the place her family lived was not home, and the Wallflower Academy could no longer be home in five weeks, then what on earth was she supposed to call home?

But Sylvia either did not notice or did not care. She was gone, her scent of lavender disappearing as the noise of the church started to dissipate.

Eventually there was just one set of footsteps.

'Miss Newell?' came the voice of Miss Pike.

She sounded nervous. It was strange, to hear her so uncertain, and Rilla almost grinned.

Well, it was good to see that Miss Pike had a heart after all.

'I am quite well,' Rilla said softly from her seat on the pew. 'I just wish for a little reflection time in the quiet of the church. That is all.'

There was silence, no answering response from the Pike, but no footsteps to suggest she had departed. Evidently she was unsure quite whether she should leave her here.

Rilla forced down a snort. It was not appropriate in church, and most of all, the Pike would scold her for it—and she wasn't in the mood for being scolded.

'Nothing is going to happen to me here,' Rilla pointed out dryly. 'This is a church, Miss Pike. I will be alone for a short while, then I will return to the Academy.'

'Yes, well…the reverend is coming to luncheon to instruct the wallflowers, but…but I suppose you have a great deal to think about.'

Rilla's throat tightened. 'I do.'

Only then did the footsteps depart, growing fainter as Miss Pike reached the door. And then there was silence.

Shoulders sagging, Rilla allowed herself to feel the weight of what she had so recently been told.

No more money for the Wallflower Academy—and no warm invitation to return home. So where would that leave her?

She was gifted with nothing more than a few minutes of solitude before footsteps appeared again. A prickle of irritation curled around Rilla's heart. Could she not be trusted to sit quietly in a church? Was the Pike truly about to interrupt her, when all she wished was for silence?

'I want to be alone,' Rilla said harshly as the footsteps grew closer.

They suddenly stopped. And then came a scent of lemon.

'F-Finlay?' she breathed.

It was a foolish thing to say. It could not be him. Why the Earl of Staromchor would have left his own church to drive or ride out of London to see her, she did not know. There was no logical reason.

'I have to work out how you do that,' came the light, cheerful voice of Finlay Jellicoe. 'Budge up, there.'

Hardly able to think as her mind whirled, Rilla obeyed, shifting along the pew what she believed was a sufficient amount. A person sat beside her. A person who smelled of sandalwood, and lemon, and whose warmth was moving powerfully through her.

His arm was pressed against hers. His leg—

Rilla swallowed.

His leg was pressed against hers, their hips connected in a way that even through several layers of clothing, a burning heat spread through her.

There was surely no need for him to sit that close to her... was there?

'What are you doing here?' Rilla asked sharply.

She had not intended the words to become an interrogation, but fear and worry were tinging her blood with every thrum of her pulse, and the anxiety poured into her words.

Besides, what could this man possibly want from this strange friendship? What did he want with her?

Oh, he had kissed her—but they had never spoken of it. Sometimes Rilla wondered whether she had dreamt the entire thing. It would not be the first time she had wished to kiss an earl.

'I came to see the church. My mother asked me to...well, look at churches. No reason why,' came the nonsensical reply.

Rilla snorted. 'You do know that makes no sense, don't you? What does your mother need a church for?'

'What are you doing here?' Finlay returned, seemingly without concern that she had been so rude.

'This is my parish church,' she snapped in return, heat blooming in her chest, rising in temperature quite beyond her control.

And she knew she was being unreasonable, but right now, the whole world was. Why should she be sent away from home, abandoned by her family? Why should she be turned out of the Wallflower Academy—had she not helped countless wallflowers find husbands? Did not Gwen owe some of her happiness to her? And Mary before her? And Sarah before her? And when Elizabeth—

'There's no law against stepping into a church, Rilla,' Finlay said sedately, evidently unruffled by her hostile tone. 'In fact, I rather think they encourage it.'

'I wanted to be alone,' Rilla said hotly, unable to stop herself.

'Then be alone with me,' came the gentle reply.

Rilla had to swallow the retort that he was being ridiculous, for two reasons.

Firstly, because her temper was about to get the better of her, and that was never a pleasant occurrence at the best of times.

And secondly because…because he was right.

She had never noticed that before. But Finlay spoke the truth—she could be alone with him, and quite happily. The heat seeping from his body into hers wasn't fuelling her bitterness; it was calming her, washing away the anxiety and leaving calm in its wake.

His presence soothed her.

'You…you are not offended? By the way I speak to you, I mean,' Rilla said awkwardly.

The chuckle beside her rustled up her arm and into her side. 'I suppose other people placate you, accept whatever you deal out to them, just because you can't see.'

Rilla blanched, but unfortunately had little in the way of retort because it was true. It had always been true. The awkwardness people felt around her as a child had swiftly led to her being treated differently, and one aspect of that was the delicacy with which she was treated.

In some cases it was welcome. A little more grace, a little more patience—who would refuse that?

But Rilla knew, even if she had never admitted it before,

that it also led to people accepting rudeness from her that they would never accept from someone like Sylvia or Daphne.

And Finlay had noticed.

'I don't pity you, you know.'

Rilla started, still staring towards the front of the church. 'You don't?'

'Not because you cannot see, I mean,' came Finlay's soft voice. 'Though I do pity you in a way.'

Already the tension was returning to her shoulders. 'And why, precisely, would you?'

'You have fewer options than me,' Finlay said softly. Despite that, the low pluck of his voice seemed to reverberate in the empty church. 'I…well, I don't have every choice set ahead of me, but I certainly have more choices than you. Your future… what does it contain? You never told me, the other day.'

Rilla swallowed back the hated tears.

She would not cry. She would not.

'You don't have to talk to me about it. But I'd like you to.'

And it was the gentleness that prompted her to speak. She had never met a man, or anyone, who spoke with such gentleness. Such understanding.

'I… I do not have much longer at the Wallflower Academy.'

For some reason, the man sitting beside her stiffened. 'What do you mean?'

'Oh, never fear, no man is about to sweep me off my feet and propose marriage,' Rilla said, forcing herself to laugh. As long as she was the one doing the laughing, then it didn't matter if others laughed, too. 'No, it's… Well…'

It wasn't a lack of money, and even that would be shameful enough to admit. It wasn't a lack of space—the Wallflower Academy was busy at the moment, to be sure, but there was plenty of space in the old Tudor manor for her.

It was a lack of care, she supposed, though wild horses would not get her to admit to such a thing about her father.

Rilla sighed, her head dropping. 'I think if I had just married the Earl of Porthaethwy, none of this would be a problem. My father wouldn't—none of my family would be ashamed. There would be no scandal—'

'It wasn't as much a scandal as you think,' came the interjection of Finlay's voice. 'I mean to say, I had never heard of it.'

'I am not sure whether to be pleased or mortified that my life has had such little impact,' Rilla said dryly.

They sat for a moment in silence, and she could not help but notice just how comfortable it was.

He made her comfortable.

And then Finlay made her distinctively uncomfortable by shifting in his seat and asking in a low voice, 'What happened between you and the Earl of Porthaethwy?'

Rilla trotted out the tried and tested formula instinctively. 'There was naught but a misunderstanding.'

'Which was?'

No one had ever asked her that. A misunderstanding was usually sufficient to ward off even the most nosey of gossips.

But this wasn't a gossip. This was Finlay. A man who absolutely should not matter to her, and by God, he mattered.

'I… He wouldn't accept my explanation, my apology, when…' Rilla swallowed. Old wounds never healed, not entirely. The scars still rested on her heart, and tugging at the injury threatened to cause an ache she was not sure she could accept.

But if she were to tell anyone, it would be him.

Sighing heavily, she tried to keep her voice light. 'It was my own fault. I can admit that now, though it was a most challenging thing to accept when I was younger. But I know now that the blame was my own.'

'Blame?'

'I was not always the paragon of virtue that you see before you,' said Rilla, trying to keep her tone light. 'I was…arrogant,

I suppose. I revelled in the idea that I would be a countess—an earl, did you know, an earl wished to marry me? And the Earl of Porthaethwy, he was coming a week before the wedding. His Lordship arrived, for the first time. A house party before the wedding, to meet me, to meet the whole family. The match had been arranged when we were young, and…'

Her voice trailed away. How could she admit this? How could she reveal just how foolish she had—

Her gasp echoed around the church.

Finlay had taken her hand. No request, no hesitation—he had just reached out and taken it in his. His warm fingers entwined with hers and he pulled her hand into his lap, holding it there as a secure anchor against the storm that was railing in her chest.

Rilla swallowed. And could somehow continue. 'Nina and I were in the drawing room. My sister, my next-youngest sister. This was two…no, maybe three days since Lord Porthaethwy had arrived. She asked me what I thought of him, and I… I was young, you must recall, and I did not know what I was about. Anyway, I… I spoke cuttingly of the man.'

'Ah,' came Finlay's voice. 'I have a sense where this is going.'

'I thought to impress, I suppose. I was almost giddy with excitement. I was getting married, and I was to be a countess, and at that age those sorts of things mattered,' said Rilla bitterly. 'I spoke in a way— Oh, how I blush to even think of it now. It is hateful indeed to look back upon the person you once were, and realize that you were unformed, unfinished.'

'What did you say to him?' came Finlay's curious voice.

Her chest tightened painfully. 'None of your business.'

'It's just, to break off an engagement…'

'I was not… Well, not the person I aim to be now,' Rilla said, heat burning her cheeks. 'It was nothing serious, of course, but he was a proud man, and I injured that pride. The damage was done.'

'Naught but a misunderstanding, I'm sure.'

Rilla laughed ruefully. The pew was cold under her free hand as she clutched it tightly. 'I think perhaps more accurately I should say that the Earl of Porthaethwy did not wish to be understanding. I had offended—nay, mortified him. He would not accept my apology, nor that of my father.'

Strange. She had not permitted herself to think of those days for such a long time now, it was as though the colour had been taken out of the memories she held. They were so distant now, yet they were a part of her. Had made her who she was.

'And so he left me at the altar.'

'He—'

'Yes,' said Rilla as lightly as though she barely cared. She would not permit the man to continue to injure her. 'Yes, he waited until the moment that would hurt me, hurt my family the most. There I was, having just swept up the aisle on my father's arm…'

'The brute!'

'He was hurt.' That was what she had told herself then. 'He wished to punish me, I suppose, and earls can do whatever they like in Society. Why not shame the entire Newell family by thrusting aside my hand when it was offered, declaring to the whole church that he had no wish to align himself to a woman with a sharp tongue and an even sharper heart?'

Finlay was spluttering so dramatically his words were almost entirely incomprehensible. 'I— The cheek— If I had— Your father must—'

'It was an arranged marriage,' she said as lightly as she could. 'He never would have chosen me, not of his own free will. And the whole thing, it should not matter, I should not care.'

'I think we're past the point of "should." You obviously cared, in a way. You must have been mortified.'

Mortification did not adequately cover it.

'And I never spoke to the Earl of Porthaethwy again,' Rilla

continued, pushing past his astonishment. She could not dwell on this story much longer. 'I attempted to apologize, but it did not matter. I had injured, insulted, and I was not to be forgiven. He married my sister Nina in the end. My father was insistent that the connection still be made, and after all, he had four daughters.'

She could well imagine the look of astonishment on Finlay's face.

'I am sorry—he merely exchanged one sister for another?'

'What did the substitution for one over the other matter? I did not attend the wedding.'

'And your sister?'

'We have not spoken since. I suppose she feels a duty, a responsibility to honour her husband, and I suppose, rightly so,' Rilla said, attempting to keep her voice level. 'I know I have not visited. No invitations have been forthcoming.'

Some things broken never mended. And it was her fault. Her pride, her arrogance, her determination to be adored, admired. To finally be the fortunate Newell sister.

It was her fault, all her fault—and by the time she'd concocted a way to make it right, it was too late. Too much time, too much silence, too much distance for too long. Too much pain, too many tears. Too many nightmares of standing there, the scent of the church candles, the shocked gasps echoing…

Finlay's hand squeezed hers. 'I am sorry.'

'Don't be,' Rilla said briskly.

'Just take my kindness, will you, and don't brush it away?' Finlay's voice was level, and there was concern, and what could be considered affection if one were seeking it. 'You don't have to always push people away, Rilla.'

Rilla blinked back tears.

Perhaps she did not—but she certainly should have done when it came to Finlay Jellicoe, Earl of Staromchor.

Because here she was, falling in love with him.

Oh, it was a disaster. After guarding her heart so well, for so long, she had managed to allow him in—and he was an earl, too.

Try as she might, Rilla could not deny the intensely emotional tie between the two of them. That connection, the soft and gentle comfort that they shared, belied the undercurrent of attraction.

And it was the thought of attraction that led Rilla to pull her hand away and rise abruptly.

'I should return to the Wallflower Academy,' she said firmly. 'The reverend is having luncheon with us.'

'Yes, I should return, too,' Finlay said. The rustle of his greatcoat suggested he too had risen. 'Would you like a hand?'

It was the first time he had offered, and Rilla knew it would be churlish to push him aside. Besides, she wanted the contact.

Desperately.

His arm was steady as he led her out of the pew and into the aisle.

'I hope you still intend to come riding with me tomorrow.'

'With you and Sylvia,' Rilla corrected, heat flushing through her chest.

But she wouldn't. Her, riding? It was the most ridiculous thing she had ever heard.

'I greatly wish to take you riding,' came Finlay's soft voice. 'Will you not give me the chance to show you?'

Give him a chance.

Had she not been giving him chances every moment she was with him? Did he not know how much she had already compromised for him? Was he unaware that she had undermined her resolve to stay away from earls, her determination never to open herself to a man like that again?

Rilla swallowed. 'I suppose I can walk with you to the stables.'

'Good,' said Finlay, his voice low and warm. It vibrated through her, promising possibilities that were simply not possible.

Their footsteps echoed on the stone-flagged church aisle.

'I suppose it is a good thing we did not meet at the altar,' Rilla attempted to jest. 'It's something neither of us will be doing anytime soon.'

The silence from Finlay suggested, much to her horror, that she had gone too far. But as he stepped towards the church door, his hand over hers on his arm, she could have sworn that he had spoken softly. So softly she could barely hear the words.

'I wouldn't bet on that.'

Chapter Twelve

'Ah, there you are,' said the disapproving voice of Miss Pike. 'We were beginning to believe you had forgotten.'

Forgotten?

Finlay could not comprehend doing such a thing. Forgetting would mean that Rilla was out of his thoughts for more than a minute, which was not something he had managed to achieve since he had deposited her on the doorstep of the Wallflower Academy yesterday.

'I was momentarily delayed in London,' Finlay said smoothly as he stepped into the Wallflower Academy hallway and bowed low to Miss Pike. 'I regret it most sincerely.'

Which was true, though perhaps not in the manner the proprietress of the Wallflower Academy believed.

Yes, he was sorry for the accidental rudeness. But he was more sorry that he had missed even a moment of Rilla's company.

She was standing just behind Miss Pike and was wearing the most splendid riding habit that he had ever seen. It was dark green, and swept down to the floor with elegant brass buttons in the military style along the shoulders and cuffs. She wore a jockey bonnet of last year's style upon her head, and there was a glare in her expression.

Finlay swallowed, his mouth dry. He should have expected it. There were times when he forgot that Rilla was also the

Honourable Miss Newell. Her family must have some wealth, with a title like that. It was entirely appropriate for her to be well dressed.

And entirely inappropriate for him to be staring with his mouth open.

Closing his jaw with a snap and hoping to goodness only Sylvia, similarly attired and clearly stifling a giggle, had noticed, Finlay cleared his throat.

'And what a lovely day you have for your ride, too,' Miss Pike was saying, though whether to himself or to the two wall-flowers, Finlay was not sure. 'I trust you will be able to assist Miss Newell in any way necessary.'

'Miss Newell has no intention of riding whatsoever,' said Rilla sharply, pushing past the older woman and striding confidently towards the Academy door. 'But I'll indulge this nonsense and accompany you to the stables. Come, Sylvia.'

Disappointment twisted in Finlay's chest. Well, it wasn't as though he could have expected anything different. Rilla had never made any declarations of her feelings. Of course, neither had he. But surely she had noticed? Surely she had guessed, after he had kissed her on the beach in Brighton, that he felt something for her.

'And how is Miss Carr, my lord?' asked Miss Pike sweetly from behind him.

Finlay whirled around, his tails flapping in the sudden breeze he had created. Sylvia had departed, racing after the swiftly disappearing back of Rilla. They were alone.

He tried to smile. 'Miss Carr?'

'Your betrothed, Miss Carr,' said Miss Pike, a slight frown puckering her forehead. 'How many other Miss Carrs do you know?'

Cursing himself for not considering this, Finlay attempted to gather his thoughts. Right. He should have expected the announcement to have been read by all. 'She…she is well, thank you.'

What else was he supposed to say?

'I must say, I think it very gracious of you to take time away from your betrothed to help some of our wallflowers practise their conversation and riding,' Miss Pike was saying lightly, as though this occurred every day. 'Marilla and Sylvia will chaperone each other, naturally, and as you are already engaged, there can be no thought of impropriety.'

Finlay's smile weakened. 'Yes. Yes, I quite agree. Now, if you will excuse me, Miss Pike…'

The Wallflower Academy stables were just to the left of the house. Finlay had stabled one of his own steeds there once, when he had come to that dinner.

That dinner when he had fed Rilla. Oh, that sensuous delight, nothing could compare to—

Well. He supposed that something could.

He would have to tell Rilla, of course. There was nothing else for it, not now Miss Pike knew about the engagement. The engagement he had thought was not public knowledge.

Swallowing hard and thanking his stars—and his valet—that his riding breeches were a little loose at the front, Finlay stepped into the stable yard.

Rilla was standing in the middle of it. She had her arms crossed. Rilla's moods were changeable, and passion ran deep in all of them. What had irritated her?

Apprehension and anticipation warred in Finlay's chest as he moved forward. Oh, but one more afternoon surely would not hurt. He would tell her tomorrow. Four and twenty hours, what difference would it make?

'I said you were being ridiculous, and this proves it,' Rilla was saying smartly to Sylvia. 'You cannot think he would believe—'

'Ah, there you are, my lord,' Sylvia said, interrupting her friend. To Finlay's surprise, she gave him a huge theatrical wink he was certain he would have seen from fifty feet. 'I find to my sadness that I have a stone in my shoe.'

Finlay blinked. 'A…a stone.'

Rilla snorted. 'Sylvia, the man wasn't born yesterday.'

'And as such, I will have to spend a great deal of time sitting here, on a mounting block, attending to my boots,' said Sylvia proudly, sticking out her leather boot from her long skirts. 'I fear it will take me most of the afternoon to—'

'Sylvia,' growled Rilla.

Finlay looked bemusedly back and forth between the two women. Evidently there was a scheme afoot.

'So I think the two of you should start on riding without me,' Sylvia said, winking again most ostentatiously. 'I'll catch up when I can, my lord, but it would be a true shame if Rilla were to miss out on a ride merely because I was improperly shod.'

Finlay grinned. It was an excellent excuse—he would have to remember to thank Miss Sylvia Bryant at a later date. For the present, however…

'Miss Pike will be furious,' Rilla said sharply as Finlay stepped to her side.

'Miss Pike believes you are being chaperoned,' he pointed out. 'May I take your hand?'

The beautiful woman shook her black curls back, but evidently did not have the heart to decline. 'You…you may.'

Heat shot through Finlay's body, as it always did when it came into contact with Rilla. Oh, these were the warning signs he should heed, and yet he did not seem able. All he wanted to do was be with her—touch her. Be touched by her.

Finlay almost tripped over a perfectly flat cobble as he led Rilla to his horse Ceres.

'And what precisely are we going to do together?' Rilla asked sarcastically as Sylvia disappeared off into the stables. 'You must know that I cannot ride. Me, sitting alone on a horse, guiding the reins? Preposterous—and in truth, I don't think you will be able to teach me.'

His heart stirred as the delightful idea of an afternoon spent with Rilla, alone—with a ready-made excuse—filled his chest.

This was far better than he could have hoped. Pushing aside the discomfort of keeping his secret from Rilla could be done for a little while longer. His feelings for Rilla, after all, were far stronger.

'That indeed would be a great challenge, and I agree that I would not be up to such a task,' he said seriously, ignoring her sarcasm and looking through it to the pain and the embarrassment beneath. 'But I do not intend to.'

There it was—the flicker of uncertainty, the nervousness Rilla was feeling momentarily expressed on her face.

And Finlay's chest ached. What must it be, to never quite know who to trust? To always be wondering when the next embarrassment would come? When someone would take advantage of your lack of sight, never knowing if one was about to be tricked?

His temper burned against her sister, the earl, the pair of them—but that was not something he could do anything about, not today.

Today, he was about to do something quite different.

They halted before Ceres.

Rilla frowned. 'So…so if we are not going riding, why am I wearing this ridiculous get-up?'

'I don't think you look ridiculous,' said Finlay without thinking. 'I think you look beautiful.'

No amount of silence could prevent him from noticing the flush on Rilla's cheeks—nor could he avoid the fact that it suited her complexion well.

So did the slow smile that tilted her lips. 'You…you do?'

'I do,' Finlay said softly, his own cheeks burning now at the intimacy of their words, matched only by the soft, private tone of their conversation.

'I… I don't know what you mean, then,' Rilla said, the sarcasm and protective anger melting away. 'What will we be doing this afternoon?'

'We'll be riding,' Finlay said promptly.

'But you said— Finlay Jellicoe, put me down!'

And he did…though perhaps not precisely where Rilla was expecting.

'Hold on here, and here,' he said, guiding her hands to the reins.

Though surprising her was a delightful achievement in itself, Finlay congratulated himself for his brilliant idea, too. It wasn't just the execution which had to be just right; it was the inspiration itself.

And seeing Rilla in that dark green riding habit, astride his mare with her head held high and an imperious look on her face?

Finlay's manhood stirred.

That was inspiration.

'You have to be jesting,' Rilla said faintly. 'You cannot—'

'You wish me to take you down?' Finlay asked seriously.

For he would, if she asked. He was no cad, would not force Rilla to do things she had no wish to merely because he could exert his will on her.

And besides, there would be a benefit to lifting her down. The movement had offered closeness and a tantalizing opportunity— which he did not capitalize on—to kiss her again. Rilla in his arms had been something he had thought about far too often. He would not be averse to doing it again.

Rilla hesitated, and Finlay grinned. There was a woman who was bold, and brilliant, and who held herself back just as often as others held her back. 'I just do not comprehend what you could possibly think is going to help. I cannot see, Finlay!'

It took a great deal for Rilla to say that, he knew. And that was why he did not explain, but merely acted on the next part of his plan.

'Finlay!'

Finlay had mounted Ceres in one easy stride. He'd been mounting horses without a block since he had come of age, even before then, and it was not exactly hard.

It was most definitely not a hardship to mount just behind Rilla, pulling her into his arms and taking the reins from her, breathing in the scent of her body, feeling the warmth of her in his chest, her head resting against his neck.

'Finlay Jellicoe!' Rilla said, her breath warm against his cheek. 'This is most scandalous!'

'Perhaps so,' said Finlay, nudging Ceres forward and speaking calmly as they left the stable yard and started to trot gently along the path towards the greater park. 'Do you want to be taken back to the Wallflower Academy?'

He knew the answer; he did not need to hear it. He could feel it in the soft languidness of her body, the comfort she was drawing from him, that they were drawing from each other.

Oh, there was nothing like this. Nothing like being with the woman you—

Finlay swallowed as he slowed his steed to a walk now that they were out of sight of the Wallflower Academy.

That had been a close one. He had almost thought there, for a moment, about love.

It was not a feeling he was going to permit himself to even think about. Not in the slightest. Not even consider. He could not love Miss Marilla Newell. He certainly did not love Miss Isabelle Carr, but that did not mean that he could go around offering his heart to others.

He was going to be married in less than three weeks.

Finlay swallowed hard, pushing all thoughts of Isabelle out of his mind. Surely it was not a betrayal if he had never promised love and affection to begin with. No one could expect anything else from him. He had done everything that had been expected—more, perhaps.

Somewhere deep inside Isabelle Carr was the woman she had once been.

Perhaps, Finlay tried to convince himself, *after they were married...*

The revulsion that stirred at the mere thought was not a good sign.

'You are very quiet,' said Rilla softly.

Finlay tried not to shrug. 'I suppose I am.'

It was not as though he could share his thoughts with her. Why he had kept the truth of Miss Isabelle Carr—the very existence of Miss Isabelle Carr—from Rilla, he did not know.

Well. He had a vague guess.

Bringing those two worlds together, those two women together, even in conversation, would mean having to face up to the fact that he wanted one but could only have the other.

That he was going to be miserable with one, and miserable without the other.

That one of them he respected, and the other he...

Finlay cleared his throat as he nudged Ceres along a left-hand fork in the path. Perhaps...well. Men had mistresses all the time, didn't they? He was in fact unusual in his circle of friends, *not* having one. He had considered it an offence to Isabelle once their engagement had been decided upon, but even before then, Finlay had never wished to engage in such a thing without...well, without his emotions involved.

But now that they were...

'You know, I feel like I can tell you anything,' he said before he could stop himself.

Rilla was silent for a moment. Then she asked, 'Where did that come from?'

'I, uh...'

'You say nothing at all, and then you say you can tell me anything?' She turned slightly in his arms. 'Do you have something to tell me, Finlay?'

His stomach lurched.

Only that I'm lying. That I'm keeping from you information that you would almost certainly want. That I'm being torn in two directions, between who I should be and who I am.

Finlay swallowed. 'No. No, nothing.'

Hell's bells, man, this can't continue.

Trying not to think about the delicate woman curled into his chest, exclaiming with delight at the strange sensation that riding provided, Finlay prodded at his conscience.

Would he, in turn, be content if Isabelle took a lover?

After a moment of introspection, he believed that he would. Well, their marriage had begun as one of convenience only, had it not? Though now he'd overheard her declarations of love, perhaps it was unlikely that Isabelle would wish to look elsewhere...

'And this is riding?'

Finlay's focus snapped back to the woman in his arms. 'I beg your pardon?'

'Well, is this...it?' Rilla said, a slight tension in her voice.

It was a bizarre question. After all, the rolling hills, the frost-tipped branches of the forest of their left, the way the sunlight glittered...

And then Finlay felt very foolish indeed.

When was he going to learn that so much of his experience was different to Rilla's? That he could not simply amaze and dazzle her with new sights, as though that would make her care for him?

Not that he was attempting to do that. Obviously.

Finlay fought the instinct to press a kiss into her hair and instead said softly, 'We are riding along a path covered with leaves. Most of them have decayed, with the winter approaching, but there are toadstools and mushrooms pushing up through the foliage, striving to reach the sun.'

Rilla's breathing changed. Unless he had been acutely attuned to it, he would not have noticed.

He took that as encouragement to continue. 'On our left is the forest—or woodland, I suppose. I never knew the difference. Trees stand tall against the sky, their branches bare. I can see the remnants of nests, the evidence of a summer well lived. There are several ravens, or crows, sitting in one tree and they examine us as we pass.'

'A family?' Rilla breathed.

Finlay chuckled, his chest pressing against her back. 'Perhaps. And on our right are the fields, soaring out into the distance, kissing the horizon. The hedgerows are brimming with berries, and birds flicker in and out, guzzling themselves full for the winter ahead. There'll be squirrels in there, I suppose, and mice perhaps. I can't see.'

'Neither can I.'

He stiffened for a moment, then softened as Rilla's laughter rippled through his chest.

'Tell me more,' she said, a giggle in her voice.

More? How could he possibly think about the countryside around them when Rilla was in his arms?

'There are clouds in the sky,' he said, his Town upbringing starting to betray him. 'Erm…big clouds. Fluffy clouds.'

Rilla snorted. 'Snow clouds.'

'Now how could you possibly know?'

'Can you not smell it?' She took in a deep lungful of air, while Finlay did his absolute best not to notice the most tantalizing swell of her breasts. 'That's snow on the air. I could smell it a mile off.'

'It's not going to snow.'

'Have it your way,' Rilla said with a grin, nestling into him. 'But I'll be proved right, you'll see.'

'You are not too uncomfortable?' Finlay said aloud, concern twisting in his chest. 'I do apologize, I have barely asked.'

'It is a most strange sensation, I will admit,' said Rilla, a laugh lilting in the air. 'I imagine it is like being at sea. The undulation, not knowing what is going to happen…it's a loss of control.'

'Not something you enjoy, then,' said Finlay ruefully.

She had never told him that she needed to be in control, but it was obvious, was it not? Anyone who spent more than five minutes in the same room with Rilla would surely know that.

Rilla shrugged. The movement tightened her in his arms and Finlay revelled in it. 'I thought I would not, in truth—though I admit, I did not think you would actually get me on a horse.'

'And I am sorry for not asking your permission,' Finlay said, regret pouring into the joy, tainting it. 'I know how much you dislike being touched without your permission.'

'You…you remember that?'

Rilla's voice sounded surprised, which was a surprise in itself to Finlay.

'Of course I remember that,' he said, startled. 'I remember everything you say.'

They continued to ride in silence for a few minutes. Finlay was not certain if the silence was awkward for Rilla, but in himself he felt nothing but contentment and satisfaction.

After all his hopes and planning for such an afternoon, he could not have conceived of such a pleasant day. Rilla in his arms, Rilla happy—what else could he want?

'I love to hear you describe what's around me. What's around us.'

The sudden lurch in his chest was most definitely not something he should pay attention to, Finlay told himself. Nor the rising affection, the warmth in his chest, the way he wanted to nuzzle and kiss that delicate neck…

'There's not much else to tell,' Finlay said aloud, partly to redirect himself from his most distracting thoughts. 'Though there's you, I suppose.'

Rilla snorted. 'I know what I look like.'

'Do you?' he could not help but ask. She was warm in his arms. They had never felt empty before, but now he knew he would be bereft once she had left him. 'Do you know how you shine, Rilla?'

She turned at that, her gaze flickering over him as though attempting to discern whether he was chiding her. 'I don't know what you mean.'

'I think you do,' Finlay said softly, trying not to think of that spectacular kiss they had shared. 'I think you know what I think about you. What…what I feel for you.'

Whether it was him who moved first, or Rilla, he was not sure. All Finlay knew was that the woman he cared about deeply had turned in his arms, lifting up her lips to him in a silent plea for his attention, and he had given it most willingly.

Oh, God, it was a challenge to stay on the horse. Rilla's lips had parted almost instantly, inviting him in, and Finlay's grip around her tightened as every part of him longed to pour himself into her.

He made do with his tongue, desperately tasting the sweetness of her mouth, the delicacy of her affection, and tried not to moan too loudly.

But Finlay could barely stand it. Rilla had somehow woven her fingers in his hair, and he had never felt so close, so intimate with a woman before.

This was it; she was it. He adored her. He—

I wager you'll feel infinitely better for a flirtation. I think it'll bring you joy, and won't betray Isabelle in any way, and you'll enter the married state far happier. If I'm wrong, you can…oh, I don't know…choose your punishment.

The memory of Bartlett's words caused Finlay to break the kiss, to lean back, panting, to look at the woman with whom he had intended to enjoy nothing more than a flirtation.

The pang in his chest suggested otherwise.

No, this had gone much further than he had intended. This had gone beyond mere appreciation, beyond respect and admiration, beyond like.

Despite having no intention to create an entanglement before his wedding to another, Finlay had fallen completely in love with Rilla Newell.

Soft flakes of snow started to fall from the sky.

Chapter Thirteen

By the time Finlay whispered in her ear that they were about to enter the stable yard, Rilla knew two things.

Firstly, she knew that Finlay had never mentioned matrimony. He had probably never even considered it—the thought would never have passed through his mind. He was an earl, a man who would marry a beautiful heiress without any hint of stain upon her character.

It was surely no coincidence that Finlay had never spoken of his marital prospects.

Her own reputation was not so marred as it could be, but the fact that she had been sent to the Wallflower Academy and never visited by her family would surely cause eyebrows to rise. And that would be before anyone discovered her shameful history with the Earl of Porthaethwy.

No, Finlay would not marry her. The idea would never occur to him; Rilla was certain. Earls with egos like that did not marry women like her.

Secondly, she knew that when Finlay kissed her, every inch of her came alive in a way that she was certain would never be sparked again.

He knew her, truly knew her, and he desired her. That much was undeniable. Rilla did not care how carefully constructed the man's persona was in Society—he may be charming and light-hearted in company, and more serious and grieving in private, but no man could pretend that sort of desire.

Which made her just like…just like any other woman.

And so with these two facts in her mind, Rilla came to a most astonishing conclusion as Ceres's shod shoes clattered on the cobbles of the stable yard: seducing Finlay Jellicoe, Earl of Staromchor, would be her best opportunity in her life to know what it was to make love.

Rilla knew she could not just suggest such a thing bluntly and without careful consideration. The trouble was, her time was running out. In a few short weeks, her sojourn at the Wallflower Academy would be over, and she would be seeking her fortune elsewhere.

Perhaps, Rilla could not help but think ruefully as the horse was brought to a stop and she lost the sensation of Finlay sitting behind her, she would end up as a governess after all, just as Miss Pike had wished.

But how precisely she made her way in the world after the Wallflower Academy was immaterial. She had this time, this moment now, to create a memory she would never forget.

And besides. She wanted him. A dull, throbbing ache between her legs told her that there was more pleasure to come, if that could be believed. More joy, more sensuality, more decadence—more of Finlay.

She wanted that.

So when Finlay said softly, 'May I help you down?' and Rilla offered her hands out into the unknown, she knew what she must do. What she had to do, if she wanted to continue without adding a regret to the list she bore in her heart.

Finlay's hands were warm, and strong, and gentle. He lifted her down carefully, almost reverently, and as her boots touched the cobbled stones beneath her, Rilla found her lungs were tight and breathless.

Oh, Lord, she was a walking cliché. He made her breathless!

Despite having her full balance now, Finlay's hands did not leave her sides. When Rilla took a step forward, pressing her breasts against him and feeling the rapid rise and fall of his chest, she knew he was just as breathless as she was.

'Is...is there anyone else here?' Rilla asked, her mouth dry.

After all, it would never do for the conversation she intended to have with the man to be overheard. Miss Pike would be the least of her problems.

She felt the brush of air as Finlay turned one way, then the other.

'Strangely, no,' he said quietly, hands still around her waist. 'I think I can see— Yes, they are all inside the servants' hall. An early dinner, perhaps? It appears that we are alone.'

Alone.

Well, thought Rilla, steeling herself for what was about to be a very bold declaration, *there is no time like the present.*

'I like you, Finlay,' she blurted out.

And immediately cast her face down.

She liked him?

Was that truly what she had managed to say, after carefully constructing a logical argument for why they should make love at the swiftest opportunity?

That she *liked* him?

Rilla felt, as well as heard, his chuckle.

'Goodness, I thought you hated earls.'

'I do not generally hold them in particularly high regard, no,' she said as heat suffused her cheeks. 'In my experience, earls are insufferably proud, indeterminately arrogant, and unable to listen to a woman for five minutes together.'

Finlay's second chuckle was deeper. 'And yet you like me?'

I don't like you, Rilla wanted to say. *I... I think—*

'My dislike of earls in general has been tempered somewhat, yes, by...by getting to know you better,' she said aloud, forcing down the declaration of affection she knew would not be returned. 'And I... I trust you.'

Why it was so difficult to admit to such a thing, she did not know—but Rilla knew it mattered.

Trusting Finlay, not only to respect her but to treat her kindly, learning to expect kindness from a man whose position and station in life suggested she would receive naught but pain...

'I am grateful for your trust.' Finlay's voice was low, his breath warm, and she could feel his fingers momentarily tighten on her waist. Then they relaxed—though they did not release her. 'Earning your trust is something I think very... very precious.'

Here they were, Rilla thought. Right on the precipice of what they wanted to say, and yet neither of them willing to be the first to admit it.

They wanted each other.

Desire was not the domain of a respectable young woman. Oh, she knew the basics—the physical mechanics of lovemaking. It had been rather a surprise to learn that that was what happened, but since meeting Finlay, Rilla had come to understand that the stirrings within her whenever he touched her were the first steps on a journey she wished to take...with him.

And now, here, standing in Finlay's arms, knowing him to be a man of passion and caring, desire and understanding, grief and love, as well as joy and jesting...

He was far more than she had presumed.

Rilla took a deep breath. And if she didn't speak now, she would always wonder, *What if...?*

'Finlay,' she said firmly.

'Rilla,' he returned with a gentle chuckle.

Deploying the intense glare Sylvia had helped her to perfect, Rilla said, 'I am attempting to be serious here.'

'I wouldn't dare stop you,' Finlay said quietly. 'Though that doesn't mean that I have to be serious in turn.'

Rilla raised a hand and splayed it against his chest—and

gasped. She had meant it as a censure, but all thoughts of that had melted the instant she had felt his heart.

Thump-thump-thump-thump...

It was racing. In fact, Finlay's pulse seemed to be just as frantic, perhaps more so, as her own.

'Rilla?'

She swallowed. Perhaps she was not about to request something that would be denied, then. Perhaps he wanted this just as much, or perhaps even more, than she did. But she knew what she wanted. Just one encounter, she was certain, would be enough. Wouldn't it?

Well, she would never know if she never asked. 'Would you make love to me?'

Shame soared through her chest at the inelegant—and painfully direct—question. What had possessed her to speak so frankly? Dear God, he would think her a harlot, a strumpet, a woman utterly devoid of—

'I beg your pardon?' came a strained voice from Finlay.

Rilla twisted in his arms, attempting to get away. She would find the wall of the Tudor manor and from there she could make her way around to the front door—and then never leave it again.

How on earth could she be so—

But Finlay had tightened his grip, making it impossible to escape. 'Rilla!'

'Forget I said anything,' she said hastily, her words almost tripping over themselves as she struggled to free herself. 'And let me go, damn you!'

And then she was released.

The sudden space around her, the sudden lack of Finlay, took her quite by surprise. Rilla almost stumbled, her head spinning.

'But just so you know, before you march off,' said the Earl of Staromchor quietly. 'Yes.'

Rilla froze after a single step.

Yes?

He couldn't mean— Surely he did not mean…?

Turning slowly on the spot to where Finlay's voice had last been, Rilla breathed, 'Yes?'

'Yes,' said Finlay matter-of-factly, as though they were discussing something no more important than the expected change in the weather. 'Yes, I… I would very much like to make love to you. Now, in fact. Damn, Rilla, I have done for quite some time.'

Heat was stirring across Rilla's décolletage, but it was not shame, or guilt, or embarrassment, but—eagerness.

For quite some time?

'I know you have no wish to marry. That is, a marriage between us would be impossible,' Rilla said, straightening herself and attempting to approach this as a simple conversation.

Simple conversation? Had anything ever been less simple?

'That is not what I am asking for,' she said, her voice stronger. 'I just… Before I leave the Wallflower Academy, I need to know…know what it is to be loved.'

A hand took hers, and Rilla could tell it was Finlay. Her body was attuned to him in a way she could never have predicted.

'Leave the Wallflower Academy?'

Rilla hesitated—but this was not the time for that conversation. She would tell him tomorrow. What harm would it do, keeping a little truth from him?

'One day,' she said, a little awkwardly. 'I ask this of you, Finlay as…as a favour.'

'I cannot offer marriage to you today,' said Finlay softly. 'And I would still very much like to…to make love to you.'

Make love. Was this what Gwen had experienced, rushed Rilla's wild thoughts? Was she finally about to experience something that she had longed for?

How long they stood there in silence, hands clasped, luxuriating in the knowledge that they were going to enjoy one of life's most delicate pleasures, Rilla did not know. A minute? An hour? She could have remained there all day, she was certain, and as long as she had the certainty of Finlay's presence, she could have endured anything.

As it was, the very worst she had to endure was the uncertainty of what happened next.

Well, it wasn't as though she proposed lovemaking frequently. What did one do, once two people had agreed that they would quite like to take all their clothes off and…?

'Is there a side door?'

Rilla blinked. 'I beg your pardon?'

'A side door,' Finlay repeated. His voice was low, molten, teasing tendrils of desire across her skin. 'I don't think Miss Pike would appreciate seeing me ascend the staircase and enter your bedchamber, do you?'

A jolt of shock rocked Rilla's body. 'But you can't mean now?'

'Why not now?' His voice was urgent, his fingers tightening around hers. 'I don't want to wait for you, Rilla. I want you now, right now. I need you right now.'

And he was kissing her, and his other hand was tangled in her hair, and pins were cascading to the cobbles but Rilla did not care.

How could she when he was kissing her like that, his lips pressing hard hot desire into her, his tongue causing ripples of pleasure that thrummed through her body and settled in that aching spot between her legs?

When he finally released her, Rilla was once again breathless, but far more decisive. 'There's a side door just here. Wait, where is the entrance to the stables?'

Finlay took her hand, made a point with her finger, and moved it. 'There.'

Getting her bearings, a miracle considering how her head was spinning, Rilla took a step forward. 'This way.'

The side door by the stables was unlocked, as it always was before night fell. And Rilla would have known that, unequivocally, if they had managed to reach it.

Unfortunately their need for each other swiftly scuppered their plan to enter the house. The side door was at least, as far as Rilla could make out, ten yards from them.

Not that it mattered. Not with Finlay's arms around her, his lips trailing kisses down her neck.

'We…we shouldn't.'

'No one is here—they are at dinner. I told you,' Finlay said, his voice somehow raw and eager at the same time. 'And I want you, Rilla.'

How was any woman supposed to defend herself against such unashamed desire? How could woman prevent herself from succumbing to such words, spoken in such a tone, by such a man?

'Here, then,' Rilla found herself saying, pulling him in the opposite direction.

'Where are we—'

'You'll see,' she said breathlessly, stepping forward confidently.

Riding may have been a diversion previously unavailable to her in the past, but Rilla had spent a great deal of time around the stables as she waited for the other wallflowers to mount and dismount their horses. She knew the cobbles well, knew that when she reached the stable door, they would become slabs of stone rather than the small, uneven cobbles that typified the stable yard itself.

And so when she reached out in confidence, she was rewarded. The door to the stables opened to her, and with Finlay's hand in hers, she pulled him through.

'You will have to tell me,' Rilla said, her breath short and her cheeks burning as she spoke so directly, 'which of the stalls is empty.'

Finlay's breath caught in his throat. That was the only indication that he had responded at all to her words.

When he finally spoke, it was with an incredulous—and impressed—tone. 'You cannot mean to—'

'You want to wait until we creep down a corridor, pause for the servants' corridor to be empty, go up three flights of stairs, ensure there are no wallflowers on the bedchamber corridor, hope we are not seen, then—'

Rilla's mouth was hushed by a passionate kiss. It spoke of eagerness, and surprise, and delight in her equal hunger.

And when Finlay finally released her, his breathing was quick and his hands warm. 'Dear God, you are magnificent.'

'I don't know about that,' said Rilla, trying to force away the shyness she felt.

She wanted this. She wanted him. There would be no time, no space in her mind for regrets.

'The stall at the end is empty,' said Finlay, his voice low. 'This way.'

Rilla allowed herself to be led along the corridor that ran between the four stalls on either side. The sound of creaking hinges rippled into the air, and she stepped forward with Finlay's hand on the small of her back.

Well, perhaps slightly lower than the small of her back.

Her lungs tight and her heart thundering, Rilla heard the squeak of the hinges as the door to the stall closed. Then she felt the warmth of Finlay's breath on her face. He was standing right opposite her.

What was his expression? Not for the first time, Rilla wished she had that additional insight into the people around her—but this time, there was no painful tinge to her wish.

Finlay Jellicoe had never hidden himself. Not since those ridiculous footman antics at their first meeting, anyway. He would tell her, show her, reveal in his movements and the shortness of his breath precisely what he was thinking.

And he was probably thinking, Rilla thought ruefully, what on earth they should do next. After all, it was not typical to make love to a wallflower in a stable.

'May I take off your jockey bonnet?'

'Yes.'

His hands were gentle. As the jockey bonnet came down, so did the final pins that had been barely containing her curls. Both pins and curls fell down her shoulders, and the appreciative sound she heard told Rilla that the effect must be pleasant.

'May I take off your riding habit?'

Rilla's chest tightened, just for a moment. 'Y-yes.'

'We can stop at any time,' Finlay's voice said, soft yet unshaking. 'Any moment you wish to—'

'I want you,' Rilla said.

Did he know just what she meant by that? Of course not—how could he? She barely knew what she meant by it, by all these feelings and emotions rushing through her, making it impossible to decipher just what she felt for Finlay.

Except love.

As her riding habit slipped from her shoulders, Rilla shivered. 'What about you?'

'What about me?'

She smiled. 'I cannot help but notice that you are still wearing all your clothes.'

'So are you. Mostly. Something I would like to rectify immediately,' came the seductive murmur of Finlay as he pressed a kiss into the base of Rilla's throat.

Unable to help herself, Rilla's head tipped back as she welcomed the intimacy. How did he make her melt under every kiss? He had a way with him that she could never have imagined—and would never forget.

'But I understand,' Finlay added. 'Here.'

Rilla frowned as her fingers were clasped in his own and brought forward. Then her brow unfurled.

'Undress me,' he whispered.

He had guided her hands to his coat—somehow his riding frock coat had obviously been cast aside—and his own hands had dropped to his sides.

She was in complete control.

'Kiss me,' Rilla breathed as her nervous hands undid the first button of his waistcoat.

There was strength under these clothes; she could feel it, and she could sense the strength of restraint as Finlay kissed her. His chest tensed as each button was undone, and Rilla tried to concentrate as his meandering lips teased that delicate spot beneath her ear, her neck, the curve of her collarbone and the swell of her décolletage.

'You're not making this easy,' she gasped, her fingers slipping on a button as his lips danced across the top of her breasts.

'Good,' growled Finlay, his hands cupping her buttocks with a groan. 'Neither are you.'

The idea that anyone, let alone an earl, would find her so enticing was unfathomable to Rilla, but she did not have the concentration to consider that. Not now she had finally managed to undo all the buttons before her.

Well. Not all the buttons. Tempting as it had been to allow her fingers to drift down to his breeches, she was not brave enough for that. Not yet.

'Take them off,' she breathed.

Finlay's hands left her body, just for a moment, as coat, waistcoat, and shirt fell to the stall floor. Rilla had sensed the straw beneath it, knew it would be soft when he…when Finlay…

Rilla swallowed. 'Now me.'

Turning on the spot and hoping to goodness they would not be discovered, she pulled her hair to one side to reveal to Finlay the ties at the back of her gown.

This undressing was not nearly so laboured. In a few quick heartbeats, Finlay had pulled loose all the ties keeping her gown upon her person. It pooled swiftly to her feet, leaving her in naught but—

'Dear God.' Finlay's breath blossomed out onto her now bare shoulder.

Rilla turned hurriedly, fear flooding through her chest. 'If you have changed your mind...'

'Changed my— I'm only regretting not suggesting this to you weeks ago,' Finlay said, his voice thick with desire.

Heat burned her cheeks as her secret place throbbed. 'You only met me weeks ago.'

'Exactly,' Finlay said darkly. 'May I lay you down? I've moved some blankets—you'll be quite comfortable.'

It was an entirely new exercise of trust, allowing Finlay to slowly guide her to the blankets that he had placed on the straw. With any other man she would have felt exposed, in danger—at every moment fearing that this had been a trick merely to make her ridiculous, or destroy her reputation completely.

But this was Finlay. She could trust Finlay.

She was not alone on the straw and the blanket for long. Heat seared along her skin as Finlay joined her, the rough, wiry hair of his thighs brushing up against hers.

Rilla gasped.

This was really happening. The pleasure of his presence, his touch, was about to take on a new meaning.

Fingertips trailed seductively along her hip. 'I... I don't want to hurt you.'

Rilla reached out without hesitation. Her hand cupped a cheek. 'Then don't.'

The answering kiss was slow, and passionate, and seemed to pour all the words neither of them could say between them. Rilla clutched at him, needing to know he was there, needing to know just how greatly he desired her.

And he showed her. As Finlay tilted her head back and worshipped her mouth, his hands were not idle.

Rilla whimpered as his thumb brushed across her secret place. 'Oh, Finlay—'

She was unable to say any more. Not merely because the kiss deepened, taking all breath away—but because Finlay had gently slipped his thumb into her slick folds, causing a spark of unimaginable pleasure through her body.

Oh, God—this was lovemaking?

How did anyone stop?

Finlay did not. As his tongue ravaged her mouth, teasing pleasure she had never known from it, his thumb and finger were stroking a rhythm in her secret core that was throwing fuel on the fiery ache that needed…needed—

Unable to help herself, Rilla tilted her head back. 'Oh, God, Finlay…'

The explosion was exquisite. Her whole body rippled with ecstasy, her limbs quivering at the pleasure which tightened her core and made every part of her glow with fiery heat.

His unrelenting fingers finally slowed. Rilla's panting breaths seemed to echo around the stall.

'That was…'

'I know.' Finlay's voice was thick with emotion, the words breathed not spoken into her ear. 'I've never seen anything more beautiful, Rilla. You're…you're so beautiful.'

Rilla blinked, as though that would steady her whirling mind. To think that such delicious sensuality was mere inches away from any pair, just under their clothes…

How would she ever be in Finlay's presence again without wanting this?

'God, I want you,' he groaned, sinking a kiss into her neck that fluttered longing once more through Rilla's chest. 'You can't know— But if you don't want—'

'I want you,' Rilla said quietly, knowing with a new sense of certainty that whatever followed was precisely what she wanted. What she needed. 'Take me, Finlay. Take whatever you need to.'

Her breath hitched as Finlay's lips brushed over one of her nipples, then tightened as his tongue laved, swirling around the delicate skin.

The ache was back.

'Take me,' Rilla breathed, and there was a pleading note there that she had not intended but could not, would not deny. 'Please.'

He did not appear to need convincing. Finlay's presence shifted, moving from her side to above her. The delicate nudge at her knees was enough. Rilla parted them, welcoming him in. Welcoming the intrusion, yet knowing it was precisely what she wanted.

There was a shift in the straw on either side of her head. Finlay was…leaning on it, perhaps?

'You can stop me at any point,' Finlay said hurriedly, pausing between words to snatch kisses from her willing lips. 'Rilla, you have to know—'

'I know,' she panted, the ache between her thighs desperate now for whatever satisfaction he could give her.

'You have to know how I feel about you.'

'I know,' Rilla said, blinking up into the vague darkness above her.

And there was a pause, and then Finlay was crushing his mouth on hers.

It was the perfect kiss. Rushed, a little raw, but perfect because of that, not despite it. It was a kiss that said they were equals in desire, equals in need—equals in all the ways that mattered.

And it was during that kiss that he—

'Finlay!' Rilla moaned in surprise as something thick and long pushed into her most intimate spot.

Her body knew what to do, far more than her mind. Swelling, shifting, welcoming him in, the stretch was uncomfortable but only for a moment. Rilla gasped, the ripples of pleasure now startlingly familiar.

Oh, this was—

Finlay blew out a sudden breath. 'God, Rilla, you feel so good.'

Good? A much too insufficient word.

'You feel perfect,' she managed, hands fisting into the straw as her back unconsciously arched, drawing him deeper. 'You are perfect, Finlay, perfect for me, perfect for— Oh, God!'

Rilla had not intended to cry out, but the gentle shift Finlay made, out and then spearing into her once more, was too much.

Pleasure roared through her, a fire she could never have predicted but now wished to light all over her body.

Burn.

'Rilla,' Finlay moaned, pulling out almost completely then thrusting back into her with a groan that suggested he was experiencing at least part of the sublime sensuality that she was. 'Yes, yes, yes…'

What words were spoken between them after that, Rilla could not recall. Words and kisses and moans intermingled as Finlay's gentle rhythm became harsher, harder, until she was floating on waves of pleasure that suddenly launched into ecstasy and it was no longer possible to hold it in.

'Finlay!' she sobbed.

The peak of her climax muffled all sound, removed all sense of place, and it was only thanks to her hands, which had somewhere released the straw and instead clutched his shoulders, that she knew Finlay was there.

With her. Beside her, within her through all this.

And then she heard him. 'Rilla, God, yes,' came the muffled grunt as he thrust, shuddering, into her.

The sudden pressure was quickly understood. Rilla felt the pressure of his shoulders on hers, the rough hair of his chest upon her breasts, his arms sinking around her as Finlay collapsed into her arms.

She held him. Held the man who had shown her so much. Held the man she loved.

And was complete. Complete and truly happy for perhaps the first time in her life.

Chapter Fourteen

Happiness was not something Rilla was particularly accustomed to. She had learned not to grow attached to it, and so now that it was here, it was rather a shock.

Sylvia and Daphne had both noticed the following morning and made sure to inform her in their own very different ways.

'You…you seem less morose,' Daphne said hesitantly as they all sat in the drawing room attending to their needlework.

Well. The other wallflowers attended to their needlework. Miss Pike had recently given them a lesson on the correct way to sit while embroidering, to best show off one's natural assets and to entice a gentleman to approach and ask what they were working on.

It sounded like hogwash to Rilla, but then it did not matter much to her. It wasn't as though she could do needlework.

'Less morose?' Rilla repeated sardonically.

It was Sylvia's laugh that filled the room. 'Less miserable, more like! You've been wandering around with a smile on your face all evening. What has got into you?'

And Rilla had flushed, for her friend could not know precisely how her words had been most suggestive.

I cannot help but notice that you are still wearing all your clothes.

So are you. Mostly. Something I would like to rectify immediately.

'Into me?' she said, trying not to laugh. 'I don't know what you mean.'

'It's that earl, if you ask me,' Sylvia said conversationally. 'Oh, would you like a glass of water, Rilla?'

'No. No, I'm fine,' Rilla said, her eyes watering as she attempted to slow her coughing fit. 'Perfectly fine. How is your father?'

It was a low blow, but desperate times called for something truly desperate. Besides, the gossip was all over the Academy: he had been seen, in Almack's, dancing with a woman. And not in a genteel, aloof manner, either.

'I haven't seen the Earl of Staromchor for a while,' said Daphne softly, her gentle voice even quieter. She must be concentrating. Rilla knew Daphne was always quieter when she was concentrating.

'But wasn't that him today?' came Sylvia's disinterested voice. 'I thought it looked like him, in the grounds, just ten minutes ago.'

Rilla stood up immediately. Then she wished she hadn't.

Sylvia's chortling laugh filled her ears as Rilla made her way to the hall. 'I knew it! You tell me all about it when you get back, Rilla. I want to know how you plan to seduce him!'

Little did her friend know, of course, that she had already most decidedly seduced the man, Rilla thought with a grin as she reached for a shawl hanging up in the hall and made her way to the front door.

And if Finlay was here, then his only reason could be that he wished to see her. Why else would he come all this way?

He had not been able to make any promises to her when he had left after their amorous encounter in the stables. And she had not expected him to.

I know you have no wish to marry. That is, a marriage between us would be impossible.

Still, it would have been nice to know when she would be seeing him again.

The cold air hit Rilla hard in the chest as she stepped out into the afternoon air. Goodness, but winter was here.

'Finlay?' she said quietly.

'I'm here,' came the expected answering voice.

Turning, Rilla beamed in the direction of the man she adored. Though the future was uncertain, her connection with Finlay was not one that could be denied. Her prospects aside, she had found what she wanted. True affection, true respect. What could be better?

'I was attempting to consider how I would find you,' came Finlay's voice, which was warm yet stilted.

Because they were in full view of the Wallflower Academy, Rilla surmised. Well, she could hardly blame him. They had done their best to keep their assignation to themselves. It would hardly be possible to keep such a thing under wraps if they were seen together.

'Rilla, I—'

'Why don't we—'

They both halted, and after a brief laugh, Rilla indicated her head to the left. 'A walk would do us both good, I think. Give us the opportunity to…to talk. In private.'

And more, she thought with a flicker of a smile.

Oh, she would hope for more, even if their encounter in the stables was perhaps to be the only time they managed to make love. Though Gwen had managed it with her duke. How precisely she had managed to smuggle the man into her bedchamber, Rilla did not know—had never thought to ask her. And it wasn't as though she could write to the Duchess of Knaresby and ask such a scandalous thing…

'Yes. Yes, a walk.' Perhaps it was her imagination, but Finlay sounded distracted. 'Good. Fine. Yes. May…may I take your arm?'

Rilla beamed, her heart skipping a beat as he once again asked her permission. Oh, it was so delightful when he did that.

'Yes.'

Their footsteps swiftly moved in time, mirroring her heartbeat as they walked around the front of the house and around the side by the kitchen gardens.

Step-step, thump-thump...

This was what she wanted. To be in step with a man she loved. To have him by her side, at all times. To know that if she needed him, he would be right there.

How had she managed to find such a man after all this time? After such a disappointment? After believing that all earls, nay all men, were unworthy of her trust?

'Rilla,' said Finlay in a slightly strangled voice.

Rilla tilted her head towards him. 'Yes?'

There was silence. No, not quite silence. Now she was concentrating, she noticed that his breathing was a little laboured. As though he had run here, which he most certainly had not. Perhaps he was nervous?

Nervous? What did the Earl of Staromchor have to be nervous about?

'Rilla, I... I need to tell you something.'

Rilla's shoulders relaxed. Oh, if that was all, then there was no concern there. This was the great declaration, wasn't it? When Finlay finally admitted that he loved her. Then she could happily tell him that his affection was reciprocated, and then...

Well, what happened after that was a tad vague. But it would not matter. They loved each other. They could overcome anything.

'I had hoped to tell you this in private, but—'

'We are near the gardening sheds, aren't we?' Rilla said, interrupting him.

Finlay stopped and she halted with him. 'How on earth could you tell?'

'I can smell the onions, and there's wild garlic that grows

just outside the potting shed,' said Rilla with a wry laugh. 'Really, it's not that difficult.'

She had expected Finlay to laugh, to admit that once again he had underestimated her. As so many people did.

Instead, Finlay grunted, 'Excellent. Let's go behind here.'

Rilla almost tripped as he pulled her forward hastily, but managed to stay upright as he tugged her around to the left. Then for some inexplicable reason, he released her hand.

Allowing her fingers to move in the space around her, she grazed her palm gently against the wood wall of the potting shed. Fine, that would give her a point to navigate by.

'Finlay,' she said softly.

He sighed heavily, then his forehead was pressed against hers. 'Rilla.'

They stood there in silence and Rilla breathed him in. Not just his scent, though the fragrance was delectable. No, Finlay himself. He was everything to her now. So much of her life she had lived without being understood, and though he had made more than his fair share of blunders, he had adapted.

He had wanted to know how to improve. To know her.

And now they had shared the most precious, the most wonderful thing.

'I have…have something to tell you,' Finlay breathed.

'And I will listen,' Rilla said softly. 'You know you can always talk to me, Finlay.'

It was the wrong thing to say. At least, that was how it appeared. The earl groaned, and suddenly crushed his lips against hers in a potent kiss that pushed Rilla against the shed wall.

It was intoxicating, being pinned against the rough wood with nothing but the softness of Finlay on her lips and the hard wall of his chest before her. Rilla splayed her fingers against his coat and felt the woollen scarf wrapped around his neck.

But she couldn't think about that. She was far more interested in the searing kiss pressing against her mouth, the tease of Finlay's tongue as it slipped along her lips, parting them, the decadent pleasure that poured through her body as he began to ravish her mouth.

Rilla moaned, and that only seemed to spur him on. Finlay's hands were on her shoulders but they slipped to her waist, pulling her closer and making it impossible to escape him.

As though she would want to.

'Rilla, I—'

'I know,' Rilla said in a ragged voice as Finlay started trailing kisses down her neck, her breasts heaving with every arduous breath. 'I know.'

Precisely what he had intended to say she did not know. But she knew what he wanted, was sure that this pressure, this aching need that was throbbing through her was undoubtedly mirrored in him.

And that was why, when Finlay released her and stepped back, Rilla reached out with a whimper of need.

'Finlay?'

'I shouldn't do this. I hadn't intended to. I meant to do something quite different,' came Finlay's voice, rough and coarse.

Rilla's heart skipped a beat. 'What are you— Finlay!'

There was no other option than to cry his name as she felt his hands somehow on her knees. Was he— Surely Finlay could not be kneeling before her?

'Finlay?' she repeated, her voice now a whisper in the hope they would not be overheard.

Being discovered like this, with a man kneeling before her... Surely he was not going to propose?

Rilla swallowed hard, but all thoughts of proposals disappeared the instant another sensation rushed over her knees. This time it was not the warm and steady touch of a gentleman who knew precisely how to please.

No, it was the movement of her skirts.

Then and only then did she get an inkling of what Finlay was about to do.

'Finlay,' Rilla said for a third time. This time her voice quavered with unadulterated lust.

She had guessed right. Kneeling before her, and probably getting damp knees in the process, for it had rained most heavily that morning, Finlay was lifting up her skirts and...

And kissing up her thigh.

Rilla tried to breathe steadily as she leaned against the shed, depending on it for stability as her whole body quaked with mounting pleasure.

Surely he couldn't—he wouldn't? Gentlemen did not do such a thing, did they?

They most certainly did. Before Rilla could even think about telling Finlay to stop—and she definitely did not want him to—his lips had reached between her legs.

And licked.

Shivers claimed her body, making it almost impossible to stand, but the solid potting shed behind her and Finlay's grip on her hips kept her steady.

Though neither of those forces could steady her mind. Whirling, twisting with astonishment at the sparks of pleasure formed with every nibble, lick, suck of Finlay's mouth, Rilla clutched at his shoulders in an attempt to remain upright.

'Oh, Finlay,' she whimpered, the pleasure overwhelming.

It was decadent, it was outrageous, it was scandalous. If they were to be found...

And somehow, the suggestion that they could be discovered at any moment only heightened Rilla's enjoyment. Which was indecent. And delicious.

Finlay's tongue darted inside her and Rilla moaned, the aching heat growing at such a fast pace she could hardly keep up.

'Yes...'

The whisper was not precisely a request, but Finlay seemed to understand what she meant by it.

The intrusion, the welcome intimacy, deepened as his tongue delved into her wet folds, and Rilla's head tilted back against the rough wood of the potting shed as her pleasure built...

'Finlay,' she choked out as her climax rolled over her.

It was short, sharp, sudden. More than she could have imagined, and yet in many ways entirely different from the roll in the hay which they had enjoyed previously. Rilla's body washed with pleasure, the ecstasy hot and burning, exacerbated and fed by the strange sensation of Finlay kneeling between her feet, his head under her skirts.

Just when she thought it was over, Finlay's tongue swirled around the nub of her pleasure and he pushed her higher, thrusting her over a peak she had never reached, and Rilla cried out just as jackdaws squawked and took to the air.

And then she was blinking as the man she loved withdrew from her body, still holding her tight.

It was a wonder, really, she was able to stand at all.

Finlay chuckled as he brought his arm around her waist. 'Steady on there.'

'You think that I can remain steady after...' Rilla swallowed.

It had been difficult enough to keep her voice down as he brought her to such pinnacles of pleasure, but her mouth was still dry and her heart still frantic.

This man—she loved him. And surely he must love her, even if the words themselves had not been uttered between them.

Love was not something one said. It was what one did, and Finlay had proved, several times now that he was a man she could trust. An earl she could trust, far more than she could have believed possible.

And as for the future...

Well, the future would come whether she wanted it to or not, Rilla reasoned as she steadied herself on her feet and slipped her hand into Finlay's arm, feeling the roughness of his coat against her fingers.

What the future would hold, she did not know. The one thing she did know was that Finlay would be in it.

What else could she possibly want?

'I had not intended to ravish you so utterly,' Finlay said in a low voice as they started to walk slowly towards the Wallflower Academy.

Rilla laughed, joy bursting in her chest. 'Oh, I wouldn't say that was utterly.'

Flirting with Finlay was as natural as breathing. So too did it seem natural that his chuckle radiated through her side, making her feel his laughter as well as hear it.

'Well, we are close to the stables.'

'Finlay!'

'Perhaps I can show you just how utterly I adore you.'

Flickers of delight were cascading down Rilla's spine and heat blossomed on her cheeks at the inappropriate suggestion.

'We were fortunate not to get caught the first time,' she reminded him, squeezing his arm.

Finlay sighed dramatically. 'I suppose so.'

'And Miss Pike has decided to ban us from the stables,' Rilla added, recalling the awkward conversation over breakfast.

There was a snort from beside her. 'Dear God, there is no possibility she suspects, is there?'

Heaven forbid.

'No, no,' Rilla said hastily, their feet moving from the grass to the gravelled path. It crunched under their feet as she continued, 'No, this is because of Sylvia.'

Another snort. 'I should have guessed.'

'She is perhaps not the wallflower the Pike envisioned for her Academy,' said Rilla with a grin.

'What has she got up to this time?'

'From what she will admit to me, I believe Sylvia was attempting to steal a horse,' said Rilla in a confidential tone.

She was rewarded by another chuckle from Finlay. 'She didn't!'

'It won't be the first time she's tried to run away from the Wallflower Academy,' said Rilla darkly, though a smile still lingered on her face.

How could it not, when she was with the man she loved?

'Sylvia and her schemes… I tried to talk her out of the last one, but apparently—'

'So it is thanks to Sylvia's antics, then, that we will have to find a new location for…conversation?' came Finlay's low, seductive voice.

A thrill rushed through Rilla as she thought of all the joy and pleasure they had to look forward to in their future. Days and days of it. Precisely what she was going to do when the month was up and her place at the Wallflower Academy was gone, she did not know…but surely Finlay would not allow her to be destitute?

And an idea, a wonderful idea, one she had barely allowed herself to consider but now sparked in her mind as bright as the sun, soared into her consciousness.

Well—they loved each other, did they not? Those words had not been exchanged but they did not need to be. Rilla knew how she felt about him, knew how Finlay felt about her.

He could not marry her—surely he would have offered for her hand if he thought her position appropriate for that of countess— but perhaps that was not necessary.

Rilla swallowed hard. Could she do it? Did she love him enough to become Finlay's mistress?

'Finlay,' she said softly, hardly sure how precisely she was supposed to broach such a topic, but knowing she must.

After all, she had been the one to proposition him to make love to her, had she not? And that had worked out splendidly. More than splendidly. Far better than she could have imagined.

'Rilla,' he said quietly.

A shimmer of need washed over her but Rilla pushed it aside. She needed to concentrate to ask this question.

'Finlay, would you…would you ever consider—'

'Ah, I thought it was you, Miss Newell! And—my good-ness. My lord. What an honour!'

And Rilla's heart sank.

Of course.

There was no possibility she could have this conversation without being interrupted. And of all people to interrupt her...

The scent of carbolic soap wafted through the air as foot-steps approached them. 'I have just been to the village, my lord, picking up a few things for my wallflowers. I trust you have had a pleasant walk? Where is Miss Bryant? I presume she accompanied you? This is more than a little unsettling, my lord. You hardly need to be schooled in the rules of the *ton*.'

Rilla tried not to permit heat to flood her cheeks, certain her embarrassment would be obvious, but there was nothing she could do to stop it.

Pleasant walk? Yes, some parts of it had been most pleas-ant indeed...

'You have some beautiful gardens and grounds here, Miss Pike,' Finlay was saying politely. 'I look forward to seeing them in the summer, when the flowers are out.'

'Oh, just a few borders of my own design,' came the im-modest voice of Miss Pike. Rilla stifled a smile. 'Gardening is, after all, one of life's most simple pleasures. I typically find...'

Rilla ceased paying attention.

Well, she had heeded the Pike's lectures on the benefits of gardening quite enough times over the years. The woman was hardly going to say something new and surprising after such a long—

'And I do apologize, my lord, I have been most remiss! I have not enquired as to your mother's health. She must be run ragged, preparing for your wedding.'

And all sound disappeared.

It was most disconcerting. Oh, there were sounds, noises in the far reaches of her hearing, but they appeared deadened, as though underwater or a long way off.

I have not enquired as to your mother's health. She must be run ragged, preparing for your wedding.

The words each individually made sense, but as Rilla attempted to weave them together to make sense of them, a dizziness rocked her head and she almost stumbled, leaning heavily on Finlay's arm.

Finlay was saying awkwardly, 'Ah, yes…erm…th-thank you, Miss Pike, for your kind—'

'I had no idea that the wedding was so soon,' prattled on Miss Pike as Rilla attempted to gain her balance. 'Just a few weeks! You yourself must be very busy with the final preparations.'

She must be run ragged, preparing for your wedding.

'Yes, yes, very busy,' came Finlay's voice.

But Finlay was a long way off. Though Rilla still had her arm linked into his, the man was suddenly distant. Unknown to her. A stranger.

Who was this man, then, who purported to be Finlay Jellicoe, Earl of Staromchor?

She had been so certain that she had known him, had understood him. Had cleverly deduced that he was a man to be trusted, a man to whom she could give herself without regret. And now here she was, being forced to listen to the man, whoever he was, talk about his…his wedding?

'I suppose my invitation has been lost in the post…they are getting careless,' the Pike was saying in that delicate tone of self-importance that was all her own. 'Well, I must be off. I have wallflowers waiting for these. Good day, my lord. Come, Miss Newell.'

Whatever 'these' were, Rilla could not tell. She presumed that the proprietress of the Wallflower Academy had showed Finlay something and had not seen fit to bother to explain it to her.

Not that it mattered. Nothing mattered, not anymore. She stepped forward, forgetting for a moment that she was trapped by her hand in his arm. There was nothing in the world that mattered, because the man she had trusted, the man she had been certain she knew—

'Rilla,' said Finlay hastily in a low, urgent tone. 'Rilla—'

'I don't want to hear it,' Rilla said, half in a daze.

She slipped her hand from his arm. It took two attempts as the brigand attempted to clasp her fingers the first time she tried to move away from him, but then she managed it and her hands were on the wall of the Tudor manor.

It earthed her, grounded her, as nothing else had.

So. Everything that she thought she knew about Finlay, as it turned out, was a lie. Once again she had thought herself in love, thought that she could be happy. Once again she had permitted an earl to matter to her, to creep into her heart and have weight with her emotions, and once again she had been disappointed.

She must be run ragged, preparing for your wedding.

Rilla swallowed hard, desperately hoping that the tears threatening to spill would not fall—would not give him the satisfaction of seeing just how hurt she was.

Finlay was to be married. Had been engaged to be married, to another woman, the entire time.

Oh, she had been such a fool.

But no longer. Rilla straightened herself up, ignoring whatever it was that Finlay was saying in a rush of words that made it almost impossible to decipher, and said coldly, 'Stay away from me, Earl.'

Chapter Fifteen

'I do apologize, my lord, I have been most remiss! I have not enquired as to your mother's health. She must be run ragged, preparing for your wedding.'

And that was when Finlay knew he was the absolute worst human being who had ever lived.

Rilla had stiffened in his arms, and though he had turned immediately to her, desperate to show her how remorseful he was, he could not speak.

There were no words.

He had betrayed her, completely and utterly—and the worst of it was that Rilla could not see the contrition on his face. No, she had to stand there in silence and suffer listening to Miss Pike.

'I had no idea that the wedding was so soon,' prattled on Miss Pike, preventing him from saying anything. 'Just a few weeks! You yourself must be very busy with the final preparations.'

'Yes, yes, very busy,' Finlay found himself saying.

Rilla had said nothing, done nothing, merely stood there. Her expression was cold, stiff, as it always was when Rilla was seeking to distance herself from what was happening around her.

And he had done that. Him, and his lies, his deception, his inability to admit the truth: that he was engaged to be married to a woman who was devoted to him.

It pained him as nothing had ever hurt before, but what could he say when Miss Pike was still standing there?

'I suppose my invitation has been lost in the post... They are getting careless,' Miss Pike was saying with a sharp glance in his direction. 'Well, I must be off. I have wallflowers waiting for these. Good day, my lord. Come, Miss Newell.'

She waved the basket under her arm which was full of brown paper parcels, and turned on her heels before walking off.

The instant he judged her to be out of earshot, Finlay brought his mouth close to her ear. 'Rilla. Rilla—'

'I don't want to hear it,' Rilla said dully.

That was when she tried to pull free of him. Finlay attempted to hold on to her, desperate not to lose the connection they had, that they shared—emblematic of the closeness he was terrified to lose.

But he could not, would not hold her against his will. He was not that sort of man. He would not demand a woman's intimacy when she so clearly wished to revoke it.

It was as though he had been punched in the gut as Rilla took a step back from him, clinging to the wall of the Wallflower Academy as though it was the only dependable thing in the world.

Nausea rose in Finlay's chest. What had he done?

She must be run ragged, preparing for your wedding.

If only Miss Pike had not been foolish enough to mention the wedding.

But no, Finlay could not blame her, much as he might wish to. It had been his choice to keep such a thing secret, his decision not to inform Rilla of his betrothal.

He had been the one to accept her offer of lovemaking. Dear God, he had been the one to lick her to ecstasy just minutes ago.

And despite his best intentions, which had been to come to the Wallflower Academy and finally admit to Rilla that he had a prior commitment and could no longer enjoy her company as he would wish…

Despite all that, it was Miss Pike who had revealed the truth. *Hell.*

Finlay's gaze raked over Rilla's face and saw the devastation he felt. Christ, she was trying not to cry; he could see the tension in her temples as her eyes sparkled.

He was the lowest of the low. He had to explain.

'I know I should have told you from the start and I had intended to but I was in too deep before I realized what I was about and it grew harder and harder to—'

The words tumbled from his mouth, almost nonsensical in their speed, and evidently Rilla was not interested.

She had straightened up, back against the wall, as she said, 'Stay away from me, Earl.'

Mortification rushed through Finlay's chest.

Oh, it was not bad enough that he had completely destroyed all faith and trust between them. It wasn't enough that he had lied, and had now been caught out in said lie in a most shameful way.

No, it was worse than that. He had manged to confirm to Rilla just what she had believed when they had first met: that earls were not to be trusted.

'I should have told you earlier.'

'You should have,' said Rilla quietly, her voice distant, as though they were discussing the weather. 'And yet you did not.'

Finlay swallowed. This would have been a much easier conversation if he could have arrived with his engagement broken completely, Isabelle Carr nothing more to him than an acquaintance he used to know as a child.

Oh, hell. How had he managed to create this situation? One bad decision after another, but each one made because he had thought it was the best thing at the time. The best thing for Isabelle.

How had he managed to get this so wrong, hurt so many people?

'Who is she?'

Finlay winced. The ice in Rilla's tone was surely merely a front, something designed to keep her true feelings at bay, but after all they had shared it was excruciating to hear all warmth gone.

Less than an hour ago, they had been happy. But that time was over.

'Her name, please, my lord,' said Rilla, as though she were merely enquiring about a pair of kid gloves.

Finlay took a deep breath. 'Isabelle. Isabelle Carr.'

'Carr?' Rilla nodded slowly. 'Ah, I see. Cecil's sister. You must care for her very much.'

'It's not like that.'

'Then why are you marrying her?' Rilla said, cutting him off.

Finlay attempted to gather his thoughts, flying about him with no consideration for his exhausted mind.

Why was he marrying her?

A fortnight ago he would have said it was nothing more than a marriage of convenience. Something required as a man of honour, not because he had ruined Isabelle's, but because she had precious little else to sustain her.

And now...

Now there was guilt. Oh, there was guilt. He should never have listened at the drawing room door, but he could not forget what he had heard.

His happiness is... It is the most important thing to me. There is not a single day that does not go by when I do not think of him.

She loved him, depended on the marriage going ahead. The true affection had been so potent that he had not needed to see her speak to believe her words. And he could not cause that woman any more grief. She had already suffered enough.

'It… She…' Finlay pulled a hand through his hair, desperately attempting to marshal his ideas. 'It was a marriage of convenience.'

'Was?'

'I offered her marriage when her brother—when Cecil died,' Finlay said, rattling on hastily in the hope it would be less painful that way.

The wind blew between them, a chill in the air. It would snow soon.

'Why would you do that?' Rilla's voice was calm, as though attempting to discover why a friend had chosen a particular hue for a painting.

If only he had time to think—if only his frantically beating heart would give him solace, rather than course panic through his veins with every squeeze!

'I— It's hard to explain.'

'You said it was a marriage of convenience.' Rilla's hands were clasped before her. 'Was. What is it now? Are you in love with her?'

'No,' Finlay said immediately. Of that, he was sure.

'And yet you will marry her.'

'I— It's not as simple as…' His voice trailed off as he attempted to think.

It was his own fault. If he had just been open about Isabelle's existence at the beginning…

Finlay's shoulders sagged. But he had so swiftly been caught up in Rilla's presence that all thoughts of Isabelle were entirely forgotten.

He swallowed hard. 'She loves me.'

'Ah, there it is,' said Rilla darkly, in a sardonic tone that cut straight into Finlay's chest. 'Of course she does! What woman would not fall in love with the charming earl?'

'It isn't like that,' Finlay snapped.

'Isn't it? You are engaged to be married, you absolute cur, and you knew that I had once—that I had almost married. Was it not enough to make me the laughingstock of the whole Wall-flower Academy? How can I ever trust—'

Rilla's voice broke off as she raised a hand to her mouth, forcing down a sob that broke Finlay's heart.

He had done this.

Rilla was right; he had known her history with the Earl of Porthaethwy and he had ploughed on regardless. He had wooed her, flirted with her, charmed her, and he had known at every turn that nothing could happen between them.

Nothing that would last, at any rate.

'I wanted to end the engagement,' he said, his voice cracking.

Rilla snorted. 'But you have not.'

Finlay closed his eyes, desperately forcing the tears away. 'No—not yet! I intended to last night, but she was out, and… I will. I will, I promise.'

Oh, God, he sounded like such a scoundrel saying that.

But Rilla had not heard Isabelle talking so passionately about her affection. She had lost her brother—they had both lost Cecil, but Isabelle was the one alone in the world.

What, was he to deny her any happiness whatsoever?

But there could only be one happy woman: Rilla or Isabelle. Finlay knew he had been forced to choose between them.

And there was only a wrong choice.

'I… I made you no other promises,' Finlay said, grasping on to that fact like a lifeboat in a storm. 'I never intended for you to care.'

'You have broken no vow, either,' Rilla retorted. 'Do you feel proud of yourself?'

Finlay's jaw tightened. 'No.'

'Oh, God, I said to you before that I was more than a match for an earl, and yet here you are, proving me wrong!'

'No, Rilla, I—'

'I am worth far more,' she said imperiously, holding her head high. 'I am certainly worth more than this.'

How could she say that? How could they even be having this conversation here, right in front of the Wallflower Academy, where anyone could see them?

Oh, God. Where anyone could see them.

Finlay turned away from Rilla for a moment and saw precisely what he had hoped not to see. There, in the large bay window that jutted out from the morning room, and therefore where there was an excellent view of the front of the house, was...

A troop of women. He recognized Sylvia and Daphne, but there were also half a dozen other ladies, all goggling. Hell. There must be an afternoon tea or something. Of course there was.

Finlay swore under his breath.

'There is no need for language like that!'

'No, it's just—'

'And I did not demand any promises,' Rilla said, countering his earlier point.

'Rilla, there are people watching.' Finlay tried to take her arm to pull her away from the window and the gawping gazes of the wallflowers, but she continued on, her voice catching as words spilled out.

'But I presumed that friends—lovers—had an unspoken expectation of honesty. More fool me.'

Finlay's jaw was tightening again, causing a throb of pain to stretch to his temple. This was all going wrong, but he had to admit, even if it were only to himself, that there was no possibility of it going right. He had made this decision. Now he was having to face the consequences.

'You should have been honest with me,' Rilla said quietly. 'You should have said... That poor woman, and here I am... I would have wanted to know if there was no future for us, of any kind.'

That sparked indignation in Finlay's chest. 'I did. You said that you knew we could not wed!'

'But I hadn't thought about marriage, not really,' she said fiercely, and Rilla actually took a step towards him, her body seeming to thrum with certainty. 'I hadn't expected *that*! When I thought about our future, I thought… I hoped…'

Finlay's stomach lurched.

Was it possible? Could it be that Rilla had considered becoming his mistress?

They could have been together in a small way. He could have found his joy and happiness with her while Isabelle…

The thought of his future bride poured cold water over that idea.

He was no rake. He could not take one woman to the altar, knowing that she was desperately in love with him, then betray her with another woman.

His stomach twisted painfully. Though hadn't he done just that? Self-loathing and regret mingled with pain in his chest. How had this gone so wrong?

Finlay took in a deep breath and rubbed his chin, his jaw tight. 'I know you probably think very little of me in this moment. I may not love her, but I have to respect her. Respect her feelings.'

'Like you respected mine?'

He hung his head, shifting on his feet. 'You…you're right. I lied to myself, Rilla. I made myself believe this whole damned situation wouldn't hurt anyone. And I've hurt you, and I'm so sorry, you're the one I would least like to hurt, Rilla, I—'

'Don't call me that,' she said sharply.

Pain flared in his chest, but it was quickly subsumed by despair. 'I was weak, Rilla, I was a fool, but you have to believe me, no one can loathe me more than I loathe myself! You've never made a mistake? Rilla—'

'I told you before, my friends call me Rilla,' she said, and now she was crying, tears gently falling down her cheeks, and Finlay's heart twisted in agony. 'You may call me Miss Newell, for the purposes of this conversation.'

A flicker of hope. 'This conversation? And after?'

'Oh, there won't be an after,' Rilla said with a sniff. 'You think I wish to speak to you again after this?'

Finlay turned away for a moment in an attempt to gather his thoughts. If only there was a way to prove his affections… but what was the point? He would be Isabelle's groom in ten days. Ten days—that was all—and he would be parted from Rilla forever.

Though he wasn't sure they could be much more parted than this.

She was closing herself off from him, distancing him from her true self, and there was nothing he could do but watch it happen. Hate it happen. Hate that he could do nothing about it.

'I… I hoped—'

'When you said that you were not getting married anytime soon, that was a lie,' Rilla said, speaking over him as a cloud shadowed the sky. 'Your friendship, our connection, whatever… whatever this is, it was all based on a lie. Did you think you could lie to my face because I can't see?'

Revulsion poured through Finlay's chest. 'No.'

'Yet you did so anyway,' Rilla said with a nonchalant shrug that cut to his very soul. 'I wasn't important enough to tell the truth to just a wallflower, no prospects, no family—'

'I love you!' Finlay blurted out.

He had imagined a completely different moment when he would tell her this. When they were in each other's arms, perhaps. When they had just finished kissing. Maybe when he had just finished feeding her strawberries, Rilla's lips stained with the juices and his own lips hungry for hers.

He had certainly hoped for a different response.

Rilla snorted. 'Don't be ridiculous.'

'I am not being—'

'A man in love doesn't hurt the person he purports to love,' Rilla said, and there was pain in her voice, which Finlay hated to hear. 'A man in love—a gentleman!—does not lie about his marital prospects!'

'I never lied. I just never—'

'Told the truth?' she said, finishing the sentence for him.

Finlay turned away for a moment, trying to collect himself, but when he turned back to her she was still standing there, still Rilla, still perfect.

'I should have known,' Rilla said softly. 'Never trust an earl.'

And the fire that flared in his chest had nothing to do with Isabelle, or his upcoming marriage, and had everything to do with Rilla's words.

'I'm not saying that I am a paragon of virtue,' he said quietly. 'But blame me for my actions, not my title. You were just as guilty of treating me poorly when we first met.'

'You made me think you were a footman!' Rilla interjected hotly.

'I thought we had moved past our assumptions about each other, but clearly I was wrong!' Finlay said bitterly before he could stop himself.

Regret soared through his heart immediately.

What did he think he was doing, speaking to a woman like that? Speaking to Rilla like that—to anyone like that?

Finlay's head hung low.

Dear God, he was just as bad as she thought he was. Perhaps worse.

But there was still something he could do, if he could just kiss her, show her...

'Rilla...'

'Rilla!'

Finlay stepped back hastily as he glanced over his shoulder to see Miss Smith, her blond hair now paired with scarlet cheeks, staring at the two of them.

'What are you doing to her?' she said, a mite accusingly.

'Nothing,' snapped Finlay, knowing he should be more patient, knowing the poor woman had no idea what was truly happening, but unable to restrain his ire. 'I'm not doing anything.'

'That is precisely right. His Lordship is doing nothing,' said Rilla with a sardonic smile. 'Go on in, Daphne. I will join you presently.'

The wallflower did not seem particularly convinced, but she did not appear to have the force of character to disagree. She turned slowly, fixing her eyes for the longest moment in a stare, then trotted up the steps to the Wallflower Academy.

Only when the door closed did Finlay take a deep breath. Now to show not tell Rilla precisely how he felt.

'And on that note, I will bid you good day,' Rilla said darkly.

She had managed to take three steps before Finlay grabbed her arm. 'Let me help.'

'I have had quite enough of your help, thank you,' she snapped, wrenching her arm away. 'Don't touch me!'

'But I can help you up the steps,' Finlay persisted, walking alongside her.

He was bound to her in honour, even if he could not be bound to her in any other way. Did she not know that? Could she not see that he adored her? Had she not listened when he had said that he loved her?

'Oh, I know this path,' Rilla said with a laugh that held no mirth. 'I know this path well. It is one I have walked for many years—alone.'

Finlay swallowed, wishing he could console her, wishing things could be different.

'At this rate, I will be walking alone for many years to come,' Rilla said as they reached the steps up to the Wallflower Academy. 'But you know what, Finlay?'

Her voice had modulated, calmed. Hope, pathetic and small, rose. 'What?'

'I would rather walk it alone than with you,' Rilla said sweetly before she turned, walked up the steps, and slammed the door behind her, leaving Finlay standing before the Wallflower Academy entirely alone.

Chapter Sixteen

Staying in one's room for three days and requesting meals to be sent up to you was the sort of thing that great ladies did, Rilla reflected as the haze of light she could just perceive moved slowly across her bedchamber.

Still. That did not prevent her from doing it.

After all, it was not as though there was anything downstairs that she wanted. Company was abhorrent to her. The well-meaning questions flying about the place were anathema to her, and Rilla had already suffered the curiosity of those who had spotted herself and…and the Earl of Staromchor arguing.

A tear crept from her eye, sliding down her face and onto the bedlinens. Rilla did not bother to contain it. What was the point? There was no one here to see it, no one to judge her for making such a foolish choice as to trust an earl.

Not that she didn't judge herself.

I should have known. Never trust an earl.

A second tear followed the first one. She had fallen in love with Finlay Jellicoe, Earl of Staromchor, and try as she might she could not just cease loving him because it was inconvenient. Because he was marrying another woman. Because they were to be separated for the rest of their lives.

Rilla swallowed. What she had expected from him, she did not know. It was all so clouded now, clouded with the confusion of pain and their argument.

A man in love doesn't hurt the person he purports to love. A man in love—a gentleman!—does not lie about his marital prospects!

I never lied. I just never—

Told the truth?

And now all she could think about was Finlay and the woman he would marry. Was she beautiful? Did she sing well, play the pianoforte, embroider cushions and dance elegantly while listening to Finlay's words?

The knot in her stomach twisted most painfully.

Because it did not matter, did it? Finlay had made a commitment to that woman, and in all honour he certainly should continue with it.

Even if it hurt.

The pain of losing him was exquisite. Rilla had known hardship, known pain, known the separation between people you loved…or thought you loved. She had known betrayal. She was hardly new to expecting the worst in people.

Yet he had somehow wormed his way into her heart and now she was crippled by the affection within it that she could no longer give. It was a physical ache in her chest, as if a heavy weight had been placed there, and no one but Finlay could remove it.

But she couldn't just stay up here moping. Rilla knew, better than anyone else at the Wallflower Academy, just what was at stake if she did not find herself a situation.

I refer, most unwillingly, to the fact that your father will cease to pay for your place here at the Wallflower Academy at the end of next month.

Taking a deep breath and propping herself up against some pillows, Rilla tried not to think about the Pike's latest recommendation.

'A perfectly good school not ten miles away,' the woman had shouted through the keyhole only last night. 'They are looking for a well-bred, elegant woman to take charge of literature and history, and I thought—'

'They won't want a woman like me,' Rilla had shot back at the proprietress through the door.

Which had been a mistake. It had only encouraged Miss Pike to rattle on about how she was the daughter of a baron and an honourable and there was nothing anyone could dislike about her.

As if she did not know what Rilla meant.

The trouble was, the idea had kept Rilla up all night. It was a good situation, two hundred pounds a year, and bed and board included; it would certainly afford her a comfortable life. She may even be able to put a little aside for the future. For when she would be no longer useful, and therefore have nowhere else to go…

Rilla had finally arisen that morning with a headache and no clear direction. If only he hadn't—

Pushing thoughts of Finlay aside was getting harder and harder. Intrusive, warm thoughts about how comforting it was to find herself in his arms, how strong he was, how she had sunk into his embraces and kisses…

Sighing heavily, Rilla turned onto her other side. Today was the last day she would permit herself to lie about the place, she promised herself.

Tomorrow she would rise and tell the Pike that—

A timid knock on the door made Rilla jerk her head in that direction.

'Go away.'

The knock was repeated, louder this time. Rilla sighed and fell back onto the bed. The Pike had been sending wallflowers almost hourly since she had flown upstairs after the argument with Finlay.

She did not want to see anyone.

But that did not appear to matter. The Pike was determined that Rilla entertain, God forbid, and that was the direction her requests—demands—tended.

Come and converse with the wallflowers.

Come and sit with the wallflowers.

Come, tell the wallflowers the pitfalls of losing one's heart to an earl...

Another knock, this time even harder.

'I said, go away!' Rilla said sharply.

'I knew you would say that,' came the wretched voice of Daphne Smith. 'I told the Pike you wouldn't want to see me. No one ever does.'

A shard of guilt slid into her heart.

Oh, very clever, she thought darkly. *Well done, Miss Pike. You knew I could not be angry at someone like Daphne Smith.*

'Come in,' she said wearily aloud. 'The door is unlocked.'

Rilla never locked her door now, not after the key was once jostled from the latch and it took her over an hour to find it. The sense of being trapped, of being unable to escape, had been formidable.

The click of the door opening, then the snick of it closing again, sounded around the little bedchamber. Rilla pulled herself into a proper sitting position on the bed and looked defiantly in the door's direction, not bothering to wipe away her tears.

She could sense the hesitation of her friend. One of her two friends, really—being a wallflower at the Wallflower Academy naturally led some to a competitiveness that Rilla simply did not care for.

But Daphne was not like that. She was a true wallflower, a woman who hated being the centre of attention for more than five minutes.

Even when it was just the two of them, she was hesitant.

'I suppose the Pike wants me to come downstairs,' said Rilla into the silence. 'Please, sit.'

The creak of the wicker chair in the corner suggested that Daphne had accepted her invitation. Her assumption was confirmed when her friend spoke, the words coming now from the corner rather than the door.

'We are all very worried about you.'

Rilla snorted. 'I doubt that.'

It was perhaps a tad cruel, but it was also the truth. The Pike would be worried, certainly, but about what on earth to do with her when the money ran out, not about Rilla herself.

'I am very worried,' came the tentative voice of Daphne. 'Worried for you. No one should feel alone.'

And some of the bitterness and resentment against everyone in the world melted away.

'Thank you,' Rilla said awkwardly. 'You… Well, you did not have to trouble yourself.'

'I am happy to do it,' said Daphne softly. 'I never had a sister, and I thought— Well, when I was sent to the Wallflower Academy, I hoped…'

The trailing off of her words was in some way worse than her actually saying them.

A twist of discomfort surged in Rilla's chest. She and Sylvia had always been close, and Gwen had joined them for a time. Daphne was always on the outside looking in. She was a naturally shy woman who could not compete with the rambunctious Sylvia or the dry-witted Rilla.

It was not a pleasant thought, to believe she had left out someone who had so desperately craved friendship.

'I would like to be a friend to you,' she said awkwardly.

There was a slight chuckle from the corner. 'I don't want your pity, Rilla.'

'I did not mean it like that.'

'I know, and it speaks well of you that you would wish to… well, make amends is not quite the right phrase, but I do not know what is,' came Daphne's quiet voice. 'And I would like to be a friend to you. I would like to help, if I could. If you wished to talk to me about…about him.'

Him.

The entire Wallflower Academy had apparently watched her argument with Finlay with open mouths, from what Sylvia had said through the door yesterday. It showed great restraint on Daphne's part, Rilla thought, that she did not say his name.

'There's not much to say,' she said swiftly.

Not much that she was willing to say, anyway.

Rilla's fingers tightened around the bedlinen, the comfortingly familiar weave of the fabric grounding her.

'I suppose not,' came Daphne's soft reply. 'And I have no wish to force you.'

And it was precisely because Rilla knew that Daphne would never consider forcing her to spill her secrets that she felt as though she might.

After all, thoughts had been whirling around her mind for days and she had gained no relief from them. It was frustrating to the extreme to think that she may never fully understand why Finlay had done what he had done. She might never get the answers she sought, never again feel the brush of his fingers along her arm...

Rilla swallowed. 'It's...complicated.'

There it was again, another chuckle from the wallflower. 'I presumed that.'

Laughing despite herself, Rilla sighed. Opening up to anyone wasn't exactly the sort of thing she typically did. It was always easier to hold herself at a distance, to allow the cold and stiff expression on her face to keep others away.

Once bitten, twice shy.

But it was more than that. Rilla had never noticed it before, but the three years she had been at the Wallflower Academy had reduced her somehow. She had squashed herself, forced down her instincts, her personality, made it almost impossible not to succumb to the fear of...

Fear of what?

Rilla could not articulate it. Fear of what had happened, happening again.

But now the very worst had happened. She had fallen in

love, truly, for the first time, and that love had been betrayed. Nothing could be worse than that, could it?

'I trusted him,' Rilla found herself saying, her voice breaking.

She sensed a creak of the willow chair, a footstep, and then a depression on the bed near her feet.

'Tell me about it,' said Daphne softly.

And she did.

The words came slowly at first. It had been many years since Rilla had been open, truly open, with anyone. Besides, it was shameful, to reveal just how easily she had been taken in.

I know you have no wish to marry. That is, a marriage between us would be impossible…

The only parts of the story she neglected to mention were…

Well. Daphne did not need to know about that particular moment in the stables, did she? Or the proposition that came before it. Or the moment of intimacy by the potting shed near the kitchen garden.

Rilla swallowed.

No. Definitely not.

Daphne was an excellent listener. Rilla supposed it was due to the fact that the wallflower was often excluded from conversations—a thought that made her cringe with shame.

And before she knew it, she was nearing the end of her tale.

'And Miss Pike enquired about his wedding,' Rilla said miserably, her chest tight just thinking about it. Her hands had moved to her lap, clasping and unclasping. 'His wedding. And it was—oh, Daphne, it was so humiliating! To know I had given my…had given my heart to him, and he had known all the while that he was betrothed to another…'

That was when her voice faded into nothing.

Rilla swallowed hard, but there was no force left in her tongue.

What else was there to say? She had been taken in, and cruelly, but there was no brother to defend her and her father would surely not disgrace the family name again by intervening.

Miss Pike would merely censure her for getting entangled with an engaged man, Rilla thought darkly, and Sylvia—

Well. Sylvia would probably bodily attack the man, which wouldn't help, either.

What she needed, Rilla thought darkly, was for Finlay to wake up one moment and realize he had changed his mind. That he could not, would not go through with the wedding. That he would—

Carr? Ah, I see. Cecil's sister. You must care for her very much.

Her stomach lurched.

What, would she take a man like Finlay away from a woman who had, by the sound of it, already gone through so much?

'I am sorry,' came Daphne's soft voice.

Rilla laughed ruefully. 'As am I.'

'It seems a most unfortunate situation.'

'Most unfortunate, yes,' she replied sardonically. 'An earl who took advantage of me—which should not have surprised me—who is going to go and marry a woman he…he doesn't even love.'

Which was another reason why the whole blasted situation was such a disaster, Rilla wanted to say, but couldn't bring herself to.

Finlay was going to be miserable.

There was no doubt in her mind: he did not love this Miss Carr. He was only marrying her for some strange sense of duty. Did they both have to be miserable?

'I wish there was an answer,' came Daphne's gentle voice. 'I suppose in times like this, there is no one solution, no way to make everyone happy.'

Rilla blinked away tears. Daphne was surprisingly astute. 'N-no. No, there isn't.'

Finlay could only wed one woman and he had made his decision. It was one he may regret, in time. She regretted it already.

Could he not see—did he not understand how happy they could be?

'Unless…' Daphne said slowly. And then she said nothing.

Impatience flared in Rilla's chest. 'Unless what?'

'Well, it was just a passing… I would not like to presume… but—'

'Really, I must insist that you— Ah, Miss Smith. Miss Newell, I see you are feeling better,' uttered the voice of Miss Pike, coinciding with the snap of the door being thrust open. 'Excellent.'

Rilla sighed.

The Pike meant well. She knew it, all the wallflowers knew it. But the woman had no sense of timing.

What had Daphne been about to say?

'Now, I have not wished to press you while you were…unwell,' said Miss Pike sternly, stepping towards the bed and halting somewhere nearby. 'But as I can see that you are now entirely better—'

'Miss Pike,' Daphne said softly, but she was entirely ignored.

'I have come here to request your decision,' Miss Pike continued firmly. 'I believe you have had sufficient time, and time is, as it were, not your friend in this matter.'

Rilla winced. Yes, the proprietress of the Wallflower Academy certainly had a way with words. Not that Rilla could deny anything the woman had said. Time was certainly not her friend in this matter, and a decision was needed.

There was not much of a choice. Teaching, or penury on the streets?

'Well, you will be delighted to hear I have made a decision,' Rilla said stiffly. 'I will accept a post anywhere away from here. Where he can't— Where I won't have to meet—'

'You will?' came the delighted tone of Miss Pike.

'You will?' repeated Daphne, evidently confused. 'What post?'

'If you had wished to teach here, I would have welcomed that, naturally,' the Pike continued, once again ignoring the shy wallflower. 'And I am confident you will make an excellent teacher at—what was it called? I can't remember, I've got it written down somewhere. Arrangements will have to be made. You can take the Wallflower Academy carriage most of the way...'

Rilla allowed the words to wash over her as a dull sensation settled in her chest.

So, it was decided.

She would be leaving the Wallflower Academy and not to be married, as her father and the Pike had so desperately hoped—but to be a teacher. To accept that she required wages now to live.

'I'm sure some of the reports of the fractious nature of the pupils are completely fabricated.'

Rilla's shoulders tensed. But she couldn't fight any longer. She had no one on her side, supporting her cause. Her father had no interest, and Finlay...

She blinked back her tears furiously. Finlay had made his choice. He would be marrying Miss Isabelle Carr, and she was certain they would find a way to be happy together.

Could she have been happy with him?

Some moments, Rilla could not understand him. A man who had everything, a title, a position in Society, a fiancée—why had he dallied with her?

And then she recalled the openness in the garden, the closeness they had shared, the knowledge, knowledge she had felt in her bones, that she was the only one he cared about.

Oh, it was all such a confusion.

'So you can be gone within a week,' the Pike finished with a falsely bright tone. 'Won't that be nice?'

A wave of nausea flooded through Rilla at the thought.

Leaving the Wallflower Academy was an inevitability—she knew that—but leaving its comforting, familiar halls would be a wrench.

'Very nice,' she said aloud.

'Yes. Well. Right,' said Miss Pike, perhaps a little rattled by Rilla's lack of fighting spirit. 'I'll leave you two alone, then.'

Footsteps sounded, and a flutter of carbolic soap wafted through the room before the door snapped smartly behind her. The departing footsteps grew fainter on the other side of the wall, and then there was silence.

Silence, that was, until Daphne cleared her throat.

Rilla jumped. Goodness, she had almost forgot that the wall-flower was still there.

'Why did you not argue with her?' Daphne asked. 'I… Well, I do not mean to presume, but I did not think you wished to be a teacher. I have heard you and the Pike argue about it before.'

'What choice do I have?' Rilla said dully.

A woman without choices—most women, now she came to think about it. Choices were made by a father, brother, husband, someone else. Or there were no choices at all.

'But—'

'Daphne, I have no choice,' Rilla said sharply. 'Finlay, the Earl of Staromchor, is wedding someone else. I don't have a home to go back to, my father won't welcome me at home, and with no money to pay for my place here at the Wallflower Academy… I have nowhere else to go.'

Chapter Seventeen

Finlay pushed open the door, ignored the bell, ignored the astonished gasps from the customers about the place, and did what no gentleman had ever done before.

He marched past the modiste's assistant and into the fitting area.

'My lord!'

'Sir, please, you cannot go back there, it is for the ladies—'

But Finlay did not care.

He had taken three days to think it through. Three days, he had reasoned, was enough time to truly sit with the decision he wished to make. Time to consider if it was truly what he wished to do. Whether it was something he could live with.

And no matter how much time passed, his resolution remained: he had to marry Rilla Newell.

The instant he had come to the decision, he had to enact it—and this was the first step. To be sure, when Turner had said that his mother and Miss Carr were out, he had presumed they were at Hatchard's, or a bakery, or Twinings tea shop.

Still. Once he'd made the decision, nothing was going to hold Finlay back. Not even—

'Really, sir!' Another modiste's assistant, an apron over her gown and a wide-eyed expression of horror on her face, attempted to bat him away. 'This area is for ladies. There is a young Miss here for the final fitting of her wedding—'

'I know,' said Finlay sharply. 'She is my betrothed.'

Or at least, she was for the moment. A moment that would not last very long.

Ignoring the startled expression on his mother's face, Finlay marched past the two sofas and an armchair which were evidently there for the friends and family of whoever it was being fitted, and approached a screen.

'Isabelle?'

There was a startled yelp, a genteel curse, and Madame Penelope's head appeared around the side of the screen.

'You have made me prick my thumb,' she said darkly. 'I hope you have a good reason for barging in here, my lord.'

'I quite agree with you, Madame,' came the dour voice of the Dowager Countess of Staromchor behind him. 'I do not understand, Staromchor, why you suddenly have lost all sense of decorum. Really! A modiste's!'

Finlay ignored them both.

Well, he ignored them both as much as he could. It was impossible to prevent his ears from pinking. Especially as now he looked around him, he could see... Ah.

His mouth went dry.

Well, it was a lady's domain, he supposed.

The chintz everywhere was not his style, nor were the delicate shades of pink and leafy green that Madame Penelope had chosen to decorate the place with.

It looked more like a boudoir than a shop.

And it was even more like a boudoir, Finlay realized with growing apprehension in his lungs, because on display just to his right were a number of garments that were designed ... well, to be underclothes.

His face was now burning.

Hell's bells, but he hadn't expected this.

What man knew anything about the attiring rooms of a modiste's?

Finlay turned to his mother, who raised an eyebrow.

'I hope you are satisfied,' she said calmly, looking up from a pamphlet with a variety of different styles of gowns printed on its pages. 'I suppose this will be the talk of the Town, you forcing your way into a modiste's and risking seeing Miss Carr's wedding gown, too.'

It was the mention of the wedding gown that stiffened Finlay's resolve.

He had to finally speak his mind about this wedding. It had gone on for too long. He was starting to think, in truth, that he should never have made the offer to Isabelle in the first place.

The instinct had been a good one, Finlay knew, but it was not one which he could surely be expected to hold for the rest of his life.

I did not demand any promises... But I presumed that friends—lovers—had an unspoken expectation of honesty. More fool me.

His shoulders snapped back and he held his head high. No, mortified Madame Penelope and irate mother aside, he had to speak his mind.

He had not expected to do so in front of so many people, of course...

Finlay looked around and spotted no less than three assistants, one holding a plethora of ribbons, another merely blinking in astonishment.

Right. First things first.

'I wish to speak to Isabelle—to Miss Carr,' he amended hastily, in a voice he hoped was both commanding and charming. 'Alone, if you don't mind.'

The three assistants scampered away, but his mother rose and drew herself up in a most impressive manner.

'I do mind,' she said sharply. 'I cannot just permit you to be alone with Miss Carr. That would be scandalous. The very idea, a gentleman and a lady together, alone—and unmarried!'

Try as he might, Finlay was unable to put aside all thoughts of Rilla. Of the time they had spent together alone, of the things they had enjoyed while alone…

Perhaps his mother was right.

'My lord?'

The voice was gentle, and nervous, and it came from behind the screen.

Finlay's stomach twisted in a painful knot but he could not turn back now. He had to act. He had to have this…this show-down, for want of a better word.

He had hoped to speak with Isabelle at her lodgings, but the housekeeper had said she was getting her wedding gown fitted and—

Well. He had rather lost his head. The idea of Isabelle, a woman painfully in love with him, having her wedding gown fitted before he could speak to her…it could not be borne.

Which had led him, circuitously, to this awkward conversation.

Madame Penelope disappeared for a moment behind the screen again, and when she emerged she was not alone.

Isabelle Carr stood there, gazing with a curious look.

Finlay's heart skipped a beat.

Not because affection had suddenly welled in him—quite the opposite. A part of him, and he had not realized it had even existed until this moment, had wondered whether he would eventually fall in love with her. Whether the Isabelle he had once known would resurface, once they were married, and they could enjoy a sort of companionable respect in their marriage.

But seeing her like this, dressed in her finery, the elegant blue silk gown delicately fitted around her bust, her hair taste-fully shaped upon her head…

It was nothing. She was nothing compared to the sight of Rilla, straw in her hair and her unseeing gaze trusting.

Finlay swallowed.

There was no easy way to do this. Best to just get it over with.

'I can't marry you,' he blurted out.

The silence that followed this pronouncement was absolutely excruciating.

At least, Finlay had thought so. It was only then that he realized that the scream of astonishment from his mother was perhaps worse.

'Not…not marry her?'

'Ah, I think I hear a customer calling,' murmured the modiste quietly. She stepped past Isabelle, past Finlay, and out into the shop proper.

At least, he presumed that was where she went. Finlay had not taken his eyes from the woman who, until a minute ago, had been his betrothed.

Isabelle's eyes were wide and her lips had parted in silent shock. Evidently his statement had made it impossible for her to speak.

Wretched guilt tore at Finlay's heart. This was his fault, all his fault. If he had not been so charming, so polite—if he had not attempted to make Isabelle comfortable in the marital decision they had taken, she would not have fallen in love with him.

And now he would have to stand here and watch her crumble.

'I know I should have said something sooner,' Finlay said awkwardly, taking a step forward and ignoring the impassioned speech from the dowager countess behind him.

'The scandal sheets! The whole of the *ton* will be filled with the news that my son has abandoned his bride.'

'I offered you marriage out of convenience. We both agreed to that—to provide you with a home,' Finlay said stoically, not taking his eyes from Isabelle. 'And though I fully intended until just a day ago—'

'Disgrace upon our name! No one will ever touch us again. We'll be forced to—'

'Once I realized that I could not marry you, I knew I had to tell you instantly,' continued Finlay doggedly.

Oh, Lord, only his mother could make this situation about herself.

'And I am sorry…truly sorry, Isabelle.'

'Why?' breathed the young woman, her face pale. 'Why won't you marry me?'

Finlay winced. But this was the decision he had chosen, and he could not back away from it now just because it was uncomfortable. 'Because…'

'I shall lose my voucher at Almack's and then what will I do? Oh, the shame of it all!'

Finlay squared his shoulders and ensured that he looked Isabelle directly in the eye as he said the words he knew would cut the deepest. 'Because I am in love with someone else.'

That cut his mother's tirade short. 'And I… Wh-what?'

He did not look around. He could console—or attempt to console—his mother later. He would have all the time in the world to do that, and to acclimatize her to Rilla, if she decided to take umbrage at the fact that he had chosen his own bride.

Oh, please God, let Rilla accept him.

Yes, the dowager countess could be calmed another time, but Isabelle?

Finlay did not look away from the young woman. A young woman who had lost her only family and had no one else to turn to. Who would now have nothing to live on, no one to protect her…

'Isabelle,' he said, taking a step forward. 'I will still help you—'

His words were cut short by such a bizarre occurrence, all words fled from his mind.

Isabelle raised both hands to her face, covered her eyes, and…laughed.

It wasn't a snort of panic or the beginnings of tears—at least, he did not think it was. No, her shoulders were shaking from the fit of giggles she appeared to be experiencing.

Finlay swallowed awkwardly. She was having a most strange reaction to the news, but then perhaps this was just her way of attempting to understand what was happening to her. It was hardly an everyday occurrence, a broken engagement mere days before the wedding itself.

Right, now, what had he decided? Oh, yes.

Finlay stepped forward, awkwardly patting the arm of the now hysterically giggling woman. 'Please do not concern yourself. I have thought long and hard about it, and I will give you a thousand pounds.'

'Finlay Jellicoe!'

'A thousand pounds,' continued Finlay, throwing a dark look at his mother over his shoulder. 'That should be more than sufficient for your needs for the rest of the Season, at least I think so, and I am sure that by that time you will most definitely have found another man to marry you.'

Which would be a relief from his shoulders, he thought woefully, hating that he had placed her in such a terrible position.

First the loss of Cecil, and now the loss of him. Would it be any wonder if Isabelle decided to leave the marriage mart and take a Grand Tour on the Continent?

Perhaps an Italian prince or a French count would take pity on her. Perhaps she would become someone else's problem.

Finlay instantly felt guilty for such a thought, but he could not blame himself. He had taken the weight of responsibility of caring for Isabelle Carr without considering just how heavily it would press upon him.

Now he had just informed her that the safety and security of marriage had been, at least from him, removed.

No wonder she was so hysterical.

'Please, Isabelle,' Finlay said in a low voice, patting her self-consciously on the arm again. 'Do not distress yourself.'

'The woman can be distressed if she—'

'I know you are deeply in love with me,' he said, hoping to goodness that she did not mind him revealing that he knew of her feelings. 'But your affections... I am sure they will fade with time, and it will be as though you never cared for me in that way. I hope... I trust that we will be able to return to being good friends. As we once were.'

As I thought we would be forever. You and me and Cecil and Bartlett. God, what had happened to us?

At his words, Isabelle dropped her hands from her face, and Finlay was astonished to see that she was...smiling?

Perhaps she was in shock. Perhaps after losing Cecil, she had no other way of accepting difficulty than through laughter. It was odd, to be sure, but—

'My dear Finlay,' said Isabelle with a broad grin. 'Please do not concern yourself.'

One may as well tell paint not to dry. 'But—'

'I am in love with someone else.'

This time it was Finlay's turn for his lips to part in astonishment.

I am in love with someone else.

It wasn't possible—no. He must have misheard.

Finlay cleared his throat as tingles of anticipation washed over his body. 'I do apologize. I do not think I heard you.'

'I am in love with someone else,' repeated Isabelle, soft pink tinging her cheeks. 'Someone who wants to marry me.'

It could not be happening.

Finlay did not understand—he had heard her most clearly, had he not? Isabelle had been effusive in her regard, passionate in her affection, far more than he could have imagined.

Oh, I could never speak to him about the depths of my feelings. Besides, I do not think it would be appropriate. He does not expect it. He would not... I do not think he would wish it.

I love him, my lady. Everything he says is music to my ears, everything he does is the best thing a man has ever done!

He could not have misheard, nor misunderstood, all that. 'But…but…'

'And why you believe that I am in love with you, I really do not know,' continued Isabelle blithely, a small line appearing between her brows as she frowned. 'I do not believe I have ever given you cause to believe that from my behaviour.'

Finlay's mouth dropped. 'But I heard you!'

It was probably not the politest thing he could say, and he was not surprised when his mother behind him snapped, 'I beg your pardon?'

'I heard you, the two of you, talking,' Finlay said, a shade discomforted at having to reveal that he had been eavesdropping. 'I assure you, I did not intend to—'

'And you heard what?' asked Isabelle.

Hell's bells, why did it feel so awkward to repeat this?

'Well, a lot of talking about…about being in love with me. How deeply you felt, how you adored me.'

Whenever I am with him, I can think of nothing but the pleasure I gain from being in his presence.

It had been strange to hear, but it was far more mortifying to repeat. Finlay hardly knew where to look, but as his gaze eventually returned to Isabelle, she…she was laughing again.

Laughing, at him?

'Look, I know this has all been very difficult for you,' he said a little stiffly. 'But—'

'Oh, Finlay, you dear sweet man,' said Isabelle, shaking her head with a laugh. 'You presumed that I was speaking of you, then?'

A flicker of uncertainty awoke in his chest. 'Well…well yes, obviously. Who else could you be speaking of?'

And the pink tinges in her cheeks darkened as Isabelle held his gaze. 'Why, George of course.'

George. George? They did not know anyone called George. Finlay blinked. 'Who the devil is George?'

'Lord George Bartlett,' Isabelle said, her eyes shining. Bartlett.

Bartlett? What the hell was going on?

And then the memory of their conversation that late night resurfaced in Finlay's mind. Bartlett had been concerned, had he not, very concerned about Isabelle's well-being? They had discussed her in depth and the man had been worried about her.

Far more worried than he himself had been, now Finlay came to think about it.

Bartlett and Isabelle?

'And I have been feeling so guilt-ridden, all these weeks,' Isabelle was saying as Finlay forced himself to pay attention. 'I have been spending every moment with him that I could, and yet my remorse about lying to you, about keeping this hidden—'

'Why on earth did you not say something?' Finlay said, a slow smile starting to creep across his face. 'Do you mean to tell me that the blackguard is in love with you?'

Isabelle's expression was warm. 'He tells me so.'

'Then why—'

'I did not know of his feelings before…well, before you offered me marriage,' Isabelle confessed, hugging herself as the evident regret of her actions rose. 'I thought— Well, I had no other choice.'

'Charming,' muttered Finlay, his smile broadening.

Isabelle shoved him hard on the shoulder, and there she was, the Isabelle he had known, the one who had pushed him about when they were younger and had thought nothing of cutting off her own hair so that she could play pirates with them.

The three of them. The three boys: Cecil, himself…and Bartlett.

'When a woman has few options, she takes the option presented to her,' Isabelle said with a snort. 'Even if it was you.'

'Outrageous!'

'And before I knew what was happening, George and I… Well, there it was. You had paid off so many of my debts.'

'I had not bought you,' Finlay said sharply.

Isabelle nodded. 'I know that, but you must admit, it put me in rather a delicate situation.'

He supposed it did. That was the trouble with money; it always ruined perfectly good friendships.

Still, it did not explain why Bartlett was so damned silent about the whole thing. 'And Bartlett never thought to say anything?'

'Neither of us wanted to offend you, and though George was certain you were not in love with me—'

Dear God, it was so obvious, Finlay thought with rising disbelief.

Had not Bartlett asked closely about his feelings for Isabelle? Had he not been most interested to discover whether Finlay had fallen in love with her?

'But I wasn't sure, and just when I was attempting to tell your mother that I was in love with another—'

'Mother!' Finlay turned around, nettled. 'You knew?'

The Dowager Countess of Staromchor shrugged. 'I knew she cared for another, but that is by the by.'

'Mother!'

'You think every marriage is made between two people who love each other? Come now, Staromchor, I raised you to be smarter than that,' said his mother in a cutting tone, seated still on the sofa and with the pamphlet open in her lap. 'Hardly anyone marries for love. I knew you would be a good husband to Isabelle, so what did it matter if she had feelings for another? Those feelings would fade.'

'They will not,' Isabelle said sharply, and Finlay grinned as the rambunctious tomboy he had known sparked back to life once more. 'I happen to believe that if love can be found, then it should be grasped as tightly as one can. How often does love arrive? Should we not seize it when it does?'

Finlay swallowed.

I love you!

She was right. Both of them. He should have offered Rilla his heart the moment he had realized it belonged to her. And now…

There was still a chance it was too late, even with the complication of Isabelle removed from him.

It was removed, wasn't it?

'Just to be clear, then,' Finlay said hurriedly, and Isabelle's attention moved back to him. 'Our engagement is at an end, and you are…happy?'

'Ridiculously so.' His previously betrothed beamed. 'No offence meant, you understand. But I wish to marry the man I love.'

There was a loud sob that filled the modiste.

Finlay blinked. He had not made such a sound, and neither had Isabelle. Which could only mean…

The two of them turned around slowly, Finlay hardly able to believe his eyes, as he saw his mother sobbing on the sofa.

'Mother?' he said weakly.

'I… I am in love with someone, too!' declared his mother, tears rolling down her cheeks. 'And I declined him b-because… a small scandal, but that was twenty years ago. I want to marry him, but I said no, I do not know why!'

'Mother?' Finlay repeated again, hardly able to keep up with all this change.

'Right, I had better go,' said Isabelle smartly, starting to pull her gown off.

Finlay snapped a hand over his eyes, now utterly bewildered. 'Where are you going?'

'Why, to find George and make him marry me, of course,' Isabelle said lightly. There was the sound of fabric pooling to the floor, and Finlay wished to God she had stepped behind the screen. They weren't seven years old anymore. 'And what about you, Fin?'

It was the childhood name they had all used, and its utterance here, at Madame Penelope's after his engagement was put to an end, was a moment of realization for Finlay.

He dropped his hand and grinned at the troublemaking Carr that he and Bartlett—he and George, heaven forbid—still had in their lives. 'Good luck.'

'You, too,' said Isabelle, pulling up a sprigged muslin gown and hastily doing up the ties.

'Me?'

She snorted and laughed as she marched out of the modiste's. 'Did you not say you were in love with someone else?'

And a moment of clarity dropped into Finlay's mind as he realized what he had to do next. 'Rilla.'

'And now he might not marry me! Why did I decline…? My fear of scandal… What was I thinking?'

After, that was, he had comforted his mother.

Good grief.

Chapter Eighteen

'Here we are, then,' said a gruff voice Rilla knew well, and strangely thought she would miss. 'The Markhall School for Girls.'

Rilla had felt the carriage slow five minutes ago, the surface of the road shifting from the rough country lane to the slightly smoother gravel path.

They had arrived, then.

'C'mon,' the driver snapped gruffly.

Rilla bit back her tongue and forced down all the explanations that she had already made to the unfeeling and unpleasant man. Her fingers curled around the unopened letter she could not see. She was depending on the driver to guide her in and out of the carriage; this was all new to her, and she did not know where she was going.

A heavily gloved hand grabbed her own.

Trying not to cry out with the discomfort of someone suddenly touching her, Rilla allowed herself to be tugged forward in the carriage, moving in a haze of uncertainty and distrust.

'Step,' snapped the tired voice.

She had tried to be patient. She would certainly not like to be a carriage driver, spending hours and hours out in the elements, freezing in the winter and baking in the summer sun. The wind was surely a cruel whip across one's face, and one's fingers and toes were doubtless ice in this weather.

But that was no call for rudeness.

'Oh,' Rilla muttered as her foot caught on the first step. Then she had her bearings and was able to descend from the carriage with relative decorum.

The instant her booted feet crunched on the gravel she gained her equilibrium, she snatched her hand away from the driver.

'Thank you,' she said ungraciously.

It did not appear that he had noticed. His footsteps, heavier than hers and faster, had moved around to the side of the carriage, and soon they had returned. The hearty thud of her trunk being dropped beside her was unmistakable.

'Nice place,' the carriage driver grunted.

Trying her best not to be sarcastic, Rilla shrugged. 'It makes no difference in the end.'

And it didn't. Whether or not the Markhall School for Girls was pleasing to look at was neither here nor there.

Even if she could see, Rilla could not help but think darkly, the place was not going to be improved by fine stonework.

No, she was here to do a job. The students of the Markhall School for Girls were the important factors to secure her future happiness, and she would not know that for some time.

She would simply have to hope, to trust, that they were not as odious as she feared.

'Y'want yer bonnet?'

Suppressing the desire to point out that if she'd had any warning that she was about to be dragged out of the carriage, she would certainly have picked up her bonnet, Rilla said instead, 'Yes, if you please.'

Her courtesy was not returned. The bonnet was thrust into her hands, the surprise at the sudden movement meaning that she almost dropped it.

Then the door snapped shut behind her, and there was a creak of wood and leather.

'Good luck, Miss,' grunted the man.

Rilla turned immediately, real panic flaring now in her chest. 'But Miss Pike instructed you to—'

'I reckon as you can find your own way in,' the driver said curtly, jerking the reins and causing one of the horses to neigh in indignation. 'Night is drawing in and I want to be on my way afore dark. Good luck, as I say, Miss.'

'But—'

Whatever words of remonstrance she had intended to utter would have made little difference, Rilla was sure, even if the man had heard them. As it was, he had urged the horses on and the rattle of the carriage made her attempts at speech completely moot.

Only when the sound of the carriage had entirely died away did Rilla swallow and allow the emotions flooding through her veins to appear on her face.

Oh, damn.

Her cane was still in the carriage.

She'd accidentally left it in the carriage when she arrived... and now it was rattling on its way back to the Wallflower Academy.

Ah, well. She would have to learn quickly, that was all.

Rilla had known, from the moment that the Pike had suggested that she go and become a teacher for a school, that leaving the Wallflower Academy would be a deprivation.

None of them could truly understand. It was like having her right arm cut off, the familiar sensations of the Wallflower Academy removed from her.

This gravel was different. It crunched at a different pitch when Rilla took a hesitant step to where she believed her trunk had been deposited. It took her three attempts to kneel and find the blasted thing, and in the end, it was only when her toe clipped the corner that she was absolutely sure.

Straightening up and holding the handle of the trunk in her

hand, Rilla rammed her bonnet on her head and turned her face up to what she presumed was the school.

And then she swallowed.

How had she managed to learn the routes and routines of the Wallflower Academy? It had all seemed so long ago now, she could barely recall. It was as familiar to her as her own limbs.

Well, she had to start somewhere.

With a sinking heart that was partly to do with her practical predicament, and partly to do with the unopened letter clutched in her hand, Rilla took a step forward. Hating that she had to do this, she put out a hand.

Then she halted.

Rilla turned, back to the direction the dratted carriage had gone, and swore under her breath.

It took five minutes of careful exploratory stepping for Rilla to find the portico, then another minute to navigate the six steps whilst holding on to her seemingly increasingly heavy trunk.

By the time she had deposited it on the stone before the front door, Rilla's shoulders ached and her temples were starting to throb.

It had been a long journey, and now…now the difficult part was about to begin.

She did not irritate herself by seeking a doorbell. Instead, Rilla rapped hard on the door with her fist.

It would have been far louder with a cane, she could not help but think, *but there it was.*

The door did not open for several minutes. When it did, a voice far sharper than Miss Pike's snapped, 'Yes?'

Rilla curtsied, hating that she had no idea if this woman was a maid or the headmistress. 'Miss Marilla Newell, at your service.'

'Miss Marilla— Dear God, you're the teacher?'

Still no real clue as to the voice's owner, Rilla thought darkly, though it was not a good sign, whoever it was.

'Yes,' she said aloud.

The owner of the voice sniffed. 'I should have informed your previous headmistress…teachers are supposed to come around the back.'

Like a servant, Rilla thought with an ever-sinking heart. That was indication enough that this place was not going to be the haven of learning and new home she could grow comfortable in as she had hoped.

Still, she was far away from everything and everyone that she knew. If there was ever a time and a place for a fresh start, it was the Markhall School for Girls.

No Sylvia, no Daphne, no Miss Pike, and no…no Finlay Jellicoe, Earl of Staromchor.

Which was all to the good. Of course. There was no reason that she would want to see them, especially not the latter. No reason at—

'Well, don't just stand there—come in,' sighed the voice. 'I am Miss Hennessy. You may call me ma'am.'

Rilla nodded, apprehension flowing through her veins. 'Shall I just leave my trunk—'

'You can bring in your trunk. Our teachers don't have airs and graces,' said Miss Hennessy curtly. 'Honestly, what did they teach you in your last position?'

It was only then that Rilla realized just what a false reference Miss Pike had provided.

Dear Lord, had the woman intimated that Rilla had already been a teacher?

What on earth was she supposed to say?

'It was…a very different establishment,' Rilla said demurely, leaning to pick up her trunk as her shoulder protested.

Miss Hennessy sniffed. 'So I see. Come on.'

Her footsteps on what sounded like hardwood floors immediately began to move away, and Rilla hastened to follow her.

If only there had not been such a large step into the building.

Careering forward and only just managing to prevent herself from smashing her nose onto the floor by whirling her arms like a windmill, Rilla's heart was thundering painfully by the time she righted herself.

'No time for fun and games,' came the distant voice of Miss Hennessy. 'Honestly, were you always larking about at your old place? We don't have much time for that here.'

Rilla swallowed her irritation as she turned vaguely in what she presumed was a hall. 'Miss Hennessy, I do not know what the Pike—what Miss Pike—told you about me in her letter to you, but—'

'Not much, scarce enough to place you with a subject.' Miss Hennessy appeared to be moving away, though where precisely, Rilla could not tell. 'Keep up, will you?'

'The reason I mention this,' Rilla continued doggedly, putting her trunk down and deciding once and for all that she was not going to cart it about like a servant, 'is because Miss Pike appears to have neglected to tell you—'

'I am sure there are many things your precious Pike hasn't—'

'To tell you that I am blind,' Rilla said, with the patience of a saint.

Miss Hennessy's voice immediately disappeared.

And there it is, Rilla thought dully as the silence elongated most painfully.

There was always the awkward silence after a statement of that nature. Next would be the frantic apologies, then the questions about precisely how it happened, and what she could see, and whether she had seen a doctor…

'I beg your pardon, I'm sure,' said Miss Hennessy, her voice growing in volume as her footsteps echoed towards her. 'Why on earth didn't you say?'

'I… I presumed you knew,' returned Rilla, slightly dazed.

Where was the apology? Where were the questions? Where were the recommendations of different eye drops, poultices, and for some reason, liquors that different people had recommended her over the years?

'Honestly, why would you presume that? I am glad you told me, though,' said Miss Hennessy briskly. 'It makes things a good deal clearer. Do you want my arm?'

Rilla's mouth fell open.

It was…refreshing.

Miss Hennessy would never gain many friends, not with that acidic nature and sharpness of tongue—but it was far pleasanter to be subjected to that than the pity she'd expected.

Despite herself, a wry smile crept over Rilla's face. 'That would be most welcome, thank you.'

It was not the softest of touches when Miss Hennessy pulled her arm into her own, but at this point, Rilla did not care. Perhaps this place, though strange and unfriendly at first, could become a kind of home.

Exhausted from her journey, Rilla did not attempt to memorize the path from the hall to whatever place it was that Miss Hennessy was taking her. Left, right, up a flight of stairs then down a few steps, the place appeared to be a maze.

'Here we are,' came Miss Hennessy's voice, accompanied by the click of an opening door. 'Your schoolroom.'

Rilla's stomach lurched as she was guided into a place that was far lighter than the corridor before it.

Her schoolroom.

Well, the Pike had been attempting to convince her to become a tutor at the Wallflower Academy for…how long now? Eight months? Longer?

Perhaps she should have known from the very beginning that she would end up here, Rilla thought darkly.

In a schoolroom, in an unwelcoming school, in the middle of nowhere.

'Most people don't want to teach here,' came the sharp voice of Miss Hennessy as she released Rilla.

Rilla raised an eyebrow. 'Oh?'

It was as non-committal an answer as she could manage, without giving offence or leading to further questions.

Miss Hennessy's sniff occurred from several feet away now. 'Yes, we are too far from London to be of interest to most.'

The words slipped out before Rilla could stop them. 'I have no wish to be near London.'

'Really,' came Miss Hennessy's wry response, no question within the word. 'I thought as much.'

Heat burned Rilla's cheeks, but there was nothing she could do about it. She was not about to bare her heart to anyone at the Markhall School for Girls, much less Miss Hennessy, who had still not clarified whether she was housekeeper, fellow teacher, or headmistress.

No, the sorrows that plagued her heart were hers alone, and she would bear them as best she could.

Even if it meant pain beyond what she had ever known.

'I suppose it was a great wrench,' came Miss Hennessy's next words. 'Leaving your previous position.'

A far greater wrench than Rilla had expected. Until the very moment of departure, she had considered the Wallflower Academy to be what it was for so many: a strange sort of prison, attempting to mould the women termed wallflowers into something that the *ton* preferred.

Only when she had left it did she realize just what a sanctuary it was from the world.

And now it was gone—or more accurately, she had gone, and now her very independence had been similarly taken from her.

'Is that a letter?'

Rilla's hand tightened around the paper. 'Yes, it is.'

'But how do you…?'

The question was left delicately on the air, as though that would make it less distasteful. In truth, Rilla could hardly blame her. It was a question borne of curiosity, not malice, and it was not a difficult one to answer.

'I cannot read,' Rilla said airily. 'I usually have a friend read my letters to me and then I memorize them. It is easier that way.'

She really should have asked Sylvia or Daphne to read it for her before she left. Rilla's finger stroked along the soft grain of the letter. There hadn't been time.

Lying to herself, now, was she?

She hadn't wanted to see them. Hadn't wanted to hear the disappointment and the disgrace in their voices. Would they treat her differently? Had they forgotten her already?

'And who will read your letters now?' came the voice of Miss Hennessy.

Rilla swallowed. Well, there was no time like the present for trying to make new friends. Goodness knew, none of them here could be as shy as Daphne nor as wild as Sylvia.

'If you would do me the honour?' she said formally, holding out the letter.

Miss Hennessy did not reply in words, but perhaps that was unnecessary. Her eager steps forward and the way she half took, half wrenched the letter from Rilla's hand suggested her nosiness was perhaps on par with Sylvia's after all.

Rilla was silent as she heard the breaking of the seal and the unfolding of the page. It had been good paper, a high quality; her fingertips had told her that much. Her father had perhaps wanted to wish her good fortune on the start of her new endeavour. It would have been more pleasant if he had visited, but—

'"My dear Rilla..."' said Miss Hennessy aloud. 'Rilla?'

Her stomach lurched painfully. 'It is what my family and some close friends call me.'

I told you before, my friends call me Rilla.

It was impossible to tell whether Miss Hennessy approved of this. With a sniff, she returned to the letter.

'"My dear Rilla, I am so sorry that I was not able to see you before you left the Wallflower Academy. It had been my intention, but as you can imagine, I have had a few important things to take care of before then.'"

Rilla forced her expression to remain still.

Of course her father would put almost everything before her. Why was she surprised?

"'Having discovered that you will be leaving before I can return, I hope you will do me the honour of receiving me at the Markhall School for Girls, and we can continue our very important discussion then,'" Miss Hennessy read.

A frown puckered at Rilla's forehead. Important discussion? It had been a good many years now since she and her father had had a discussion of any description. What on earth did he mean?

"'Your very faithful Finlay.'"

Rilla staggered, the weight of the name Miss Hennessy had just read unsettling her to such an extreme that her knees buckled. 'Wh-what did you say?'

"'We can continue our very—'"

'After that,' Rilla snapped.

She was undoubtedly offending Miss Hennessy, the only person at the Markhall School for Girls she knew, but that did not matter. Not with those words ringing in her ears—words she could not have heard.

"'Your very faithful Finlay,'" repeated Miss Hennessy in a bemused voice. 'Who is that—a brother?'

There had never been anyone less like a brother in her entire life.

Despite the fact that her head was ringing and her knees felt as though they were about to collapse at any moment, Rilla managed to say, 'No, a…a friend. Thank you, Miss Hennessy, I will have my letter back now.'

The accompanying sniff was unwelcome, but expected. 'Well, I'll leave you to get accustomed to your schoolroom. Just ring the bell by the blackboard, and I'll send someone to show you up to your room. Good evening, Miss Newell.'

'Miss Hennessy,' Rilla said in a hoarse voice.

The door snicked shut behind her, and Rilla staggered back until her fingers found a wall. Then she leaned against it and closed her eyes.

He was being cruel.

All that talk about continuing their discussion—there was nothing more to discuss! Finlay was not truly in love with her, and though he was not in love with Isabelle Carr, he was about to marry her.

What else was there to say?

'He is not coming back,' Rilla said into the silence of the room. 'And you would be a fool to wish for it.'

A fool to wish for greater heartache. A fool to hope for something that simply could not be.

The door to the corridor clicked open.

Rilla straightened as best she could. Well, she did not want Miss Hennessy to think she could be so easily exhausted. Her place here was only secure if she could teach all day, after all.

'I am quite well,' she said firmly in the direction of the door. 'In fact, I do not believe I have ever been better.'

'Excellent,' said the voice of Finlay Jellicoe, Earl of Staromchor. 'I am delighted to hear it.'

Chapter Nineteen

Finlay had to put the past behind him and attempt to make those things right. He had already given Bartlett and Isabelle their wedding present—an impressive gold clock—and had managed to calm his mother sufficiently, though he had still not gained a clue as to who this gentleman was that she was supposed to have fallen in love with.

Now it was time to tend to his own affairs.

Swallowing hard, wishing to goodness he had a speech prepared and certain that merely seeing Rilla would thrust it out of his mind anyway, Finlay opened the door.

When he stepped into the room, his breath was quite literally taken away.

There she was. Rilla. The woman he loved.

He had never seen her quite so downcast. Her travelling pelisse was stained with mud at least three inches deep, and her bonnet was askew, as were her dark midnight curls. There was a look of pain in her expression that even her straightening up against the wall she had been leaning against could not distract from.

And then Rilla spoke.

'I am quite well,' she said, turning to him and evidently presuming he was someone else. 'In fact, I do not believe I have ever been better.'

And Finlay's heart stirred as it had never stirred before.

She was so brave. Here she was, to all intents and purposes alone, with a new life ahead of her—one Rilla had not chosen.

And still she was determined to face it head-on.

It was all he could do to keep his voice steady. 'Excellent. I am delighted to hear it.'

Finlay was gifted a brief moment of satisfaction. There was nothing quite like the woman you loved gawping at you, utterly confused, her jaw dropping and her fingers tightening on—

Was that his letter? Was the fact that Rilla was still holding it a good sign?

No, it could not be that simple. Within a heartbeat, Rilla's expression had transformed into one that was stiff, polite, and worst of all, aloof. He knew she only put on that appearance when she wanted to be distant from the person with whom she was conversing.

So, he had a great deal of ground to cover. There was a chance, perhaps, that she would not forgive him at all.

Though the thought of being separated from Rilla forever was bitter bile on his tongue, Finlay had to accept it was a possibility. There was nothing he could do here, save tell the truth.

And apologize. Dear God, she deserved an apology.

'Rilla, you have to let me explain,' Finlay said hurriedly, launching into a declaration that his mind managed to drag up from the depths of his imagination. 'I know you probably don't want to hear it.'

'You're right,' came Rilla's curt reply. 'I don't.'

Finlay only hesitated for a moment, then forced himself to take a step closer. If he could only tell her everything he had done since he had last seen her, then surely she would understand.

She may still not wish to have anything to do with him, but she would at least understand.

'I'm afraid I'm going to tell you anyway,' said Finlay, cringing at the inelegance of his behaviour. Most unsuitable for an earl. 'The moment you left me standing outside the Wallflower Academy—'

'Which you rightly deserved.'

'Which I deserved,' Finlay accepted, trying not to allow himself to get drawn into a debate.

He could see what was happening. All Rilla wanted to do was protect herself, prevent herself from ever feeling hurt again.

And he knew why. Finlay had hurt her. He had hurt himself, too, but that had been different; he had been in possession of all the facts. It had been Rilla who had been thunderstruck by the revelation that he had been engaged to another.

Now he had to make it right, push through Rilla's defences one last time, make her see his bruised and battered heart, and…

Wait for her to make her decision.

'I wanted to tell you everything, but I had to—'

'What are you doing here?'

'I'm trying to tell you,' Finlay said, his voice rising in volume. 'If you would just let me—'

'Are you the new footman?'

Finlay whirled around. There stood a woman who could only be a teacher at the Markhall School for Girls. She was wearing a very masculine-styled gown with a sort of fitted waistcoat around the bodice, and her spectacles were topped by a pair of frowning brows.

'F-footman?' he spluttered.

Then a noise caught his ear—a noise he had not expected, but nonetheless lifted his spirits magnificently.

Rilla was laughing.

Finlay turned to her, delight soaring through his chest as he watched the woman he adored giggle with unrepressed laughter.

'I do not see what is so amusing,' sniffed the woman who had stepped into Rilla's new schoolroom. 'I only asked—'

'Miss Hennessy, this is the Earl of Staromchor,' said Rilla with a grin, managing to stifle her laughter long enough to speak. 'I apologize for laughing, but the misunderstanding—'

'Oh!' Miss Hennessy went scarlet.

Finlay waved a hand and cast her a charming smile. 'Please, do not concern yourself. It happens all the time.'

Rilla snorted with laughter behind him.

'Well, I— Right, so… Your Lordship is an acquaintance of Miss Newell?' spluttered the teacher.

Finlay swallowed.

An acquaintance?

Oh, they had shared so much more than mere acquaintance-ship…but at the same time, he could hardly describe Rilla as a friend. Not in this moment. Not when he was uncertain whether or not she would even permit him to attempt to explain…

'Something like that.' Rilla's dry voice held no hints as to whether she would let him continue, but her next sentence did. 'Please excuse us, Miss Hennessy. I believe the earl has some-thing important to tell me. If you would be so good…'

It was delicately done, and Finlay had to remind himself once again that Rilla, far from being an abandoned wallflower in the Wallflower Academy, was the Honourable Miss Newell.

Dear God, there was so much of her he still had to learn. So much more of Rilla to discover.

If she would let him…

Miss Hennessy was all awkward apologies, curtsies, and kowtowing. By the time she had shut the door with as genteel a click as she could manage, nerves had once again seized Finlay's heart.

He turned back to Rilla, who was now staring with a bold-ness typical of the woman he cared so deeply for.

For a moment, silence hung between them.

Then their mutual laughter echoed in the otherwise empty room.

'A footman,' Finlay said dryly. 'I must just give off that sense.'

'I think it more likely that anyone in my presence immediately becomes more servile,' Rilla said dryly.

Finlay winced, but only for a moment. Rilla was a woman, he knew, who could quite happily laugh at herself. If she were saying such things, it was because she felt comfortable doing so.

'Look,' he said quietly.

The laughter left Rilla's lips, but her openness appeared to remain.

Finlay took a deep breath.

Well, here goes—everything.

'It is true that the initial flirtation I enjoyed with you was never meant to mean more,' he said quietly, then hurried on, 'but I promise it was not nearly so bad as you probably think.'

A sardonic eyebrow rose. 'You have no idea how bad I think it was.'

'Oh, I can probably guess,' Finlay said darkly.

After all, had he not heard some of the lewd things the members of White's had suggested about innocent and largely unprotected ladies of the *ton*? There was a reason he had moved clubs.

'Was that all I was?' cut in Rilla, her voice once again harsh. 'A bit of fun?'

'Not in the slightest. Well, yes,' Finlay said, stepping forward and wishing to goodness the woman before him could see how contrite his expression was.

Her frown deepened. 'Well? Which is it?'

'Both, I suppose,' he said awkwardly, twisting his fingers before him as his heartrate started to quicken again. 'It *was* fun, talking to you. I had never experienced so much joy in the presence of a stranger.'

It was difficult to admit such a thing, but far more difficult to see the complete distrust on Rilla's face. 'I find that hard to believe.'

'I am telling you nothing but the truth,' Finlay said simply. 'Bartlett's encouragement to flirt with someone before I was chained to Isabelle…it was the perfect excuse. I already wished to know you better.'

That was clearly not something she had expected to hear. Rilla's expression softened, just a mite. 'You…you did?'

'I did,' said Finlay, taking another step forward. A great expanse still separated them from each other, an expanse he did not believe he could yet cross. But perhaps, with enough time, enough trust…

'And our conversations swiftly became so much more than that—more to me, at any rate.'

'You think they did not mean anything to me?' Rilla's whisper was full of heartbreak.

Finlay swallowed, crushing the instinct to pull her into his arms and kiss away all the misunderstanding, the mistrust.

He would not do that to her. Rilla would not be touched by anyone, including him, without her permission.

'Our conversations, our time together… I have never felt so…so seen,' Finlay said, conscious of his poor choice of words. 'Dammit, I cannot explain.'

'I know what you mean. At least, I think I do,' said Rilla quietly.

Her hands had left the wall, as though it was no longer required to sustain her. Was that a good sign? Finlay's head was spinning so rapidly, the room almost swaying before him, he could not really tell.

He swallowed. 'Our connection has meant so much to me that I have… I have broken off my engagement.'

His heart rose to his mouth as he waited for Rilla's response.

It did not come. She merely stood there, still as a statue, as though she had not heard his words at all.

Finlay cleared his throat. Rilla said nothing. He shifted from one foot to the other, certain she would be able to hear the movement. Still she was silent.

When he could endure the silence no longer, Finlay said, 'It was really only a marriage of convenience, as I told you. Yes, I paid off her family debts, and I felt a debt of honour, but… but that is nothing compared to you.'

He had presumed such words would inspire a response, but still Rilla remained taciturn.

And though his instinct was to speak, to fill the silence, Finlay forced herself to remain quiet. This was all new information for Rilla, information she surely could not have been expecting. The very least he could do was give her the chance to absorb it.

When he truly felt as though he would burst with the unsaid words rolling about his chest, Rilla said quietly, 'Will… will Miss Carr…will she be able to live? Without the money and protection, I mean, of your name?'

'If anything, I believe I was holding her back,' Finlay said wryly, a spark of mirth in his lungs. 'She had already fallen in love with someone else. Their engagement will be announced tomorrow.'

'But…but you said…you said she was in love with you!'

'No need to sound so surprised,' Finlay said, a dart of pain searing his heart. 'I had thought, but I was mistaken. It appears that another man, a better man in my estimation, captured her heart months ago. It was only our arranged marriage that was preventing them from being together and now…now that is at an end.'

And his heart leaped as Rilla did something he could not have imagined when he first entered the room.

She took a step towards him.

'This…this bet. Was it to bed me?'

'No!' Finlay was horrified at the insinuation, that she could believe such a thing of him.

Dear God, had he proved himself to be the rake he had never thought he was?

'Absolutely not!'

'Because I can imagine two gentlemen, an earl and a…?'

Finlay winced. 'A viscount.'

'An earl and a viscount, from my experience, would have few qualms in—'

'Bartlett—Lord Bartlett—is not like that,' Finlay said firmly. 'In truth, I cannot think of anyone less likely to do such a thing, or even think such a thing. No, it was…it was to charm you. To flirt, to enjoy a woman's company.'

Rilla breathed a wry laugh. 'And we have done so much more than that.'

'And I want more,' said Finlay, his mouth dry as he tentatively approached the crux of the conversation. The centre, the part that mattered the most. 'So much more.'

He took a step towards her, making sure his footstep was heavy. She did not blanch or move away.

Finlay's heart skipped a beat.

He was going to do it.

'Rilla— Marilla, I suppose I should say—'

'You're not going to…are you?' Rilla peered in his direction with flushed cheeks.

And that was when he knew. Finlay could not have known beforehand, not in advance of turning up at the Markhall School for Girls and hoping to goodness that whoever opened the door would let him in.

But in this moment, he knew.

She loved him. She wanted him, had been devastated not just because of the lies, but because Isabelle Carr's existence would make it impossible for them to be together.

And the affection he felt for her stirred so powerfully, it

was almost as though it was pouring out from him, invisible perhaps to the naked eye but perfectly evident to Rilla Newell.

'Goodness, I love you,' Finlay said simply.

Rilla's pink cheeks turned red, but she took a step towards him. 'And I love you.'

The simplicity of it all—that was what he loved. The fact that loving each other did not have to be difficult or complicated. Life might make it so, but at the very centre of who they were was love. Love for each other. Love for what mattered.

Finlay grinned as he caught Rilla's hands in his own, and she did not pull away. 'When we are married—'

Rilla snorted. 'I never had the impression you were particularly fond of the married state!'

'I did not want my life chosen for me, dictated by honour and forced down a particular path,' Finlay quipped, warmth spreading from the connection of their fingertips. 'And it's not. This is my choice—you are my choice. And yes, it may perhaps shock the *ton*.'

'Oh, good,' said Rilla darkly. 'Another scandal.'

'But as long as I have you, I don't care,' Finlay finished seriously. 'Rilla, you said before that you were more than a match for an earl.'

'Oh, don't repeat what I—'

'And you were right. You're more than a mere match—you... you are everything,' he said, taut emotions finally pouring out of him. 'My better half, my best friend—the one woman in the world who makes me laugh and makes me think, usually at the same time. More than a match? You're more suitable a match for me than anyone I've ever met.'

The woman he loved tilted her head as she laughed. 'You were never going to take no for an answer, were you?'

'I would always take no from you, if you do not wish it,' he said quietly. It was important she knew that. 'Even as my wife, you will never get dictated to, Rilla.'

Her twisting smile aroused his manhood. 'And what would you have done, then, if I had rejected you?'

Finlay stared. Then he pulled Rilla into his embrace and she stepped willingly into his arms. 'You know, it did not even cross my mind.'

Their kiss, when it came, had been awaited forever—and as Rilla melted into his passionate affection, Finlay was certain he would never see the world the same again.

Epilogue

Her hands were shaking as they carefully smoothed her gown, but there was a smile on Rilla's face that had been there from the very moment she had awoken.

It was, after all, her wedding day.

'Such an exquisite gown,' Daphne said softly just behind her. 'You look wonderful, Rilla.'

Rilla's smile did not shift as she shrugged. 'I suppose so.'

What she looked like did not matter, not really. Not when she was going to become the wife of the best man she had ever met.

'And the service! Oh, it will be beautiful,' continued Daphne in her soft, shy voice. 'I have stuffed not one, but two handkerchiefs up my sleeve, just to be sure.'

And it was indeed most pleasant.

Finlay had surprised her with some careful planning that had brought such joy, Rilla had been unable to express it as they had left the church. Only when the wedding party had entered the Wallflower Academy and stepped through to the ballroom, where the wedding reception was being hosted, had Rilla managed to find time to thank her husband.

'You were so thoughtful,' she said between two hasty kisses.

Finlay had laughed. 'Well, I thought you deserved to have a little beauty in your day, Lady Staromchor. Your special day.'

'It is special because I am marrying you,' Rilla pointed out, splaying her hand on her husband's chest and being rewarded by the *thud-thud-thud* of his heart.

Lady Staromchor—she was the Countess of Staromchor. Now, that was a strange thought.

'You're the reason this day is just perfect.'

But his decisions had not hurt. Instead of going for the traditional roses, he had told her as they had walked from the church to the Tudor manor of the Wallflower Academy, he had instead instructed the florist to select those with the headiest scents.

Oh, the church had smelled divine.

'Isabelle helped,' Finlay said, his voice quavering as he said his previously betrothed's name. 'Which was to her credit, I must say.'

Rilla's stomach lurched, but only slightly.

It was perhaps fate that the two of them should find each other after both exiting an engagement—although of course, for very different reasons.

From the little Rilla knew of Miss Isabelle Carr from the single meeting they had shared, she seemed a very pleasant kind of person. It was natural, surely, for there to be awkwardness between them. They had, after all, both been engaged to the same man.

'I hope she will be happy,' Rilla said aloud.

'Oh, she will be.' Finlay's voice was confident, with none of the wavering that had accompanied it when he had been asked by his mother days ago whether he preferred the cream linens or the champagne for their wedding reception. 'Bartlett will take good care of her. Far better care than I could—that is certain.'

Rilla was not sure about that, but then she was hardly going to argue.

'And…and Nina? Your other sisters, your father? You have spoken to them to your satisfaction? I had no wish to intrude when I saw you together…' Her new husband spoke quietly so that, in the hustle and bustle of the ballroom, only she could hear him.

Trying her best not to disturb the pins Sylvia had dug into her midnight curls, Rilla nodded. 'And they were most gracious in their congratulations, too. I think… I hope that this is the beginning of a renewal. Of an understanding between us that has been lost for many years.'

It had been an awkward conversation. Rilla had almost been surprised that her family had bothered to come—but then, an earl was an earl. She had finally done what they had wanted, but she had done it on her terms, and to an earl who was far superior to the one they had initially chosen.

And Nina had listened to her apology.

Rilla let out the breath she had not known she had been holding. A new beginning.

'Oh, dear, it looks like one of the hired footmen is lost,' Finlay's voice said wearily.

Trying to stifle a grin, Rilla said, 'Well, you had better go and assist him, my love. After all, you were a footman the first time we met.'

His hasty kiss was followed by a snort of laughter, one that grew quieter as Finlay stepped away, leaving Rilla to stand alone.

But this time, she did not mind.

Finlay may not be standing right beside her, but she was still strengthened by his love, his adoration. Knowing that he cared about her so, that she had nothing to prove to anyone, to the world, was enough to keep her head as high as her spirits.

'I have an announcement to make!'

Rilla knew that voice, and tried not to groan as silence filled the ballroom of the Wallflower Academy.

The Dowager Countess of Staromchor. Finlay's mother. Her new mother-in-law.

She was a difficult woman to be around, to be sure, but as

she now had a lifetime of being her daughter-in-law, Rilla supposed she would have to attempt to get used to her, if she could.

If she could.

'I have an announcement,' repeated the dowager countess. There was another sound, something that sounded like tinkling glass. Was she tapping on a champagne glass?

A hand slipped around hers, and Rilla squeezed it immediately. She knew that hand.

'What on earth is my mother doing?' Finlay breathed into her ear.

Rilla ensured to keep her expression steady. 'I have absolutely no idea. I thought you would.'

'There is no announcement as far as I know,' he said softly as curious chatter rose up around the room. 'Isabelle and Bartlett have eloped.'

'Eloped?' Rilla repeated, perhaps a tad louder than she ought.

She did not need to see to feel the stares pressing against her skin. Well, she could not help it—anyone would have responded loudly to a remark like that.

Besides, it was her wedding. Her wedding, to Finlay—a man she loved, and who she had never believed could love her in the same way she loved him. It was understandable that people would be looking at her.

Staring at her, no doubt.

Finlay's chuckle was light. 'I should have known they wouldn't be able to wait for the preparations of a wedding. They had kept their affection hidden for so long, they simply could not prevent themselves from heading in a carriage to Gretna Green.'

A slight tinge of envy crept through Rilla's heart. 'What an excellent idea. We should have done such a thing.'

Her new husband nudged her shoulder. 'Don't be daft—and miss whatever spectacle my mother is going to make of herself?'

Rilla groaned, but kept it as quiet as she could as her new mother-in-law cleared her throat loudly.

'This is a splendid day for the Staromchor family,' the dowager countess said in that grand voice she had. 'But I could not let this moment of happiness go by without revealing…without saying… Well, I am to be married!'

Somewhere in the ballroom, someone dropped a glass. It smashed, the sound a mixture between tinkling and shimmering, and Rilla's mouth fell open.

The Dowager Countess of Staromchor…was engaged to be married?

'What the—' breathed Finlay.

He was not the only one. A great deal of consternation appeared to be fluttering through the ballroom, from what Rilla could sense.

'Mother!' Finlay hissed. The dowager countess must be close to them, then. It was hard to tell, since the woman always spoke so loudly. 'What are you saying?'

'I am saying, dear boy, that there is no reason why Lord Norbury and I—'

'Father!' gasped Daphne from just behind them.

Rilla could hardly breathe.

Finlay's mother—and Daphne's father?

She turned, eager to assist her friend in what must be a mortifying and astonishing situation, but without the knowledge of precisely where she was there was no chance of finding Daphne. There was almost a stampede of well-wishers marching on the dowager countess, pushing past Rilla, jostling her, making it almost impossible to stay upright.

Panic welled in her chest and she instinctively cried, 'Finlay—'

He was by her side in an instant. 'I have you.'

His steady, comforting hand was already on her waist and Rilla reached out for him, love blossoming once more in her chest. 'Did you have any idea—your mother and Daphne's father?'

'Not a clue,' Finlay said darkly. 'I suppose I was too wrapped up in my own complicated romance that I became blind to my mother's.'

Rilla snorted.

'Ah— I mean…'

'I know what you meant,' Rilla said hastily. 'Of all people in the world, I know to trust your intentions. Can you see Daphne? Is she quite well?'

'She…' Finlay's voice trailed off.

Concern gripped her stomach. 'Well, is she?'

'She has left the room,' her husband murmured in her ear, lowering his voice. 'Looking quite distressed, I think. Sylvia has gone after her.'

Rilla relaxed. It wasn't as though she could do much for her friend, and Sylvia was far better at comforting people than she was. The young woman would soon have Daphne laughing again.

It was a shock, to be sure. It would also make Daphne her… her step-sister-in-law?

All thoughts of attempting to calculate just how the Staromchor family would now be formed were scattered, however, as Finlay pressed a kiss to her temple.

'You look radiant.'

'You know, I feel radiant,' confessed Rilla with a shy smile.

'And that is the most important thing,' Finlay said, his voice full of pride.

Pride in her.

She could hardly believe it. There was such joy in her heart it was overflowing, spilling out whenever she spoke to anyone, making it impossible for dour worry to overcrowd her heart.

She was loved. She loved a man who was good, and noble, and who felt things so deeply. Finlay was a man not made for her, but who had made himself what she wanted, what she needed.

A life full of richness and meaning was ahead of her, a life Rilla could never have imagined, let alone presumed to claim.

She would be leaving the Wallflower Academy after all, but she now had a home, a heart quite given over to her, to fill her life.

'Miss Pike appears most disconcerted,' Finlay said, narrating the room's surroundings as he knew she appreciated. 'A few guests have accosted Lord Norbury, who looks pleased yet red-faced. My mother is adoring all the attention, as you would expect, and I—'

'Yes, how are you?' Rilla said, a teasing lilt in her voice.

Another kiss was brushed against her temple. 'You know full well that I would much rather take my wife home and ravish her than stand about with all these people.'

Rilla shivered. She was quite aware of her husband's mind, in truth, but she knew what was expected of them, even if neither of them wished it.

They would remain here, at the wedding reception, for another hour at least. Then, and only then, would they be permitted to depart.

Depart, and start the beginning of a happy life together.

'Ah, I see Miss Pike wishes to distract people,' came Finlay's laughing voice. 'She's about to instruct the musicians to— Yes, there they go.'

Music expanded just to Rilla's left. She had attempted to convince the dowager countess and Miss Pike that a dance at their wedding reception was most unnecessary, but they had both discounted her objections. The dowager countess said she wished to dance, and Miss Pike said it would be a wonderful opportunity for her wallflowers to gain practice.

'After all, the gentlemen your future husband will be inviting to his wedding will doubtlessly wish to dance with my wallflowers,' Miss Pike had said only the previous day. 'Will they not?'

Whether Rilla herself would dance apparently had not occurred to either of the women. In truth, it had not occurred to her.

But she smiled broadly as Finlay squeezed her hand and said, 'My darling wife. Will you give me the honour of this dance?'

This dance, and the next, and the next, she wanted to say. *All the dances of my life, for the rest of my life. And all the days, and all the nights, all the griefs and all the joys. The moments I never thought I could share with another. And all the rest.*

'Yes,' Rilla breathed. 'With all my heart.'

And as they stepped forward, her arm in Finlay's, Rilla did not care whether anyone was watching. The whole wedding celebration party could have melted into thin air and it would not have mattered.

What mattered was the man beside her. The man who would be by her side for the rest of her life.

Being safe, being loved, being adored in his arms was the only way she knew how to live—and as Finlay placed her in the set and whispered, 'I love you,' Rilla knew nothing could compare to this. Nothing.

Except, perhaps, the next dance. And the next. And the next…

* * * * *

If you enjoyed this story,
then make sure to catch up on the first book in
The Wallflower Academy miniseries,
Emily E K Murdoch's debut for Harlequin Historical

Least Likely to Win a Duke